I0653725

The Victorian Erotic Romance Trilogy

Take a trip back to Victorian England with three erotic stories of sex and love. A young widow seeks a tutor to discipline her nephew but learns her true nature at the hands of a dominant lover. A strong-willed woman refuses to be married off and instead plans an indiscretion, but will she succumb to the charms of the man she thought was only her pawn? A lonely vampire falls in love, but will his sire stand in his way of finally finding happiness? The repressed world of Queen Victoria has never been so sexy!

The Victorian Erotic Romance Trilogy

NEW YORK TIMES BESTSELLING AUTHOR

K.M. SCOTT

WRITING AS GABRIELLE BISSET

2013 Copper Key Media, LLC
Copyright © 2013 Copper Key Media, LLC

Published in the United States
Second Edition
ISBN-10: 1941594204
ISBN-13: 978-1-941594-20-9

Cover Design: Cover Me, Darling

Interior designed and formatted by

www.emtippettsbookdesigns.com

TABLE OF CONTENTS

Love's Master

One

London, 1853

Lily sat in the parlor attempting to read a book and tried to tune out the din caused by her eight-year-old nephew. Repeatedly, he raced back and forth from the kitchen to where she sat, yelling and chasing the cat his parents had given him for his birthday one month earlier. In his wake were toys strewn all about that he'd discarded in favor of whatever else had attracted his attention. At the moment, it was the cat, which luckily could run faster on four legs than William could run on two.

While she loved her brother's child, she silently lamented the events of her life that had caused her to move in with him and his parents.

If only...

But recriminations wouldn't bring her husband back. Taken from her just three years into their marriage and before they could be blessed with a child of their own, he'd been a victim of the cholera epidemic that had ravaged the city. Now a widow, she had few choices but to look to her family for support and a place to call home.

Her brother Richard and his wife Elizabeth had welcomed her with open arms, a fact she now suspected had hidden their happiness at the prospect of having an additional adult to tend to their son. The reality was that no one had ever truly tended to William, and as a result, the child was incorrigible. Nannies came and went with alarming speed, as did tutors who simply refused to deal with the child whose temper tantrums were legendary on Frederick Street. Few of their neighbors in the London suburb of Regent's Park had escaped the scene of the young boy's misbehavior.

"William!" she snapped as she caught him by the arm.

Stunned into stopping for a moment, he stood in front of his aunt and stared up into her eyes in surprise. Lily looked at the deceptively angelic face looking back at her, knowing the façade was just that. Beneath his rosy-cheeked expression was the terror of her new home.

Holding him, she said, "William, I want you to sit down this minute. I will not tolerate this behavior any more."

Smiling, the child replied sweetly, "All right, Aunty Lily," and when she released her hold on him, he promptly ran away screaming after the cat.

Two hours later, Lily was sure she couldn't stand another day of her nephew's behavior but was just as sure she'd have to be the one to tackle the issue if it were ever

to be solved. Scouring the newspaper advertisements for willing participants to replace the nanny and tutor, both of whom had recently left as their predecessors had, she recognized the names of many of the men and women who sought employment and knew no amount of money could entice them to return.

Sadly, she was forced to admit the solution to her problem wouldn't be found in the employment section of the Times. She continued to peruse the paper, at least hoping to find some diversion from the noise around her.

William walked up to her and tapped his hand on the newspaper. "Aunty Lily, play with me!"

Looking down at him, she wondered if a little guidance from her might do the trick. "If I do, you must promise to behave. Do you understand?"

"Yes, I promise."

With a great deal of direction, she found some measure of success in making him behave. When his parents finally returned from their time away nearly an hour later, she was set on broaching the discussion of what would have to be done with her nephew. If she didn't, she was convinced she'd soon go mad.

After a dinner that included more of William's bad behavior and a temper tantrum over the suggestion he eat his vegetables, his mother took him to prepare for bed and Lily took the opportunity to discuss the situation with her brother.

"Richard, I think something must be done with William."

Her brother looked past her, his face a practiced

expression of feigned interest. "Everything will be better when we hire a new nanny and tutor."

"Please excuse my interference, but nothing is going to be better if William doesn't learn to behave."

The silence that met her statement along with the continued stare past her told Lily he knew she was right. It also told her that her suspicion was correct—if anything were to change, she would have to change it.

Touching his hand, she continued in a far softer tone. "Richard, I appreciate how much you've done for me since Jeremy's death. Let me help you with this."

Her brother sighed and seemed to admit defeat. "Fine. You may be in charge of finding a new nanny and tutor for William."

Lily rose to leave the table, but Richard stopped her. "I want to discuss something with you. I have someone I want you to meet. A gentleman."

"Why?"

"Lily, your mourning period has been over for months. You need to rejoin the world."

"I'm not out of the world, Richard."

"I invited Captain Mason Danvers to join us for dinner soon. He's a wonderful man, a veteran of the Army. I'm sure you'll like him."

Quietly, she said, "I'm not sure I'm ready."

"I understand how difficult this is for you, but you're a young woman who shouldn't be stuck living with her relatives."

Lily knew what her brother really meant was that as much as he loved her, he didn't want to be forced to baby-

sit a grown woman for any longer than society dictated. And that meant he was actively searching for a potential husband for her.

All she hoped was that his choice was someone she could grow to like.

For hours, she thought about the surprise life had thrown her. Married at nineteen to a man who had swept her off her feet, she had taken to the role of wife easily, believing the rest of her life had been plotted out for her as it was for other women lucky enough to be successfully married.

Jeremy had been the perfect husband, kind but with the ability to handle her stubborn streak. And as a lover, he'd been patient and devoted—just what any young woman would want to initiate her into the world of marriage.

She watched as the day faded into darkness remembering the feeling of having someone close as the night settled in. Sadness came over her as it always did when she thought about her husband's passing before they'd had the chance to have a child. Reconciled to a life without Jeremy, she'd turned to Richard for help.

But could she deal with the type of help he now offered? She sympathized with his desire to have her settled with another husband. Who wanted a twenty-three-year-old sister hanging about, especially a willful one? She couldn't change who she was, but would this Mason Danvers want her as much as Richard wanted him to?

Lily remembered meeting Captain Danvers once

before when Richard and Elizabeth had insisted she attend the Jarret's Christmas party. Still in mourning, she'd relented and joined them, but looking back now, she was sure she hadn't made much of an impression dressed in her mourning clothes and wearing a look of sadness she'd accepted as fitting for a widow, even a young one.

He'd struck her as confident, if not a little too brash, and a man who probably wouldn't look twice at a woman like her, dressed in mourning garb or not. Tall and suntanned, with hair the color of caramel, he looked like a man who'd seen the world outside of England — the quintessential military man of the Empire. Lily, on the other hand, had always seen herself as the picture of English womanhood, with porcelain skin and brown hair. The only thing that set her apart from every other pale skinned brunette in London was the color of her eyes. Deep green, they told of an exotic ancestry long buried in the Scott family.

She'd never thought of herself as a beauty, no matter what Jeremy had said, and as the memory of Mason Danvers grew in her mind, she wondered if Richard's efforts to entice the man to marry her were all for naught. For what men like him preferred were women to compliment them. And she was not that woman in any sense of the word.

Lily sat with the newspaper in her lap, praying that someone new could be found among the advertisers she'd already been forced to dismiss as possibilities. A fitful night's sleep tossing and turning while her mind raced over having to meet Captain Danvers caused her nerves to be on edge, and she was embarrassed to admit she dreaded William's impending arrival in the breakfast room. Desperate to find a new nanny or tutor, she buried her nose in the paper and began what she hoped would be a fruitful search.

The advertisements offered nothing, and as she sat dejected, she turned to the Agony Column, knowing at least she'd find kindred spirits in the lost lovers and desperate souls searching for that which life and circumstance had taken or failed to provide.

Even a brief perusal of the notices in this part of the Times provided a reader a glimpse into the often lonely world of the strangers who inhabited London and its suburbs. With any luck, Lily hoped to get lost in the world of these strangers so as to forget the one she'd been thrust into and which seemed to offer only one way out: marriage to a certain Captain Danvers.

As the chaos of the day began with William's appearance at breakfast, she strived to block it out, focusing instead on the suffering of those outside the house. The column was a particularly long one, with notices of long lost relatives urgently seeking their family members and lovers conveying the details of their illicit meetings. She came upon the last advertisement and her heart skipped a beat in excitement. Worried she'd misread it, she read it again.

"K. is a strict disciplinarian and not afraid of a rather

unruly pupil."

Could it be? Had she found a tutor for William? As she attempted to ignore his stomping and temper tantrum over his mother's timid request he finish his oatmeal, Lily read and reread the notice, her anticipation building at the thought of someone finally disciplining the child properly.

"Elizabeth," she said as he stormed out of the room to abuse the cook, "how would one find a person who advertised in the Agony Column?"

Her sister-in-law looked relieved at the idea of discussing other people's distress. "I don't know for sure, but you would likely have to advertise a reply."

Lily almost leaped from her chair, thrilled by the prospect of hiring William's newest tutor—a strict disciplinarian!

"Elizabeth, please have John arrange the carriage for me. I'm going into town."

As the carriage rolled toward London, the steady rhythm of the horses' hooves hitting the road relaxed Lily. Closing her eyes, she shut out everything but the sound and allowed herself to fantasize about the mysterious stranger she hoped would soon bring calm and order to the house.

My mid-morning she'd placed her reply to the potential tutor and was on her way back home. As her carriage pulled up to the house, she congratulated herself on being such a take charge woman. Her triumph was cut short, however, by the vision of Mason Danvers she spied through the carriage window. Taking a deep breath, she resigned herself to the fact that what she'd dreaded had begun. As he helped her out of the carriage, she felt his gaze roam over her. Ever the military man, he was surveying the prize he sought to capture and devising a plan of attack, she thought to herself.

"Miss Scott, how are you today?"

Lily immediately felt irritated by his negation of her three years of marriage. Pretending he was a stranger, she asked in an indignant tone that was only partially false, "Do we know each other, sir?" as she haughtily took back her hand.

Bowing, he said, "Pardon me, dear lady. I understand you may not remember me as I do you, but I'm here at your brother's request. I'm Captain Mason Danvers. Please let me escort you into the house."

Lily looked at the man her brother had chosen for her intended. As appealing as she remembered, he appeared to be genuinely interested in her, she realized to her surprise.

"Thank you, Captain. That's very nice of you," she answered more politely than genuinely.

She let him take her hand once more and felt the strength of his hand press gently against her skin. The power he possessed seemed to exude from his very pores, and she decided perhaps she should try to like him.

The problem was just as his every movement seemed to convey a very attractive strength, his speech conveyed a far less attractive overconfidence at times that she found more and more distasteful.

"Richard, I look forward to discussing that business deal with you. I believe I can help you as much as you may help me."

Lily watched as he strutted into the parlor with her brother. Her first real meeting with Captain Mason Danvers had left her with mixed feelings for him. True, he seemed to have some fine qualities, but as she watched him staring at her from an entire room away, she sensed she was the business deal he'd wanted to discuss.

Well, if he thinks closing this deal will be easy, he's definitely overestimated himself.

"Master Kadar, your newspaper and tea."

Kadar watched as his servant placed a tray containing the items next to him on the small table that stood beside his chair. "Have there been any letters this morning?"

The servant reached into his jacket and retrieved two letters. "These just arrived."

Taking them from him, Kadar excused him with a wave and began reading the first of the two letters. What he found pleased him, and he made a mental note to arrange a meeting with the letter writer in the near future. A quick skim of the second letter produced the same pleasure and another reminder to meet that person also.

After a sip of tea, he opened the newspaper to find out the news of the day. Eventually, he came back to the Agony Column and reading through the brief but tortured listings for that day, his eyes came upon an unexpected ad responding to his own.

"L. is in need of a strict disciplinarian. Please advise to allow a meeting."

His focus was riveted to the words as he read them. Who was L? Quickly, he thought of all the "pupils" he'd hoped to reach with his notice and none possessed a name beginning with the letter L.

"Akil!" he bellowed to the servant, who hurriedly ran into the room in response.

"Yes, Master."

"Did you deliver the exact advertisement I gave you the other day?"

"Yes, Master. The exact one. 'K. is a strict disciplinarian and not afraid of a rather unruly pupil.'"

"Get me yesterday's Times."

As he waited for Akil to return, he wondered who the mysterious L. could be. Known only to a few people in London, he'd used the Agony Column many times before to meet people like him. Always reliable, it had offered him an anonymity he desired but a trustworthy method of reaching out to his kind.

"Here is the paper, Master," the servant said as he nervously handed him the Times of London for May 16, 1853.

Running his finger along the page, he traveled over notes for secret lovers' meetings and ads from those who longed to find estranged loved ones in code and foreign languages. Finally, at the bottom of the column, he saw his advertisement exactly as he'd ordered Akil to submit

it and exactly as his servant had just recited it back to him.

Who was this new "pupil" looking to join the two who'd already responded as he'd expected they would?

"Well, L. wants to meet," he muttered as the servant stood waiting to take the previous day's newspaper.

"Will there be anything else, Master?"

"Yes, Akil," he said as he rose to walk to his desk. When he'd written out a note, he handed it to the man.

"Take this and make sure it's in tomorrow's newspaper. Now hurry and get this to the Times."

Alone again, Kadar sat back in his chair by the window to drink his morning tea and decide on the details of where and when to meet his two letter writers. However, the possibility of a new person looking to join him preoccupied his thoughts, and he began to plan for the meeting he hoped would occur soon.

A new acquaintance would be a welcome, if unexpected, change. He'd advertised to replace the "pupil" he'd lost—in fact, lost would be the wrong word, he thought to himself. He'd willingly given her up when she'd decided to relocate to America, realizing their time together had come to its natural end.

Such was often the case in the world he traveled in. His "pupils" were more often than not curious ladies frustrated with the austere structure of their lives who frequented the underground sex scene. They sought him and others like him out, looking for a way to express what Victorian society hypocritically demanded stay hidden, buried under modest dress, meticulous manners, and a general fear of anything different.

Kadar stood and stretched his muscular frame. While he waited for a response from the mysterious L., he'd keep himself busy with the two who'd answered his advertisement. Summoning his maid, he readied himself for his day.

"Yes, Master?" the petite, dark skinned woman said as she appeared in front of him.

"Prepare my case. I'm going to be spending some time at the country house."

"Yes, Master."

Turning back toward the window, he watched in boredom as his Regent's Park neighborhood began to come alive for the day.

Lily awoke early and hastily dressed, eager to search the newspaper for a response to her ad. She attempted to tamp down her excitement, reminding herself that it had only appeared the day before and it was quite likely that K. was a busy person who may not have answered so quickly.

But she could hope.

As she entered the breakfast room, she was treated to a painful reminder of how desperate she was for K. to agree to her offer. William sat on the floor next to the table obstinately refusing to do as his mother requested until she agreed to take him out.

"Aunty Lily, tell Mother to take me for a ride in the carriage today," he whined.

She saw the frustration on her sister-in-law's face and for a moment forgave her for years of poor parenting. Lily pitied her, for as unfortunate as her life had recently been, she could console herself with the idea that at least she wasn't forced to face the result of her shortcomings each day. And as uncertain as her future was, at least she'd leave this house at some point. Elizabeth could look forward to no such reprieve.

Sitting down at the table, Lily casually dismissed his suggestion. "William, your mother has many things to do as the lady of this house. Perhaps if you'd stop misbehaving and chasing away your nannies, you'd get to enjoy trips in the carriage or even time at the park."

Before she'd finished, her nephew had shifted his attention to the cat, which had made the mistake of walking past the doorway. Racing after it, William left the two women in peace, if only for a few moments.

Lily watched Elizabeth sigh deeply, looking far older and more haggard than her twenty-six years. She hoped K. had answered the ad as much for her sister-in-law as for herself.

Opening the paper, she immediately turned to the Agony Column with high expectations. Her eyes flowed over the words until they stopped abruptly at the answer she'd waited for.

"K. instructs his new pupil to appear in blue at the S.E. pavilion in Regent's Park on Thursday noon."

Lily could barely contain her exhilaration. The tutor had seen her notice and wanted to meet his new pupil! In her joy, she heard William stomp his feet at the suggestion he leave the cat alone and let out an ear-piercing scream.

"No! He's my kitty!"

She couldn't take him to meet the tutor or the man would immediately refuse the appointment! In a flash, her joy turned to despair. No tutor, not even one who believed in strict discipline, would ever agree to work with the child if he acted like that.

But the ad had specifically said the pupil was to appear the next day in the park, and Lily knew no manner of cajoling would change William into the kind of child any tutor would agree to teach in just one day. She'd just have to go by herself and hope to convince him to take the position.

Right before noon, Lily reached the southeast pavilion in Regent's Park. The focal point of the London suburb that shared the same name, the park was an oasis from the effects of the city that often spilled over into the carefully planned neighborhood that skirted the capital. On this mid-May day, the sun shone brightly, and she immediately entered the pavilion to avoid getting any unsightly coloring from the sun. Suntans may have been permissible for Army men, but a proper English lady would never allow such a thing.

Lily scanned the area in search of the man she hoped would be her nephew's next tutor and her savior. People walked by, enjoying the pleasant spring day. A rainbow of colored parasols danced against the deep green lawn. She looked down at her blue dress the color of robin's eggs and nervously worried another would wear blue

and steal her tutor out from under her nose, but no one else appeared in any shade of blue nearby, and Lily smiled to herself at her needless concern.

Church bells announced the arrival of noon, and as she listened to the deep chimes, she heard someone enter the pavilion behind her. Turning to face the stranger, she saw a man she identified as a foreigner, probably from Arabia.

"Miss, pardon me. I am sent to give you this note."

Taking it from his hand, she asked, "Are you the person who placed the notice for pupils?"

The man shook his head. "No, miss. All will be answered in the letter."

Lily read the note and looked up to see the man waiting for her response. What had seemed like a simple meeting in the park had quickly become more complicated. K. requested she meet with him at his country home in Hertfordshire.

Propriety should have strictly forbidden her from going any further, but desperation trumped caution and proper etiquette. Lily wrestled briefly with the decision but quickly nodded.

"Please tell your employer I will arrive within the next two hours."

Bowing, the man thanked her and left her standing alone in the pavilion. After steeling herself against the idea that what she was about to do was entirely improper for a young woman, she left to arrange a carriage to take her to Hertfordshire.

"What did she look like?"

Kadar watched as his servant appeared to carefully consider his reply.

"Very English, Master. Dark hair worn in the style popular with young English ladies. Pale skin but very green eyes."

"Green?"

Akil nodded slowly. "Deep green, like a precious emerald."

"And the rest of her?" Kadar asked, his interest already piqued.

"Very much to your liking, if I am any judge of your preferences."

"And she agreed to meet here?"

"She will be here within the hour, Master."

"Then I will soon meet the mysterious Miss L. Be sure to obtain her full name and inform me before escorting her to the parlor."

"As you wish."

Kadar sat down and tried to relax, but the anticipation of a potential new "pupil" made it next to impossible. As the minutes ticked away, he fantasized about her with the information Akil had provided. While he thought about the pleasure someone new would give him, he spied out the window a figure exiting a coach at the end of the lawn.

Her beauty hit him like a thunderbolt, but immediately something about her looked familiar. He watched as she

walked up the path to the front door and realized with a shock that the woman coming to meet him was one of his Regent's Park neighbors.

"What on earth is Richard Scott's sister doing here?" he muttered in amazement.

A minute later, Akil confirmed what he'd seen outside. "Mrs. Lily Norville is waiting, Master. Shall I show her in?"

Kadar weighed his options and smiled. He'd never known Richard's sister to be anything but the proper English lady she was expected to be, but if she were here to become someone's "pupil", there was obviously more to her than what she appeared to be.

"Show her in, but instruct her to stand with her back to the window. Tell her I refuse to see her if she doesn't follow my explicit instructions."

Akil returned to the hallway to retrieve her, and Kadar slipped behind the decorative screen near the window to wait.

As she entered the room, she untied her bonnet and removed it to reveal beautiful dark brown curls fastened in the fashion of the day. Kadar thought how incredibly sensual it would be when he freed them and her from her restraints.

But other restraints would replace those.

He watched as she dutifully positioned herself as instructed and waited. How trusting she was!

Silently, he moved behind her and before she could protect herself, he had his hands around the column of her neck, his fingers holding her chin and forcing her head to remain facing forward. He felt her tremble in fear as he pressed his body against her back.

"Please don't hurt me," she pleaded in a frightened voice.

Whispering, he said, "That's not what this is about. Force is for brutes and blackguards."

"Then why are you holding me like this?" she asked, her voice shaky.

Kadar brushed his lips against her ear and inhaled the sweet fragrance of her perfume. "You're lovely, my dear."

He felt her body stiffen against his when he kissed the soft skin of her neck, but there was excitement in her too, evidenced by the slight heaving of her breasts and her gentle panting. One hand released her chin and slid down to caress the tops of her milky white breasts.

"Lovely."

As he trailed his fingertips over the skin above her breasts, he felt her push against his hand holding her jaw.

"Eyes forward, my dear," he whispered into her ear.

"There's been some mistake," she began.

"What you want isn't a mistake. You don't have to be frightened. I would never hurt you," he assured her in between gently kissing her neck.

"Please let me go. This is a mistake. I came here for a tutor for my nephew."

Kadar lifted his head from her shoulder and stared at her, stunned at the realization that she'd taken his advertisement literally. She hadn't wanted to experiment as a submissive. She had believed she was meeting a

child's tutor!

Closing his eyes, he inhaled her fragrance one last time, disappointed by the misunderstanding. Just touching her for that brief time had excited him, but he wouldn't force her.

"Take care, my lady," he whispered and then quietly slipped away behind the screen.

Released, she ran for the door and in seconds she was gone, running to her carriage to escape. Watching from the window, he saw her throw herself into the seat and order the driver to leave. She sped away, and he slumped into a chair, still excited but disappointed by the all too brief encounter.

"Too bad," he mumbled to himself.

The ride back to Frederick Street seemed to take twice as long as the ride to Hertfordshire as Lily struggled to understand what had happened. Her fingers caressed the path his lips had taken over her neck, and her face grew warm at the memory of him holding her as he began his seduction.

Emotions that had lay dormant since her husband's death bubbled up inside her. Deep in the pit of her stomach an ache she barely remembered settled into her.

Who was he? Who was the man whose touch had ignited such feelings of desire in her?

Quickly, she chastised herself for such a baseless infatuation. "Whoever he is, he's obviously a man whose tastes run far differently than mine," she said aloud, as if to convince herself. But the feelings he caused in her remained.

For the rest of the day, Lily worked to banish the thoughts of the stranger from her mind. Whatever he was, he wasn't the answer to her problems.

Three

L ily knew as soon as she hit the main floor that her brother had taken the next step toward encouraging a union between her and Captain Danvers. The kitchen staff scurried from stove to counter preparing the finest pheasant and wild herb meal, and the Scott's maid and head man obsessed over seating placements and dinnerware as if the Queen herself was to grace the household.

"Elizabeth, are we to entertain guests?"

"Oh, yes! Richard has invited Captain Danvers, Jeremiah Needham, and his business partner, Joseph Cranston. And their wives, of course. Now you must go back to your room and get ready. The guests will be arriving soon."

Three couples and a single man. Richard wasn't aiming for subtlety, it seemed. It was perfect, wasn't it? Lily saw all too clearly that she was in for an evening of matchmaking. She consoled herself with the fact that at least her brother wasn't arranging an engagement with a man as old as Mr. Needham, who was at least sixty.

"It could be worse," she reassured herself as she climbed the stairs back to her room.

By six o'clock, all the guests had arrived and Lily was enjoying old Jeremiah Needham's stories of his days fighting Napoleon.

"Sir, your tales are some of the most exciting I've ever heard," she said after he'd finished telling of his time at the Battle of Waterloo.

"And they're all true, young lady. Bonaparte was every bit the rascal I make him out to be," the older man boasted.

"Well, thankfully, England had fine soldiers like you ready to give their all to defeat him."

Having flattered and impressed Richard's guests, she deftly moved to find a quiet spot near the front window in the parlor, but found Mason Danvers at her elbow.

"Do you enjoy old Needham's tall tales, Miss Scott?"

Turning to face him, she stared intently into his eyes. "As a widow, Captain Danvers, I still retain the last name of my husband."

Instantly, she saw his face register her offense to his mistake. Something in his eyes telegraphed his regret even before he spoke.

"Please accept my sincerest apologies. I thought it better not to remind you of your sadness."

Lily knew his intent hadn't been to offend and let a smile soften her expression. "Captain Danvers, please

simply call me Lily and all will be forgiven."

All worry left his eyes and at once they seemed to sparkle, gold flecks dancing through the soft brown color. "Then I hope you'll call me Mason. Captain is for old men who try to flirt with young women by telling stories they hope will impress them."

Chuckling, she said, "Mason, I think you're too hard on Mr. Needham."

"I can only hope I don't behave like that when I reach his age."

"Do you have exciting military stories from your time abroad?"

"How do you know I've been abroad, Lily?"

Motioning with her eyes toward the rest of the party, she explained, "Quite simply, you have the look of someone who's seen sunnier regions. Look at my brother, for example. An Englishman if there ever was one. Look at his pale skin. Now look at yourself. It's obvious from your coloring that you've been abroad. Was it India?"

"No. I was in the Afghan wars."

Lily sensed by the darkening in his expression that his days at war weren't something he wanted to discuss and tried to lighten the conversation. "The peace and quiet in the house is quite nice, isn't it?"

Mason looked around the room. "It is indeed. Where is your nephew tonight?"

"Exiled to my sister-in-law's family for the duration of the party."

"He is a spirited one, isn't he?" Mason said with grin.

"You are most kind in your description of him."

"Boys are meant to be spitfires, Lily. That's where our military leaders come from."

"Well, while the military may benefit from his high spiritedness years from now, we would benefit from some better behavior now. In fact, I'm actively looking for a new nanny and tutor for him."

"Any luck finding one?"

Lily's mind momentarily returned to her afternoon adventure. Shaking her head, she said, "No, no luck yet. But I'm not giving up. Our sanity depends on my succeeding in finding someone to discipline the boy."

They heard Elizabeth call them to dinner, and as they returned to the dining room, Lily felt like she'd seen a different, more appealing side to Mason Danvers.

Alone in her bed, she thought of the man's hands, strong yet gentle, holding her exactly where he wanted her that afternoon. The memory of his control over her nagged at her, like an idea that haunted her into thinking something she shouldn't.

Everything about her experience in Hertfordshire should have frightened her so completely as to cause nightmares for days.

But it didn't.

Instead she found herself slipping into a fantasy about the man—the seductive smell of spices that had teased her nose as he dipped his mouth to her neck.

The power in his strong fingers as they controlled her movements.

The husky whisper of his voice in her ear reassuring

her he wouldn't hurt her.

Lily blushed in the darkness as her body came alive, reacting to the pictures her mind conjured up. It had been so long since she'd felt anything for another she'd feared she'd never again respond to a man's touch.

As she lay there, her Victorian propriety scolded her for her wanton thoughts.

"That's not how a lady is supposed to be treated," she told herself. "A gentleman never places a hand on a young woman, unless he's a brute."

Everything she'd been brought up to believe told her to forget the incident and be thankful for escaping without harm. Everything was no match for the feelings he'd stirred in her, however.

But ingrained beliefs refused to leave her so easily, and by the time she began to drift off to sleep, she'd convinced herself that the afternoon's excitement was a memory best forgotten quickly.

By morning, Lily had decided all her energy should be focused in the hiring of the desperately needed nanny and tutor. Attacking her task with a newfound vigor, she scoured the Times, careful to avoid the Agony Column. Luck seemed to be on her side and two potential nannies were her reward.

Feeling flush with the potential for success, she decided she owed it to her brother to keep him abreast of her efforts. As he sat at the head of the breakfast table dreamily looking out the window at the bright spring day, Lily explained what she'd done so far to solve their dilemma.

"Richard? Did you hear me?"

He seemed to come out of his haze at these words and looked at her blankly, obviously unaware of everything she'd said. "I'm sorry. Did you say something?"

"I was explaining that I have two fine leads for a nanny, but I've had no luck so far finding a suitable tutor for William."

A smile slowly formed on his face, but he looked away past her. "Lily, you're going to make a fine mother. I'm sorry Jeremy died before you were blessed with a child."

A tiny stab of sadness hit Lily. "Thank you, Richard."

The two sat in silence until he turned toward her again. "I'd never noticed how noisy this house is until this moment. I guess I'd just gotten used to it."

Reaching her hand out to touch his, she said, "I don't plan to give up until I find William both a nanny and a tutor. Not only for his sake, but for yours and Elizabeth's."

"We're going to miss you when you leave, Lily."

"Have you married me off already?"

"No, but Mason was very impressed with you last night. He told me you two had a thoroughly interesting conversation."

Lily watched as her brother's paternal side took over. She knew he was right: this was a woman's only choice. And as far as men went, Captain Mason Danvers wasn't a bad choice. A little brash, a tad bit bold, but not a bad choice in many ways.

But something deep inside her whispered its desire for something else. Something darker and more foreign

than anything she'd ever experienced in her life.

"Thoroughly interesting?"

As she asked the question, she heard the disdainful tone she'd attached to it. Richard's expression told her he'd heard it too.

"Lily, I don't want you to think I'm trying to get rid of you because I'm encouraging Mason. He's a good man, and he can give a woman a great deal."

Suddenly feeling ungrateful, she lowered her eyes. "I don't feel like you're trying to get rid of me, Richard. I just don't know if he's the kind of man for me."

"He thinks a great deal of you, sister."

Smiling her agreement, she wondered if it mattered at all what she thought of him.

"And he can offer the security and comfort you deserve."

"I know. And I know that you only want the best for me."

Lily listened as he listed all of Mason Danver's assets, all important things people like her brother considered when arranging a match. All his money and prestige meant little to her, though. She'd never been as concerned as all those around her about wealth and social position, much to the chagrin of their parents, who'd hoped to see her married to someone far higher on the social ladder than Jeremy Norville. But he'd always been the one for her from the moment she met him.

Memories of those days made her sad now. She'd had everything she'd ever hoped for and in the blink of an eye, it had all been taken away. What if that happened again? Could she bear caring about Mason, falling in love with him, and then losing him too?

"And after his time abroad, he's ready to settle down and live the life of a proper English gentleman."

Lily nodded her understanding. "I promise I will give him a fair chance, not only for his sake but for yours."

"That's all I ask."

By dinnertime, Lily had great news to tell. One of the nannies had agreed to accept the position and, in fact, possessed the necessary qualities to be William's governess, both nanny and tutor. Everyone looked forward to the new addition to the household, and even William seemed to enjoy the idea.

Days went by and her hopes for Miss Allen proved true. With a caring yet firm hand, she immediately began to affect change in the child, much to the rest of the household's relief. Lily watched as her nephew began to morph from a petulant tyrant of a child to one who still seemed to have a very spirited side but was also capable of being polite and behaved.

William's transformation made life better for the entire Scott household, but Lily couldn't shake the memory of the man who seemed to be causing a change in her. Every night, as she lay in bed wishing for sleep, she was tormented by memories of his touch, his lips on her skin, his powerful presence behind her commanding her to be something she wasn't.

Or was she? As she relived the brief time she'd spent with him, she wanted more. Feelings of need and desire

spiked between her legs as she thought of his long fingers replacing hers on the spot she touched and bringing her an even more exquisite release.

By the eighth day, she was back at the offices of the Times of London with another notice for the Agony Column. Unsure if she was entering a world she would eventually run in fear from, she placed her ad and hoped more than she understood that he would answer with his own beckoning her back to him, for she'd realized after nights full of thoughts of him that she would be in her own agony until she was with him again.

That night, as she lay awake in bed, she fantasized about her own potential tutor. Her delicate fingers caressed her tender thighs, over skin that hadn't felt the touch of another for far too long. The thought of his hands—his mouth—touching her there, excited her like she'd never been before, sending heat racing over her skin. Timidly, she touched her soft folds, imagining his mouth between her legs. Her other hand excitedly squeezed her thigh with each stroke of her excited nub as her mind wandered back to the feel of the man's hands on her, the way he held her so completely in control. She imagined his fingers trailing over her neck as his lips gently teased her earlobe, his voice whispering erotic words of seduction. And domination. Silently, as she felt her orgasm overtake her, she prayed he would call to her soon and show her if her desire was reciprocated.

Four

K adar sat in the study of his Regent's Park home preparing for his day. As he sipped the very black chai tea his Afghan servant had delivered, he inhaled deeply, enjoying the sweet but spicy scent of the cardamom added to it. His mind traveled back to the world where he'd first experienced the food and drink he now regularly enjoyed. Thoughts of the desert sands and his life there contrasted sharply with his current life in England.

"How different it is here," he mumbled as he sat back in his chair. In England, he was essentially a man of leisure, each day attending appointments with other men like him. There he'd been anything but that type of man.

But one similarity existed between the two very different worlds. Just as in the wilder world of his past, he still enjoyed the underground sexual world of domination and submission. And to his surprise, he'd

found many more willing participants here in England.

Reflecting on his most recent time with a new submissive, he causally thumbed through the newspaper and drank his morning tea. He read through the Agony Column, even though he no longer advertised, because like so many other Londoners he couldn't resist the mystery the column offered in the staid and responsible days of Victoria.

Before he'd made it halfway through, he saw it.

"L. misses her tutor and wishes to resume her studies."

Kadar's heart beat wildly against his chest as he reread the message he knew was meant for him. Lily had drifted in and out of his mind since the day he'd watched her run from his house. He'd accepted, albeit with disappointment, that what he'd hoped for had no chance of occurring. She was a proper society woman through and through.

But as he ran his fingertips over her words, he saw that he'd been mistaken. She was certainly a lady on the surface, but like so many of the women he'd met, she craved something more than the bland sexuality mid-nineteenth century restrictive morals forced her to accept.

No, she's different than those women, he thought to himself as his mind replayed her sweetly innocent response to him as she stood naively in his Hertfordshire home.

Her ad had given little evidence of the passion he suspected he'd find within her. His fantasy of that passion raced through his thoughts, building upon itself with each new desire he conjured.

Just as he believed her passion to be far deeper than the façade of a perfect English lady let on, he also knew he'd have to be patient and gently initiate her into the world she timidly approached. Too much too soon and she'd run.

No, he'd need to take his time.

As he considered how sweet her surrender would be when it finally came, his growing erection pushed against his trousers. His body preferred to move much faster than he should.

A knock at the door roused him from his fantasies, and as his servant entered to refresh his drink, he said, "Akil, I will need you to take another letter to the Times just as before."

The man nodded. "Will there be anything else, Master?"

Kadar rose from his chair to retrieve a pen and paper. When he was finished composing his ad, he handed it to him. "After you deliver this to the paper for tomorrow's edition, I want you to go to the market."

"Yes, Master."

He handed Akil another sheet of paper with a list of items he desired. "Make sure you obtain the ingredients for Qabili Palau. And I want the best chocolates, so go to the confectionary near Hyde Park. Do you know the one I mean?"

Akil smiled a knowing smile and bowed. "I know exactly the one, Master."

"Then go. And when you retrieve everything on that list, take it to Hertfordshire. We'll be going there

tomorrow morning."

"Will there be anything else?"

Kadar thought about his question and quickly scribbled another note. "Have this delivered to the young woman named Violet. And send Nuha in."

Bowing deeply, Akil took the paper and left to begin his errands. With his exit, Kadar's maid and sometimes cook entered the study. She stood quietly waiting for him to give her orders, her gaze directed toward the floor.

When he'd finished writing another note, he looked up at her. "Nuha, you'll be going to Hertfordshire in the morning. I'll need you to cook for a gathering I'll be having tomorrow. I sent Akil to get all the ingredients you'll need for Qabili Palau, and I want you to make baklava."

"Yes, Master. I will require rosewater. Do you prefer I purchase it or make it myself?"

"Do whatever it takes to ensure the baklava tastes like it did when you first made it for me."

"As you wish. I will need roses then."

Handing her money, Kadar instructed her to find Akil to add the flowers to his list. When she'd left, he relaxed at his desk and returned to his fantasy of his next meeting with Lily.

Lily awoke from a night filled with decadent dreams, her entire body humming with excitement. She'd submitted her ad in time for yesterday's paper and anticipated his answer today. Butterflies fluttered in her stomach at seeing something meant especially for her.

Everyone else in the house had finished breakfast, so she was able to search the paper in private. But as she began to read the Agony Column, Mason Danvers was announced and led into the breakfast room.

"Captain Danvers, this is an unexpected surprise," she said with frustration as she folded the Times in her lap.

"Good morning, Lily. It's wonderful to see you again. I'm here to meet with your brother, but I don't see him. Is he here?"

"I'm not sure where he is, but please take a seat and feel free to wait."

"That's very kind of you. Thank you. Please don't let me interrupt you. I saw you were reading the paper as I entered."

"No, that can wait. I wouldn't be much of a hostess if I read the paper while you sit here with me."

Lily accepted that she would have to wait just a short while longer to find out if her mystery man from Hertfordshire had answered. She and Mason conversed about goings on in Regent's Park and William's new nanny until Richard returned for their meeting.

"Thank you for another lovely time, Lily," Mason said as he stood to join her brother.

Smiling, Lily eagerly returned to the newspaper and the Agony Column. Three-quarters of the way down the page she found her answer. As her heart pounded against her chest, she read each of his words with delight.

"K. welcomes his wayward pupil L. at three o'clock at

his home on Saturday."

Instantly, her face felt hot and the flush traveled over her body as she reread the enticing words. He would welcome her that very afternoon!

Looking up, she saw Mason staring at her as he spoke to her brother. Embarrassed, she meekly smiled and was greeted by Mason's full grin, which only served to heighten her discomfort.

Turning away, she looked out the window and tried to calm herself so as not to attract any undue attention. Every cell in her body felt alive as she thought about what may begin in just a few hours. She would finally meet her stranger face to face. The idea of what they'd do afterward made her heart begin to pound again, and her breathing quickly became labored, her breasts gently rising and falling as she closed her eyes to envision the delights that awaited her in Hertfordshire.

Her reverie was broken by Mason's voice. "Are you feeling all right, Lily?"

Confused and flustered, she turned to see him standing near her. Quickly, she closed the paper to conceal the source of her excitement.

"Yes, yes. I'm fine. Thank you."

"Did you read something in the paper that upset you? It seems like every day the news becomes more filled with the depravity so many in our fine city wallow in."

"No, I'm fine."

Was what she planned to do that afternoon depraved? Just months before, she may have answered yes with little doubt, but now she was far less assured of her answer.

Nothing had ever excited her as much as the feel of the man's hands controlling her.

Standing from the table, she hastily excused herself, leaving the men to continue their discussion. Alone in her room, she excitedly prepared for her journey to Hertfordshire, unsure of everything but her desire to see the man again.

It was nearly three o'clock as her coach rambled to the designated meeting place. Lily fought back the urge to instruct the driver to turn around and return to the safety of her brother's home on Frederick Street. Twice before on the trip, she'd almost lost her nerve, fearing what she was about to do. But just as she had in those moments of doubt, she once again steadied herself and admitted that she wanted this, no matter what society would think.

She'd worn her most flattering dress, a pale pink that flattered her more than any others she owned. Nervously, she fixed the stray curls that had escaped her bonnet, wishing she possessed hair that behaved as it should.

Exiting the carriage, she looked around but saw no one. The country home of K. was thankfully private she noted as she approached the front door. Her knock was answered by the same man who'd greeted her on her first visit, and just as before, he showed her into the room and instructed her to wait with her back to the window. As she stood waiting for the stranger to come up behind her, Lily was sure she'd never been as excited in her entire life as she was in these moments anticipating his first touch. When he finally ended her tortured wait, she reacted with a start.

Gently, his hands held her head so she remained eyes forward, and his words reassured her. "There's no need for fear. I would never hurt you, Lily."

The way he spoke her name sounded like a secret whispered only to her. It thrilled her, and instantly she felt her nipples harden into tightened pearls pressing against the fabric covering them.

He began his sweet assault on her neck, planting kisses in a path from her ear to her collarbone as he held her fast with his hand on her jaw. Gradually, the flick of his tongue was added to his kisses, exciting her even more. Lily was powerless to stop a small moan from escaping from her throat when he spoke again.

"You are so lovely, my pupil."

Before she could think of what to say, his body moved away from behind her, only his hand left touching her as he held her chin firmly. When he returned, she felt the warmth of his body press against hers and his free hand held something in front of her face.

"Lily, I want you to wear this whenever we're together. You may refuse, but if you do, there will be no more meetings."

Each word on its own was said in a purely seductive whisper, but the meaning of them together unnerved her. Would she never see him? And why was she forbidden from seeing his face?

For a long moment he remained still, as if waiting for her answer. When she quietly acquiesced, he positioned the blue silk blindfold over her eyes and fastened it in a tie behind her head. Then he released her face and moved away from her once again.

Immediately frightened by her newfound helplessness, she lifted her hands in defense to feel for safety in front of her.

"Don't be frightened. I'm right here," he said as he slowly pulled her to him, pressing his broad chest against her gently heaving breasts.

Lily waited in sweet anticipation for him to begin his assault on her mouth, eager to finally kiss him with all the desire inside her, but instead he only very softly brushed his lips against hers, increasing her need.

Parting her lips to encourage him to intensify his kiss, she felt his soft breath as he whispered "lovely" against her mouth before pulling away. Lily pressed her lips together and bit her lower lip in frustration. How much she wanted to feel his lips on hers, devouring her passion and giving her his!

"I have something for you."

He took her by the hand and led her away from the window. After only a few steps, he stopped her and gently eased her down to the floor. Unaccustomed to sitting this way, she began fidgeting and smoothing the front of her dress.

"Don't move. And no fidgeting," he quietly commanded.

She heard his footsteps move away from her but was unsure if he left the room when he opened the door. She sat still as a statue but fearful of what he had for her. Was it a gift, she wondered as she sat waiting for what could bring her pleasure or pain?

Five

The door closed and a mixture of aromas wafted across the room. Sweet and spicy smells filled her nose, along with other fragrances she couldn't place at first. The variety was pleasantly overwhelming, and she breathed in deeply trying experience each of them.

She sensed him sitting in front of her, but she remained still as he'd ordered. Her fear had faded, and now she waited for him to hand her a plate and fork to eat the delicious food he'd kindly prepared for her.

"Lily, have you ever been fed by a man who wants to make love to you?"

The effect of his frank words left her speechless, and she merely shook her head. Was he going to feed her before they made love? Just the thought of it was more erotic than anything she'd ever heard of, let alone done.

"Open your mouth," he said in his softly commanding

tone that made her wish they were already finished with the meal and moved on to what was to follow.

She obeyed and tasted something sweet on her tongue. A wedge of orange exploded juice into her mouth as she bit into it. When she'd finished, his lips pressed against hers, and he kissed her, slipping his tongue into her mouth and tasting the remaining juice from the fruit.

As he pulled away, he whispered against her lips, "Delicious."

She heard him open something, possibly a jar, and then he returned to her and ordered her to open her mouth again. When she did, he stuck his finger in and she closed her lips to suck sweet honey from it. Never before had honey tasted so incredibly good! Aroused, she playfully flicked her tongue against his fingertip as he slowly withdrew his cleaned finger.

Lily licked her lips and waited for the next taste she'd experience, but as she sat there, she realized she'd never learned the name of the man who was feeding her and soon would be inside her.

"What's your name?"

She heard him stop what he was doing next to her, and for a tense moment, she worried she'd done something wrong by asking.

"I'm sorry. I didn't mean to..." she began, but let her voice trail off when she felt his lips brush the shell of her ear and his hand encircle her neck.

"Kadar."

As his hand glided down her neck to rest on her collarbone, she said, "Kadar," repeating his name as if to

seal it in her memory.

Again, he kissed her, his tongue sensually gliding over hers and tasting the sweetness he'd just given her. His kiss, long and passionate, tasted better than any food she'd ever eaten.

He pulled away too soon, and she wished he would end his feeding her and proceed to making love to her. When he began to speak again, she sensed he saw the disappointment on her face.

"When a man truly makes love to a woman, it's more than just thrusting his cock in and out of her, Lily. To truly make love to her, he needs to show her he can take care of her every need."

As he spoke, his fingers lightly caressed her cheek below the blindfold. Leaning in to kiss her, he reassured her, "When I finally make love to you, every other need will have been met."

Lily wasn't sure how much more she could handle. Every touch, every kiss increased her arousal, as evidenced by the growing dampness between her legs. She was glad for a respite when he began asking her questions about herself.

"Tell me about your life, Lily."

Hesitantly at first, she began to explain how she's been married young but happily for just a few short years before her husband was taken by cholera. Overcome by emotion, both from memories of Jeremy and the sweet assault on her senses by Kadar, she began to cry.

"I'm sorry. I should be past crying by now," she said as she lowered her chin to her chest. She may not have been able to see him, but she was sure he was watching her and she didn't want him to see her face.

Silently, he lifted her chin and forced her to face him. Then, very tenderly, he kissed where her tears had fallen on her cheeks but said nothing about her sadness.

"Drink," he ordered as he put a china cup to her lips and tipped it toward her. Slowly, she tasted a very strong tea and its warmth as it flowed down her throat eased her.

"Thank you. That's quite delicious. What kind of tea is it?"

"Chai. It's served black with cardamom. Did you taste that?"

"I thought it was cinnamon."

"No, cardamom is sweeter with a spiciness. Like many great things, it's a mixture of danger and comfort. Like the love I intend to give you."

Lily's eyes grew wide behind the blindfold. So now they'd move on to the lovemaking like she'd had with Jeremy. But his description of love sounded nothing like what she'd done as a wife. There'd been no danger of any sort then.

Tensing, she waited for him to begin, almost afraid of the danger he'd mentioned but desperate for him to ease the ache inside her. But instead of undressing her, she felt his fingers at her mouth ready to feed her again.

"What I'm feeding you now is called Qabili Palau. It's raisins, carrots, and lamb with brown rice. Let it sit on your tongue a few moments before you begin chewing."

Lily did as he said and let the flavors of each ingredient

dance over her taste buds before she finished the helping he'd given her. Each individual taste exploded into her mouth in a mixture just as delicious as the previous flavors but distinctly foreign tasting.

"Did I taste pistachio nuts in that too?"

"Very good. You're quickly becoming my best pupil."

His words brought her back to the reality she should have known but hadn't fully admitted. She was likely one of many women he had. One of many women he treated like this. And not special at all.

She didn't attempt to hide the unhappiness she felt at his words and merely answered, "Oh."

"What's wrong with my Lily?" he asked as he ran his fingers over her pouting lips.

What could she say? That it bothered her that what had been the single most erotic experience of her life was likely commonplace to him? That she was embarrassed that she'd been so naive as to believe he thought of her as she thought of him?

"Do you do this often?" she finally asked.

The pain of hearing the silly plea in her voice was matched by that of the silence that met her question. How foolish she had been to return to him!

Kadar traced the outline of her lips and in a voice that couldn't have more perfect, said, "Whatever I've done or whomever I've done it with, it wasn't like this or with anyone as special."

Lily had never felt as wonderful as she did at that moment. When he fed her another helping of Qabili Palau, she made sure to kiss his fingertips before he moved his hand, for he had said exactly what she'd hoped to hear.

After he'd finished giving her the main entree, Kadar sat silently and Lily wondered if something had happened to change the mood. Before she could ask, he said, "What made you change your mind, Lily?"

After a long moment, she admitted, "I couldn't stop thinking of how it felt when you touched me. How you were so powerful."

"Is that what you want? A man to take control? To dominate?"

Even the way he asked it sounded delicious, and Lily closed her eyes to imagine his strong hands on her as he dominated her. But all this was so new to her. Would he force her to do things she couldn't? He'd said force was for brutes when he'd first touched her. Would he still abide by that when they moved past mere touching?

In a voice as unsure as she was, Lily answered. "Yes."

He touched her hair, wrapping his finger around a stray curl. "When you're sure, I promise to give you what you want. But for now, I want to give you something else."

Parting her lips slightly, she felt something like a pastry enter her mouth, and she slowly chewed the delicious dessert, savoring each bite.

"Kadar, what is it? It's wonderful. I'd love some more."

Feeding her another piece, he explained, "It's called baklava. It's made with honey, dough, rosewater, sugar..."

"And pistachios!" she said excitedly.

She heard the smile in his voice when he told her she was correct. Then he pressed his lips to her ear and whispered the words that nearly made her melt inside. "I promise not to do this or anything else with anyone else if you promise to return to me."

The feel of his warm breath on her skin was as arousing as his feeding her and then promising he'd only be with her. She prayed he'd give her some release from the need that was becoming difficult to manage.

"Yes. Please..."

"Please what, my Lily?"

Unable to tell him what she desired, she merely whimpered as he ran his hand up her neck to her chin. For a long moment, he held her silently, and she knew he was staring at her. Then as if something had switched off in him, he moved away from her, leaving her lonely and cold.

"Time to go, Lily. Take my hand."

Confused and her feelings a little hurt, she held his hand as he helped her to her feet. Almost too weak from unmet need, she stood on shaky legs as he guided her back to her place near the window.

Standing behind her, he whispered in her ear, "After I'm gone, take off the blindfold and place in on the chair. Your bonnet is near the door."

"Kadar..."

"I promise when you're sure, I will give you everything you want."

"Please kiss me," she pleaded.

From behind her, he moved to stand facing her and

bent down to gently place a kiss on her lips. So controlled, his lips barely brushed hers, but she wanted more—needed more. Arching up to press her mouth against his, she urged him to intensify the kiss, and their tongues moved passionately together. Lily pressed her body to his and let him feel her excitement. Her breasts pushed against his strong chest, the closeness only increasing her passion. In her desire, she reached up to encircle his neck, but he caught her by the wrists and held her tightly.

"Time to go. Come back Monday at one."

As she began to respond, he moved away from her and vanished, leaving her to remove the blindfold and leave on her own.

Six

K adar watched as Lily left, disoriented and confused by the abrupt end of their rendezvous. Her taste remained on his lips, and he licked them hoping to have just a bit more of her with him before all he had left were memories. The tightness in the pit of his stomach from the effect she created in him remained, evidenced by his swollen cock pressing against the front of his trousers.

He'd wanted her more than he'd ever wanted a woman. Seated in his chair, he stretched to release the tension of unfulfilled need. Closing his eyes, he let the memory of Lily take him over.

A knock at the door interrupted him, and he was forced back to reality as Akil joined him.

"Yes?"

"Master, will we be staying here or returning to the city?"

"I'll be returning to London for a day, so I'll need you to accompany me. Nuha can return and stay. I'll need to be back here for Monday."

"Yes, Master. Will you need anything additional for that meeting with Mrs. Norville?"

Kadar arched one eyebrow. "Were you eavesdropping at the door, Akil?"

The servant grinned. "No. I simply assumed your return to this house would be because of another meeting with this new lady."

Remembering his promise to Lily, Kadar said, "Only lady from this time on."

"Yes, Master. Does this mean you will need something special for Monday?"

"The velvet ropes."

Bowing, Akil left after he was excused and Kadar sat regretting his inability to daydream about his time with Lily before setting off on his trip back to the city.

By the time she arrived back home, Lily had run the gamut of emotions. Frustrated as she left Hertfordshire, she'd angrily pledged never to return to Kadar again. By the time her carriage had reached the halfway point of the trip, she had reconsidered her prior decision, thinking herself rash, and had pledged to return when he'd ordered.

But her basic levelheadedness won out over her extreme emotions so that by the time her carriage arrived at Frederick Street, she'd acknowledged Kadar's effect on

her body and soul but restrained her feelings enough to face her family.

As she entered the house, she stopped to listen to the newfound calm William's governess had created. In the parlor, he played with a puzzle quietly as Miss Allen looked on with a watchful eye.

"Aunty Lily, come look at my puzzle! Can you tell what it will be?"

Lily crouched down to examine what looked like a picture of a giraffe on the African plains. Teasing him, she answered, "Is it a hippopotamus?"

"No!" he cried with a squeal. "Guess again."

Pretending to examine it more carefully, she stared at the obvious neck of a giraffe and said, "Is it a squirrel?"

Both William and the governess laughed. "Aunty Lily, you don't know much about animals, do you?"

Chuckling, Lily shook her head. "I guess not. But do you know what I do know about? Wonderful nephews."

Leaning in, she kissed the top of his head and pulled back to tap him gently on the nose.

"What's that smell? It smells like something delicious. Did you bring me a treat?"

Lily recalled how delicious Kadar's baklava had tasted and for a moment became lost in the memory of him feeding her.

"No, but I promise next time to bring you some."

Walking into the dining room, she found Elizabeth arranging the table. Instantly, Lily hoped she wasn't going to have to attend another dinner party. Her emotions were under control for the moment, but she couldn't predict what would happen if she had to pretend to be carefree and sweet after what she'd experienced with Kadar.

"Elizabeth, you aren't entertaining again, are you?"

"Heavens, no! This is simply for us."

Relieved, Lily turned to retreat to her room.

"Lily, there's a letter for you in the hallway."

Her heart leaping in her chest, Lily wondered if Kadar had sent her a message. She quickly walked to the hallway table, anticipating what might be waiting for her. *Is it possible he knows where I live?* She knew she'd told his servant her name, but had she given him her address?

Opening the letter, she saw it was from Mason and relief quickly turned to disappointment. Of course Kadar hadn't sent anything. How silly of her to think he would!

The letter formally requested a carriage ride the next day with Mason, and as much as she was sure it would at the very least be pleasant, she knew she had little reason to decline. As Richard had said, he was a good man.

The next day came all too quickly for Lily, and at one o'clock, Mason promptly arrived for their official first date. Lily knew she should simply be thankful that an eligible man was interested in her. At almost twenty-three, she was no young girl and every day she spent as the widowed sister of Richard Scott instead of the fiancé of some gentleman, her chances of securing the blessing of a second marriage grew slimmer.

Not that she believed any of that. More and more in the recent days she'd become less the proper English lady she'd always believed herself to be. But what she was changing into she didn't know.

Mason took her hand to help her into the carriage and she felt his strength press into her hand. He truly was a fine man, and as she opened up her parasol to shield herself from the midday sun, she slyly studied him.

"Lily, the afternoon is yours. Wherever you'd like to go, your wish is my command."

"Surprise me, Mason."

"Very well. And while I do that, I hope we may get to know one another better."

For almost an hour, Lily and Mason enjoyed a beautiful spring day and the sweet conversation that's found between two souls at the brink of romance. For Lily's part, she began to find many appealing parts to the captain's personality and the recent events with Kadar slipped into the recesses of her mind.

Leaning toward the far side of the carriage, Mason uncovered a box of fine chocolates, each beautifully wrapped in its individual special foil. "Please, let us enjoy a chocolate. They're handmade from the finest confectioner in town."

Lily took a candy and eagerly unwrapped it to find a milk chocolate and almond treat. Placing it on her tongue, all the wonderful feelings she'd experienced the day before with Kadar came flooding back, and she closed her eyes, afraid if she met Mason's gaze he'd see she was far different than the proper lady he believed her to be.

"Do you like it?" she heard him say in a voice that sounded very far away.

Opening her eyes, she turned to face him and smiled. "Yes, very much. Thank you, Mason."

His smile in response reached all the way to his eyes, and her attention was drawn to their warm brown color. In the sun, it seemed like golden flecks swam in the deeper color, creating a very handsome effect. She couldn't help but think he was a very attractive man.

"What kind did you get?" he asked.

"Almond and milk chocolate."

"Oh. I prefer pistachios to almonds, I think."

"Do you?" she asked, pleased to find something they had in common. "I do too. But they're difficult to find, even in our empire's great capital."

"I know. I had them often when I was in Afghanistan. There the natives use them in many dishes, often as a topping."

"Do they? That sounds wonderful."

A long silence grew between them, and Lily was conscious of Mason staring at her. Suddenly uncomfortable, she let her gaze fall to her folded hands in her lap.

"Lily? Is something wrong?"

Her gaze fixed on her lap, she shook her head. She couldn't explain that just the mere mention of pistachios had made her think of another man, a man she'd never seen and who she intended on allowing to do things to her most would denounce as depraved.

"I hope you know I'm very fixed on you."

"Fixed?"

"Yes," he said with a broad smile. "I like you a great deal, Lily."

Feeling her face grow flush, she inwardly found

amusement that his innocent words could make her blush after what she'd done in the past week.

"I'm sure you know I look forward to a time when you'll agree to be my wife."

As he spoke, he gently placed a hand on hers.

"I'm flattered Mason. And please know I think highly of you. I just don't know if I'm ready to marry again."

Lily knew in her heart this wasn't entirely true. Despite not even knowing what Kadar looked like, she knew no man, not even her dear Jeremy, had ignited feelings in her like the ones she experienced when he was near. Kadar she would be ready to marry.

Mason lightly squeezed her hand and nodded. "I'm willing to wait until you're ready, Lily. I'm a patient man who understands that good things in this world often require waiting. And you are very much a good thing."

As she thanked him, she wondered if she was, in fact, such a good thing as she spent the afternoon with one man while thoughts of another delighted her mind.

Seven

Monday morning seemed to drag on indeterminably and as the minutes slowly crept by, Lily's anticipation grew and her fear lessened. In mere hours, she would be in Hertfordshire again with the man who lately took up more of her thoughts than any other person in her life.

Would he feed her sweet delights and foreign treats as he had two days ago? Would they make love, his strong hands possessing her as they did in the fantasies she rejoiced in nightly? Would he take her to even more fantastic and sensual heights than he had simply with his drugging kisses?

The wait finally over, she left shortly before noon to insure she wouldn't be late. Just as each time before, her trip to Kadar's house was made all the more thrilling by the mystery of what she would find there.

She'd specially chosen a blue dress, believing blue to

be his favorite color, and her most flattering white bonnet, which she hoped highlighted her brown hair. Everything had to be perfect.

It was enough for him to like her. She wanted him to feel for her what she now felt for him. She wanted him to think about her every day, wishing she were near him, wanting her kiss—her touch—more than anything else. Needing them more than anything else.

"Akil, I want you to show my guest to the usual room."

The servant looked up from what he was doing and his expression showed his confusion. "Not your bedroom, Master?"

Kadar let a slow smile settle into his features. "Not yet."

Bowing his head in obedience, the servant resumed his chores silently as Kadar delicately fingered the black velvet ropes, twisting them around his hands and wrists.

As Akil made his way out of his master's study, Kadar added, "And I want you to make sure there are pistachios in the room. Nuha had some for the baklava, so find them."

"Yes, Master."

Alone, Kadar's excitement grew as he waited for her to arrive. This time, now that he'd begun to earn her trust, he'd move her closer to submission.

He brought the ropes to his lips, kissing them as he imagined them around her delicate, white wrists, just tightly enough to restrain her but never hurting her.

The sound of her carriage arriving drifted in through the open window, and Kadar moved to watch her approach his home. She looked so sweetly innocent in her pale blue dress and white bonnet.

Concealing himself from her view, he watched as her deep green eyes, wide with eager excitement, studied his home's façade. How he wished to kiss her after gazing lovingly into those eyes! Soon....

In the short time since she'd entered his life, she'd became almost all he thought of, day and night. She'd enchanted him as no other woman on any continent had ever done, and he hadn't even made love to her yet. But his desires leaned in ways other than simple lovemaking. Would she agree and ultimately submit to his unique proclivities? Or would fear of the unknown stop her before he could show her the sensual delights he preferred?

From behind the screen, he watched her carefully position herself just as she knew to, back to the window and eyes forward as she waited. Carefully, she removed her bonnet and tucked stray curls into place. Something in her movements seemed so sweet and his body tensed, stopping him. For a moment he questioned if he should continue taking her to that place of pain and pleasure. Almost as if a sign to let him know the answer, he heard her whisper his name.

"Kadar, I'm here."

He silently approached her, already almost overcome by the desire to have her, and as before, encircled her neck with his one hand as the other held her face forward.

"My Lily," he whispered as he pressed his lips to her neck.

The way she leaned back toward him, melding to his body, told him she yearned for him as he did her.

Swallowing hard against his hand, she said in a shaky voice, "I missed you."

The statement seemed unfinished, as if she'd wanted to say more but was too timid.

Kadar ran his hand up the front of her neck to join the hand holding her jaw. "Are you ready for your blindfold?"

Her voice still shaky, she nodded and answered. "Yes."

He ensured her blindfold fit snugly and stood in front of her watching as she tentatively sought him out. When she found him nowhere close, she formed her mouth into the adorable pout he loved.

"Come to me, Lily."

Hands forward, she walked toward him until her fingertips touched his broad chest and she pressed her body to his. Looking down at her, he waited for her to present her upturned face to him to kiss.

He held her face in his hands and bent his mouth to hers, deliberately pausing just inches from her. He'd thought of little else than this meeting but reminded himself that he needed to go slowly so as not to frighten her. Today would ensure she trusted him if he proceeded with the utmost care.

"Lily," he whispered against her lips barely touching them.

In her desire, she craned her neck, desperate for the kiss he knew she waited for. Unable to deny her any longer, he greedily took her mouth, running his tongue over hers. Her lips urged him on to satisfy her need, and he began to lose himself in the warmth of her. A quiet moan passed between her lips and he took it inside him, like a pledge she offered.

Before she could try to wrap her arms around his neck, he broke off the kiss and pulled out the ropes. He placed them in her hands, and confused, she dipped her head as if to look at what he'd just given her.

Tenderly stroking her check, he asked, "Have you ever been tied up?"

As the velvet ropes sat in her trembling hands, she silently shook her head. He had to carefully introduce restraints or he'd risk losing her right here.

"Follow me," he ordered as he began to back up toward the couch. As he sat, she remained standing in front of him.

"Turn around, Lily."

Lily rotated for him and returned to face him.

"You look beautiful. Blue is my favorite color."

Smiling broadly, she fidgeted over her dress, smoothing it from the waist. "Thank you! I'm so happy you like it."

Her words were met with silence. Kadar sat back on the couch and gazed up at the innocent creature in front of him. Now it would begin.

Standing up, he kissed her lips softly and quietly announced, "I want to see what you are under this pretty

blue dress."

He saw her stiffen in fear and whispered, "I would never hurt you, Lily. Trust me."

"I do," she said softly.

Kadar made swift work of her dress and undergarments and in seconds Lily stood before him naked. His breath caught in his chest, and he had to restrain himself from opening his trousers and pulling her down on his lap to bury himself as deeply as possible inside her.

Astonished by her beauty, he muttered "lovely" as he softly kissed her, explaining, "I'm going to bind your wrists together. Hold your arms out in front of you."

Taking the ropes from her, he expertly wrapped them around her wrists, making sure she wasn't hurt. Restrained, she was forbidden from holding him.

Slowly, he lowered himself to sit on the edge of the couch and pulled her to him. Unable to hold back any longer, he took a nipple in his mouth and gently sucked, feeling the tender skin harden into a peaked point against the flick of his tongue.

Pulling away, he looked up into her face now full of desire. "Beautiful Lily."

He moved to the other one and began giving his attention to it, eliciting a soft moan from her. Just as with the other nipple, it grew hard in his mouth and he tenderly fastened his teeth to bite down, knowing he had to take care not to frighten her.

Cupping her full breast, he latched on and softly bit her nipple as he gently squeezed the supple skin around it.

"Ow!"

Looking up, he saw a frown on her face. "What did you say?"

"That hurt, Kadar."

He slowly stood and stroked her face. "You told me you wanted to submit to me, Lily. Do you?"

Nodding, she bit her lower lip nervously, and he knew she feared she'd done something to displease him.

"It's all right. But you will have to be punished now."

Instantly, he saw a look of terror cross her features. How wide her beautiful green eyes must have been when she heard she was to be punished!

"Please, no, Kadar."

Cradling her face in his hands, he felt emotion tug at him. Most of the time when he announced to a woman that he intended to punish her, he had to fight to ensure he was seated before they flung themselves across his lap. Lily simply stood trembling in front of him.

"I promise it won't hurt for long, love."

Reaching down behind her, he ran his hand over one cheek, then the other, loving how full and firm they felt under his palm. Then he drew back his hand and let it land with a hard slap on her skin.

Kadar held her upright as the shock of his slap wore off, leaving only the warmth growing where his hand had landed. Although he couldn't see her eyes, he was sure tears began to well up in them.

Gently, he rubbed his hand over the skin, soothing her. "See? Not so bad."

"That hurt!"

Again, he pulled back his hand and smacked her skin just as loudly. He knew she wanted to fight as every muscle in her body tensed, but with her wrists bound and his arm holding her, all she could do was bury her face in his chest and whimper.

He soothed her skin with the hand that had just reddened it, whispering, "Someday you'll ask for this, my Lily."

"Never!"

Holding her to him, he began to repeatedly spank her, ignoring her soft cries and pleas to stop. Each time he inflicted pain, he followed it with the loving caresses she needed to know he cared. Slowly, she stopped protesting and pressed next to his body, grasping at his shirt to find the closeness she craved.

Finally, she reached up to kiss him, aroused by the sensations he was inflicting on her. Unable to hold him, she tugged desperately at his shirt to bring his mouth to hers.

Kadar let her devour his mouth as she pressed against his swollen cock, grinding against it with her moist cunt. She was reacting just as he'd hoped — even more so, to his surprise. She was opening for him, her body begging his to fill her.

But he wasn't ready for that yet. Her body may desire him, but her mind still didn't trust him. He needed her body to convince her mind, and that wouldn't happen if he took advantage and merely fucked her.

He stopped the spanking knowing that one or two more would send her over the edge, and he wanted to prolong this moment. Gently, he stroked her skin with his hand, easing the sting out.

"That's my Lily," he cooed in her ear.

"Please, Kadar," she begged.

"How quickly someday has come," he teased.

She was so responsive that he didn't want to stop. But he could give her what she wanted and still be in control. Sitting on the couch, he guided her onto his lap.

"Sit on top of me, legs apart."

She did as he commanded and positioned herself on his legs, straddling him. His hands glided up and down her sides and over her back, carefully avoiding her still pinkened cheeks.

Just as she became relaxed, he landed his palm on her warmed skin, harder than before. She didn't cry out or plead for him to stop but returned to kissing him, her mouth desperate to express her need. Sure she was close, he caressed her and then slapped her skin one last time.

Then he waited.

His hand tenderly rubbed the skin and he slid a finger between her pinkened globes. Her body tensed and her lips began to tremble against his. Moaning into his mouth, her release began to take over. Her body sought his as she pushed her pulsating clit against his hard cock to extend the sensations he'd created in her.

Her reaction was one of surprise. "Don't fight it, Lily. Let it take you," he said as he pulled her to him and encouraged her to ride him.

God, he wished at that moment he was deep inside her feeling her body milk him to his own climax! He

watched as her beautiful body was wracked by shock after shock from her release.

Up and down she slid over his cock, still covered by fabric, until his pants were drenched from her. She gave in to her abandon so completely, and he urged her body on, squeezing her breasts as she came.

"Kadar...please...yes..."she cried over and over.

Her pleas excited him more, and it took everything in him to not strip off his own clothing and make love to her at that moment, making her come again and again. Her climax receding, she slowed her body against his, making long, slow strokes against his cock

That he'd given her what was likely her first climax without being inside her or enjoying her with his mouth made it all the better. Holding her as she slumped against him exhausted, he waited until she stopped softly panting.

"How's my Lily feel now?"

Her head buried in the crook of his neck, she moaned her answer. "Perfect."

"Would you like to lie down?"

"Is it....was I okay?"

"You were perfect. Open, responsive, sensual. What every man secretly desires."

"Is that what you want?" she asked as she kissed the skin near his collarbone. "Is that what the others are like?"

He stroked her hair knowing she was looking for reassurance. He wanted to give it to her. "I have no others now that I have you. And you're exactly what I want."

Her sigh told him he'd succeeded in showing her how much he cared. But had he succeeded in fully gaining her trust? That he wouldn't know until their next meeting.

"I think it's time you left. Your family will wonder where you are."

Nuzzling his neck, she pleaded, "Please don't make me leave, Kadar. Not yet."

Her voice touched him and he relented, silently wishing neither one of them would be forced to leave the other.

"Very well. For this, you can be the master."

He let her doze on his chest for almost an hour before waking her. The feel of her naked body pressed against his enthralled him, and as he listened to her sleep, he wondered if she would ever truly accept him for longer than a few hours in the afternoon.

After he dressed her, he sat next to her on the couch feeding her pistachios. Still blindfolded, she asked, "Why do you feed me?"

Placing a nut in her mouth, he explained, "I told you that for a man to truly make love to a woman, he needs to show her he can satisfy her every need. I feed you because that's how I can ensure you're not hungry."

"You don't have to do that."

"Yes, I do."

They sat in silence for a few minutes and then he asked, "Would you like me to tell you what I fantasize about when I think of you?"

Almost shyly, she answered, "Yes. Please tell me."

"I imagine lying back naked with you between my

legs and my arms around you as I feed you baklava. We've just made love and I've been inside you for so long you feel as though a part of you is missing when I leave your body."

"How I wish that could be!"

They both fell silent and then Lily asked him a question that caught him by surprise. "Do you make me wear this blindfold because there's something wrong with your face?"

"No."

"Well, you wouldn't have to." Dropping her head, she quietly added, "I'd love you no matter how you look."

Kadar was stunned by her admission and said nothing, which he knew made her uncomfortable as he watched her begin to fidget.

"It's time for you to go, Lily. Come back on Thursday."

She stood and silently let him lead her back to her spot near the window. As he untied her wrists, he kissed each of them and then her lips.

"Your bonnet is on the table. That's where you can leave your blindfold."

Kadar moved behind her and gently wrapped his hands around her slender neck. Leaning in to kiss her behind the ear, he whispered, "Next time I'll show you how much I love you, my Lily," and slipped behind the screen to watch her leave, already missing her.

Eight

Lily closed her eyes as the carriage slowly made its way back home. She replayed every moment of her time with Kadar that day, relishing the memory of each touch of his hands on her body. Never before had a man treated her as he had. Everything about him, so sensual and different, delighted her.

She adjusted her position as the carriage rambled its way over bumpy country roads. Her bottom still stung from his spanking, and each bounce of the carriage seemed to be a renewed assault on her body, without the exquisite sensations his had produced.

What had been fearful at first had quickly transformed into pleasurable, so much so that she'd silently prayed for him to continue his sweet attack on her. Each slap had increased her desire, and each caress afterward only made her more aroused. The sweetly potent combination of pain and comfort had made her want him more than

she'd ever thought possible.

Everything Kadar had introduced to her increased her love for him. Not even Jeremy had made her feel as he did. When she was with Kadar, every part of her felt alive, like she'd awakened from a lifetime spent in a numbed daze, finally able to feel and experience life so acutely.

The reality of her life meant soon the sensations she craved would go unfulfilled, subordinated to a life her brother and society would impose upon her. She would be a proper wife again, the epitome of Victorian grace and manners.

But would she ever truly be able to be that person again after her time with Kadar?

Lily began to despair at the idea of life without him. He'd become central to her happiness. How could she leave behind everything he was for any other man?

Perhaps Kadar could marry her. The thought of spending the rest of her life with him delighted Lily. As the carriage entered the city, she sat daydreaming out the window of a life as Kadar's wife and the sensual joys he'd introduce to her.

Lily's fingers traced the outline across her cheeks where her blindfold lay earlier and closed her eyes to remember the feel of Kadar's palm landing on her delicate skin. Never before had anything like that excited her. She felt herself run wet just thinking of his effect on her.

Lost in her memories, she leaned back against the seat and let her fantasies take her away to places where Kadar was hers and she was his. And the sexual part of her was able to be free.

"Mrs. Norville?"

Lily's eyes flew open to see the driver standing outside the carriage and peering in at her.

"Yes?"

"Is everything all right? We've arrived back home."

"Yes, thank you," she stammered.

Straightening in the seat, Lily gathered herself and moved to exit the carriage. As the driver opened the door, she looked up to see Mason standing on the sidewalk.

"Lily, how are you this afternoon?"

Her bottom still tender, she gingerly exited the carriage with his help.

"Very well, Mason. And you?"

"Delighted to see you again." As he spoke, he gentlemanly offered his arm to escort her into the house.

Taking it, Lily smiled and said thank you. This was to be her life from now on, and she had to accept it. Full of restraint and manners, Mason would make a suitable husband to her suitable wife.

It was all so...suitable.

Nothing she did, nothing she felt with Kadar was suitable.

"Captain Danvers, do you ever crave more excitement than what Regent's Park has to offer?"

Mason smiled and for the briefest of moments, Lily thought she saw a look of something resembling satisfaction in his eyes.

"I'm afraid I've no desire for more excitement in this lifetime, Lily."

Dejected, Lily nodded mechanically. "Oh."

They climbed the stairs in silence as Lily thought about the rest of her life with a man who preferred to abstain from excitement, audibly sighing her disappointment. As a servant let them in, they found the house empty of the Scott family and William's governess.

"Where is Richard?"

As Lily removed her bonnet, she explained the family had left to visit Elizabeth's family for the day, "Did he mistakenly schedule an appointment with you? He must have forgotten that this day was planned weeks ago."

Mason shook his head. "No. I have no appointment with him."

He found a seat in the parlor as Lily made her way through the room to find a servant. "Would you like some tea?"

Smiling, he said yes and she left to inform the staff. When she returned, Lily sat down beside him.

"Would you like to hear of my time in the war? You seem interested in excitement today, and I think you might enjoy the stories."

Lily plastered a smile on her face as she inwardly hoped Mason wasn't becoming like old Jeremiah Needham, full of war stories but little else. She might be able to withstand an uneventful existence, but one in which he became old Captain Danvers who droned on about boring tales of battles long forgotten? That she was sure she couldn't endure.

But Lily knew polite manners required her to answer yes, so with a smile she answered, "Of course."

For the next hour, Lily heard stories of the desert and the mountains, of battles won and lost, of bravery and treachery. Mason's usually genteel demeanor morphed into one of power and much to her delight, excitement. As she listened, she watched him with growing admiration.

Maybe life wouldn't be so bad with him after all.

Mason finished his story and sat silently for a moment before he said, "What I saw made me understand how much I wanted someone to come home to, Lily."

He lightly touched her fingers, stilling them against her leg. Lily was surprised when her body reacted to his touch, her heart beating faster. She looked down at his hand on hers. Its masculine power covered her small fingers but his touch was gentle.

Would he be like that as a lover? Thoughts of Kadar flashed through her mind, and she abruptly looked up, her wide-eyed gaze meeting Mason's. Snatching her hand away, she quickly stood up.

"I'm sorry, Mason. I'm feeling a bit tired. I hope you understand."

Mason stood and flashed a sympathetic smile. "Of course."

At the door, he leaned down and kissed her hand. "Rest, Lily. It's been an eventful day."

"Yes, I guess it has. Thank you, Mason."

Once he'd left, Lily made her way to her room, truly tired after her time in the country. She lay back on the bed and closed her eyes as fantasies of a life with Kadar danced through her mind as she drifted off to sleep.

Nine

Kadar pressed his lips gently against her nape and whispered, "Today I show you how much I love you, my Lily." He fastened her blindfold and then slowly slid his hands down her neck. She swallowed hard as he pressed his erection into her back, though he knew her reaction was one of arousal, not fear.

"Today I show you how a man truly makes love to a woman."

The gentle heaving of her breasts told of her thoughts even before she spoke. "Please. Yes. Make love to me."

As he had before, he stood in front of her to watch her. "So lovely. I love you in pink. Come to me, Lily."

Lily walked toward him, arms outstretched in front of her. As was the ritual, he let her reach him and rewarded her obedience with a kiss. While he enjoyed her mouth, she pressed her body to his to feel his stiff cock.

Her hands drifted over his stomach, but he grabbed

her wrists before she reached her goal. Looking up at him, she cooed, "Please let me, Kadar."

His erection twitched at her words and although he hadn't planned on this part, he would improvise. "Follow me."

Standing near the couch, he stepped out of his trousers and removed his shirt. Seated, he reclined back to watch her do as he ordered.

"Kneel next to me, Lily."

She stepped toward the couch and tentatively felt around for him. Her hands found his bare thighs, and she lowered herself to the floor.

"Use your hands to explore my body as I have yours," he hoarsely commanded.

Ever compliant, Lily slowly learned about him through her hands. Kadar watched in rapt excitement as her delicate white fingers trailed up his legs to his hips. Her touch was whisper soft, and she seemed to hesitate before moving toward the center of his body.

"Touch me, Lily."

Even more cautiously, she slowly slid her fingers to the V between his legs. Kadar stared in anticipation as she began to tease the nest of brown hair at the base of his cock. Her hands met as they reached the hardness of him, and she wrapped one ladylike hand around him, barely able to hold him.

His cock kicked in her hand, evidence of his desire and delight at what she was doing. She recoiled for a moment, frightened by the movement.

"Don't back away. That's just the effect you have on

me. Don't be afraid."

Lily returned to her position and began gently stroking him, her motions unsure but delightful all the same. Sighing, she moved her hand from the base to the mushroomed cap. "It's so soft, yet hard as steel," she said with almost a tone of wonder in her voice.

Reveling in the touch of her hand on his skin, he moaned and thrust his hips from the couch to encourage her.

"Go faster, Lily."

She obeyed, and he watched as each stroke of her hand moved him closer and closer to that delicious moment of release. But this wasn't what he wanted. When he came, he wanted to be inside her, buried to the hilt, truly joining with her.

Grabbing her hand, he ordered her to stop and undress. Obviously disappointed, she pouted as she did as he directed, and in moments he was looking at her naked body before him.

"Now it's my turn. Lay down on the couch."

Settled between her legs, he maneuvered her into position to get a perfect view of her sex. A dark triangle at the apex of her legs, it glistened with moisture. Licking his lips in anticipation of the taste of her sweetness on his tongue, he began to tease her with his fingers.

"Lily, has anyone ever touched you like this before?"

Shaking her head, she pressed her lips together as he circled her swollen nub.

"Have you ever touched yourself like this?"

To his delight, she nodded. Curious to know more, he

asked, "When? What did you think about?"

He watched as her facial expression changed to show her embarrassment. He wasn't going to let her off that easily, though. Removing his finger, he repeated his question in a far darker tone.

"I can't, Kadar," she whimpered.

Slowly, he dragged his tongue over her inner thigh, stopping just as he reached her cunt. Looking up, he saw her nearly overcome by desire. She'd answer now.

"Tell me."

"At night. When I'm in bed," she said on a sob.

"And?"

Lily hesitated, but the touch of his finger tracing her wet seam convinced her. "You. I think of you."

"That's my Lily. Thank you for telling the truth."

To reward her for her candor, he slid up her body and kissed her sweetly. Propping himself up on his elbow, he lay next to her and let his hand drift over her soft stomach before returning to where it had been.

She spread her legs wider, beckoning him to do more than merely teasing her. God, she was responsive! Everything in his body wanted to plunge into her, but he resisted the urge to rush.

Pressing his mouth to her ear, he began seducing her with words, both scandalous and sweet.

"My Lily, your cunt is so beautiful. Such a delicate pink flower, moist and opened for me. Waiting for my tongue to taste your sweetness."

"Your tongue?"

"My tongue. No man has ever run his tongue over

your cunt making you feel the way you did the last time you were here?"

"No, never," she answered breathlessly.

"Then I will introduce you to a brand new world of pleasure, my love."

Kadar planted soft kisses on her breasts and stomach before positioning himself over her dark curls. Closing his eyes, he inhaled and then licked his lips.

"So beautiful."

With his thumbs, he opened her silky soft folds to see her swollen nub. He gently sucked it, taking it into his mouth and slowly teasing it with his tongue. His cock stiffened rock hard as the first taste of her entered his mouth.

"Kadar..." she began and then her voice trailed off, overcome by passion.

He loved the way her innocence and desire mixed to create a sweet wantonness he hadn't encountered in years. She didn't know not to trust him and her needs wouldn't let her deny him, even if it occurred to her he could hurt her.

Not that he would. He'd long passed the point where he could be careless with her. She was everything to him now.

Slowly, he dragged his tongue over her tender skin, as his thumbs moved to stroke her inner thighs. Her skin quivered under his touch, and with each swipe of his tongue and lips, he inched her closer toward sweet oblivion. He grazed her clit with his teeth ever so gently and heard her whimper his name as she begged for more.

Sensing she was close to the edge, he slid his finger into her. She tugged at his hair and cried out, "Kadar... please...don't stop. Oh my God! I..." as she slid over the edge.

Her body tightened around his finger as she climaxed, her hands clutching his head to her body, as she moaned about wanting more. He lapped up her juices, as desperate as she to please.

When her body ceased its trembling, he returned to her mouth to kiss her and to give her the taste of her body on his tongue.

"Oh Kadar! I never knew a man could make me feel this way. I'm not even ashamed."

Stroking her cheek, he marveled at how she looked even more beautiful than before at that moment. "A woman should never be ashamed of making love. To bring you happiness makes me happy."

"I want to bring you happiness. Tell me what to do."

Kadar's cock moved against her leg as a myriad of thoughts of what he'd like her to do danced through his mind. The more adventurous ones could wait, however. For now, what would make him happiest would be the simplest thing of all: burying himself inside her and making her as happy as she made him.

Sitting up, he took her hand and pulled her to him. "I want you to come with me, Lily."

"Where? I have no clothes on."

"Take my hand and follow me."

Holding his hand tightly, Lily followed him up a secret staircase that led from that room to a bedroom

upstairs. He led her to the bed and sat down, guiding her to sit with him.

"What room is this?"

Kadar began to undo her hair, letting it fall in waves over her shoulders and back. "My bedroom. That couch is fine for foreplay but nothing short of purgatorial for much else."

Turning her face toward him, he kissed her softly. "I've longed for this moment, Lily."

Kadar pulled her onto his lap and she straddled his hips. "I have too. I love you, Kadar."

"Do you trust me?"

"Yes," she said with a smile.

"Even though you've never seen my face?"

"I don't need to see you to know I love you."

"And you know what I want from you?"

"Yes."

"You're willing to submit to me?"

Lily nodded. "Yes, I will do as you say."

Fisting his hand gently in her hair, he tugged slightly. "I won't ask again. If your answer is yes now, it's yes forever."

"Yes, Kadar."

Kissing her deeply, he slid into her. "Ride me, Lily."

The sight of her body taking his into it over and over as her dark waves bounced around her beautiful face almost overwhelmed him. In just a short time, she'd transformed from a shy Victorian woman to a woman who sought to please him sexually in any way possible.

His release inched closer and closer with each slide

into her wet cunt. The feel of her body joining with his, welcoming him into her, was exquisite. He could live forever just as they were now, one with each other. But the reality of their world forced him to question the consequences of their love. Grabbing her by the waist, he stopped her, burying himself as deeply as he could and then stilling both of them.

"Lily, if I stay inside you, I may make you pregnant. I'll ask once: do you wish for me to stop?"

"No! Don't stop!

With her answer, he released his hold on her waist and began to thrust deeply into her as she rode him. When he came, he held her tightly to him and filled her just as she came, her body milking his in complete physical ecstasy.

"Muh tú ra dost darom," he said in a husky voice as she went still in his arms.

"What does that mean?" she asked into the crook of his neck.

"I love you."

He opened his eyes and saw a tear roll down from underneath her blindfold. Wiping it away, he kissed her cheek. "Don't cry."

"I'm sorry. I've just been so lonely since my husband died."

"No more loneliness, my love. You have my undivided attention. I have no one but you."

Kadar eased himself out of her and placed her on the bed. "Stay here. I'll be back in a minute."

When he returned, he stood for a moment to watch her curled up on his bed so innocent and sweet.

She turned toward him and sat up. "Kadar, is something wrong?"

"No. Nothing is wrong."

He sat down next to her and kissed her softly on the cheek. "Do you remember my fantasy?"

Smiling, she nodded. "Is that baklava I smell?"

He placed the plate of pastry next to him and pulled her to him. "Sit between my legs and lean back against me."

Kadar wrapped his arms around her and fed her a piece of baklava, just as he had the first time she'd tasted the dessert. As she ate, he explored her body as if it were his to own.

"I'd like another piece, please," she said sweetly, her face turned toward his.

"Of course. Anything for my Lily. And you'll need your strength in a few minutes, so enjoy."

After licking his fingers, she asked, "Need my strength?"

"Yes. We're not finished."

He heard a small moan escape her lips. "You like that?"

"Yes," she crooned. "I like the idea of you making love to me again."

"Good."

Nuzzling her neck, he kissed her behind the ear as his hand made its way to the dark triangle between her legs. He stroked her softly and loved how her legs fell open to provide him better access.

"I love this...its softness and pinkness. The way you

moan when I rub your clit."

Lily placed her hand over his to show her agreement. "I love the way you talk about my body as if it brings you joy."

"It does. Every part of you brings me joy, my love."

Kadar continued to stroke her until he was sure she was ready. "I want you on your hands and knees."

He knew she had no experience with this sexual position, but her willingness to obey his wishes pleased him. When she'd done as he'd said, he sat up behind her, gently placed his hands on her hips, and leaned forward to kiss her.

"Lily, don't be afraid. This is just another way for me to make love to you."

"I'm not afraid. I love all the ways you make love to me."

Slowly, he entered her from behind, careful not to plunge in too fast and frighten her. Reaching around her, he returned to stroking her slick folds above where they were joined.

Lily tentatively pushed back against his body, his cue that she was ready. He held on to her hips and began to move in and out of her with more passion. He pumped in and out, his flesh slapping off hers.

Her moans filled the room, exciting him more. "Take all of me, Lily."

"Yes," she said in a whimper.

Kadar backed off from her body to allow himself room to slide a finger between her cheeks. With his fingertip, he massaged her virgin hole and felt her body respond,

tightening around his cock.

She was close. Just a little more...

With a gentle nudge of his finger, he breeched her virgin passage and pushed in slowly.

"Kadar! I can't hold on!"

"Come for me, Lily. Come now."

In the next moment, her body was milking his cock and squeezing against his finger, softly grasping and releasing. It wasn't long before his own orgasm exploded into her, flooding her with his hot liquid.

Kadar held her tightly to him, their bodies pressed against one another as each one took and received from the other. Never before had he felt so completely joined with another.

As he lay with Lily in his arms, her head on his chest, he marveled at how much he adored her. Never in his life had he wanted—no, needed—a woman like he did her.

She'd submitted her heart and trust to him. Everything he'd ever wanted in a woman she offered him. Now he wanted more, though.

Now he wanted her solely as his forever.

Gently, he nudged her awake. "Lily, it's time to go home."

"I don't want to leave, Kadar."

"The afternoon must end. But you'll come back to me tomorrow."

Kissing his chest, she looked up at him and innocently asked, "Will there ever be a time when I may stay?"

The reality of her life provided them the answer to

that question.

"You're a young widow. Has your brother chosen a potential suitor to be your new husband?"

Lily laid silently, her head above his heart.

"Your silence tells me the answer. But we'll enjoy one another until then."

Lily sat up and faced him, her blindfold still fastened on her head. "Is that all this is? Enjoying me? I love you. You're all I can think about. When you make love to me, I feel like you care about me. Don't you?"

God, how much he wished he could see her eyes, even though he was sure they were filled with pain at that moment. He caressed her cheek and cupped it as she leaned into his hand.

"More than you know, my Lily. No other woman can claim my heart like you can. I think of little else but you. You've enchanted me, and when I make love to you, I feel like I've finally found home. You are everything I've ever desired in a woman."

"Then ask my brother for the right to take me as your wife!" she cried. "Don't let another man take me away!"

Lily slouched, her shoulders rounded in sadness. Kadar pulled her to him and held her close. Rubbing her back, he whispered, "Don't be upset. Everything will end up for the best. I promise."

Ten

Lily dressed for her date with Mason but couldn't stop herself from reminiscing about her time with Kadar almost twenty-four hours earlier. The sensations his touch created in her! For the first time, she thought of herself as desirable, and she loved the feeling.

Fixing her hair in the mirror, she stopped as she caught a glimpse of herself. Something in the way her green eyes looked back at her showed a change in her. No longer did she present the appearance of the proper Englishwoman she always had. Something in her face told of her experiences with Kadar.

Running her fingertips over her cheek as he had, she studied the newly sensual face staring back at her and wondered if anyone else saw the change that had begun in her.

Noises from downstairs told her Mason had arrived. Lily took a deep breath and left the safety of her room to begin their date. Mason waited for her at the bottom of the steps and watched her move toward him, his eyes fixed on her as if there were no one else on earth at that moment but her.

"Lily, you look beautiful," he said as he took her hand in his. "I thought we'd take a walk through the park today. Would you like that?"

Smiling, she nodded, but in truth her heart wished she was in Hertfordshire in the arms of the man she loved and feared she would soon have to give up.

"That would be very nice. It's a lovely day for a stroll around the park."

Lily walked beside Mason as they wound their way through Regent's Park and the dozens of other local citizens there to enjoy the spring weather. The colors of the season showed in the pink cherry blossoms that hung from the trees and the purples, reds, and yellows of the flowers that lined the walkway. In the green, children played and an artist painted at an easel.

He could be painting her future. A perfectly respectable future. She'd move from her brother's home in Regent's Park to Mason's. She'd become the lady of his home — Mrs. Mason Danvers — and the mother to his children, who a nanny would push in a carriage along the very pathway she walked now as she stayed at home and planned dinner parties and other affairs people of their station attended.

Until recently, this would have been enough for her. But everything had changed.

Mason's voice roused her out of her daydreaming. "Lily, let's sit at the pavilion and talk."

He guided her by the arm to a bench inside the pavilion and sat beside her, his face the look of anticipation. She knew what was on his mind and prepared herself to accept his proposal.

"I'm sure you know how I feel about you, Lily. I've made no secret of my affection for you."

"I do know, Mason."

"Then you surely know what I'm about to ask. I know I'm not the kind of man you may find appealing at first glance. I'm a military man, trained to fight, but I swear I'm no brute and promise to take care of you for all our days together."

Brute.

Mason's choice of words made her moments with Kadar flood her mind. *Force is for brutes.*

Was it right to agree to be Mason's wife when she loved another? As Lily listened to him give his well-rehearsed proposal, guilt gnawed at her conscience. Mason may be exactly what he said he was. He may even be that brash man she'd believed he was when they'd first met. Whatever he was, did he deserve to marry a woman whose heart belonged to another?

"Will you marry me, Lily?"

Mason's deep brown eyes searched her face as he tried to interpret the silence that met his proposal. Looking into them, she found it impossible to tell him she loved another man, a man who had awakened feelings in her that would have to be forgotten if she became Mrs.

Mason Danvers.

Sadness tugged at her heart. Kadar would have to be forgotten also if she agreed to be Mason's wife. How could she forget the one soul who had touched her deeper than any other in this world?

But life gave her no choice.

"Are you sure you want me, Mason? I can be quite stubborn and willful."

A sly smile spread across Mason's lips and a sparkle she'd never seen before appeared in his eyes. "Stubborn and willful? I've never witnessed that in you."

"Well, I can be. You should know that before I agree to marry you."

Mason bent down to kiss the top of her hand and seductively looked up at her. "I'm sure you're exaggerating. Something tells me you are far less willful than you claim."

Lily felt her face warm in a blush at the reality she'd discovered with Kadar. No, she wasn't stubborn or willful but, in fact, craved the permission to be exactly the opposite.

"There's no need to be embarrassed, Lily. I love you just the way you are."

"Then I say yes, Mason. I will marry you."

Lily's guilt grew with each person who congratulated them on their engagement. Mason beamed with each retelling of how lucky he was to be marrying such a fine lady, while she secretly planned on meeting Kadar one last time. When Mason announced to her that he had an

appointment he must attend to, a sense of relief came over her. She'd be free to go to Kadar.

All the way to Hertfordshire, she wrestled with her feelings for Mason and Kadar. As much as she wished she could marry Kadar, the reality of her life dictated that she marry the captain, a respectable man accepted by society.

In some way, she did care for Mason, but those feelings were dwarfed by what she felt for Kadar. She'd marry Mason knowing that the only man who'd ever made her truly feel sensual and beautiful wasn't her husband but someone whose face she'd never seen.

In his study, Kadar eagerly waited for that day's meeting with Lily. Their last time together the day before had proven to him that she was ready. Not only did she desire him, but she trusted him. Now she was ready to explore his world.

"Will you require anything this afternoon, Master?"

Kadar's daydreams about what that day's rendezvous promised receded at the sound of his servant's voice. "Yes, Akil. Bring me the cat o'nine tails."

"Will that be all?"

"And make sure to brew tea and have it in my bedroom."

"Yes, Master. Should I show the lady to that room instead today?"

"Yes."

Moments later, Akil returned with the cat o'nine tails.

Taking it from him, Kadar excused him and returned to planning for Lily's arrival. Today they would explore their relationship in ways he knew she'd never even thought of, let alone experienced. Today's events would be a drastic test of her trust in him. Would she still trust him afterward?

The soft leather of the whip he dragged across his palm excited him. His favorite sexual toy, it delivered the perfect mixture of pain and pleasure in his hands. Just the thought of its sharp caress touching Lily's soft skin made his cock stiffen.

He heard her carriage rumble to a stop in front of the house and stood to watch as she walked to the door. These few moments in which he could see her eyes thrilled him each time she visited. The blindfold was a useful prop, but he longed for a day when he'd gaze into those expressive green eyes that at that very moment seemed so full of emotion.

From the doorway of his study, he spied Akil escort her to the second floor. Through the secret staircase, he made his way to the bedroom. There he watched her carefully place the now commonplace blindfold over her eyes and tie the silk strings behind her head. He hadn't instructed Akil to tell her where to stand, so she stood next to the bed, her hands on a bedpost for security.

Padding up behind her, Kadar spoke in his usual whispered tone. "How is my Lily today?"

"I missed you so," she answered sadly.

Her voice touched him, and he wrapped his arms around her shoulders. "Why so sad?"

Twisting in his hold, she turned toward him and buried her face in his chest. "Please don't make me talk about it. I don't want to cry."

Kadar gently rubbed her back to soothe her. "There. Nothing can be so bad if we're together."

"Oh, Kadar!" she cried as tears began to roll over her cheeks from under the blindfold.

Brushing away her tears, he said, "Shhh. No more crying. Tell me what's wrong."

"Please, no. All I want is you to make love to me so I can forget everything but the time I get to spend with you—my life, the expectations of everyone, what I'm supposed to want. I want to get lost in the world we create here."

He cradled her face in his hands and kissed her, desperately wanting to replace her sorrow with happiness. She responded as she never had before.

"Make me forget, Kadar."

The sharp sound of need in her words made him want her more than ever. Quickly, he removed her dress and undergarments as she tore at his shirt and pants to reach his bare skin. He fed off her sadness and took it from her as he worshipped her body with his mouth. As she moaned her pleasure, he trailed kisses over her skin, licking and nipping her breasts and stomach, all in the hopes of making the world that had upset her fade from existence, even if only for a short time.

"I love you, Kadar. Please tell me you love me. Tell me this isn't all a dream I'll forget when I'm forced to wake. I don't want to forget this."

He released her nipple from his mouth and returned to kiss her. "Muh tú ra dost darom, my beautiful Lily," he whispered against her lips.

"Take me, Kadar. Show me your love and let me show you mine."

Scooping her up in his arms, he placed her on the bed and covered her with his body. Needing her as much as she needed him, he fought to restrain his desire, but it was too great. He plunged into her, searching for that sweet moment of release they could provide one another.

Her nails raked over his back as he thrust into her, and her moans pushed him on to give her that moment that would allow her to forget the world. Her body met each invasion eagerly, welcoming him over and over into her.

"Kadar...oh, Kadar," she groaned in a voice that sounded desperate and sad.

"Forget the world. There's only the two of us. Let me take your sadness, Lily."

Like one wanting to push away what threatened the one he loved, he worked to force out all the things that had upset her, as if the act of making love could eliminate her unhappiness. At some point—he didn't know when—the physical act transcended every experience he'd ever had with women, and he was sure he couldn't stand to be away from her for another day.

When he came, he took her body with him over that delicious edge and for a few, brief moments, he knew he'd succeeded in making her forget everything but him.

They lay silently for a long time, still joined as one

comprised of two separate beings who longed for nothing more than to be with one another.

"You've changed me. I saw it in the mirror today," she said quietly near his ear.

Softly stroking her back, he said, "Changed you? No. You are as you've always been."

"I'm different now, and it's because of you. You've brought out something in me, Kadar. I crave the feel of your touch. I dream of the things you do to me, and I want more."

"You've always wanted those things, Lily. If you didn't, you wouldn't have come back to me after the first time you came here."

Lily buried her face in his neck. "Who am I? What am I becoming?"

"The sensual and desirable woman you were meant to be. The woman who threatens to undo the control of this man."

Lily crawled on top of him and moved to fit her body onto his. Wiggling her behind, she asked sweetly, "Control?"

Kadar knew what she meant and slapped his palm against her bottom. "Control."

"No one's ever done that to me before. I had no idea I liked it."

Squeezing both cheeks in his hands, he moved her cunt over his swelling cock. She was wet and open for him, but he wanted something else before he returned to that.

"Lily, I want to try something new with you. I promise

you'll like it as much as when I spank you."

"Okay. What?"

"I want you to stand on the floor and hold on to the bedpost."

Kadar saw a slight trepidation in her movements and hugged her from behind as she stood by the corner of the bed. "Trust me."

He grabbed the cat o'nine tails from a nearby table and ran the whips through his fingers. Standing behind her, he lightly dragged the leather toy over her hip.

"Do you know what this is?"

Lily stood silently for a few moments, as if she were trying to figure out what she'd felt move across her skin. Shaking her head, she said quietly, "No."

Wrapping his arms around her waist, he dragged it over her stomach while he kissed a trail up and down her neck. "It's called a cat o'nine tails, Lily. And when I use this on your soft skin, the sensation will be exquisite. Tell me you want me to use this on you, my Lily."

Breathlessly, she answered, "Yes," as she pressed her back into his body. "But please let me take off the blindfold. Please let me see you."

He knew he should deny her request, but he so much wanted to see her eyes wide with passion after that first moment when the leather hit her skin. Placing the handle of his toy in his mouth, he untied the ribbons of the blindfold and slipped it off her head.

As he waited for her eyes to adjust, he readied himself behind her, cat o'nine tails in hand, ready to introduce her to another part of his world.

Eleven

Slowly, Lily's eyes adjusted to the light and she saw the deep reds and browns of Kadar's room. The bed where they'd just made love stood in front of her, its dark crimson sheets wrinkled and disheveled from their passion.

The man she'd waited to see stood behind her with something he promised would delight her. She'd smelled the leather of it a minute earlier and a tiny fear had spiked in her brain.

But she trusted him.

"Hang on to the bedpost, Lily."

As always, she'd obey him, but she wanted to see his face before they began. She needed to see the man she loved. Like a child eager to see a surprise, she spun around to see his face for the first time and was dumbstruck.

"No! No! It can't be!" she wailed.

She saw him begin to explain, but all she heard was

the word "No!" screaming in her brain.

"How could you do this? You lied to me! You called yourself Kadar. Your name isn't Kadar! Your name is Mason!"

Slowly, he put the cat o'nine tails down on the bed and moved toward her. "I didn't lie, Lily. I'm also called Kadar by those I knew in Afghanistan."

"You tricked me! And don't talk like him! No more whispering. Use your own voice."

"I didn't. You came to me wanting what I had to offer."

Kadar touched her arm lightly, but she quickly backed away. Confusion grew in her as the look on his face signaled his hurt. How could he be hurt? She was the one who'd been deceived!

"But you knew who I was and intentionally kept your identity a secret. I'm such a fool! What an idiot I am! Letting a total stranger blindfold me and do the things you did."

Suddenly she remembered she was stark naked and rushed to regain her modesty by covering herself with her hands.

"I admit I knew who you were, even though I hadn't begun courting you. I wanted you as much as you wanted me."

Lily frantically struggled to get into her dress. At least being clothed might lessen the humiliation, she hoped.

"I didn't want you! I wanted Kadar!" she cried. "You're just the man my brother believes can take me off his hands. But Kadar was different."

All at once the emotion of the situation came over her and she began to cry, covering her face as she sobbed.

"Lily, don't cry. I am Kadar. Even though you know me as Mason, the man you know me as here loves you. Please sit down with me."

"No, I will not! And I won't marry you! How could I knowing who you really are?"

"You won't marry me because of my sexual preferences—preferences you just told me you want more of?"

"That's not what I meant and you know it!"

He was twisting her words and she wasn't going to let him get away with it. And then the entire truth occurred to her.

"Oh my God! Just how many pupils have you had?"

Smirking, he answered, "I don't understand. It was fine when I was Kadar that I'd been with other women, but now as Mason, it's not fine?"

Wiping her tearstained face, she screamed, "It wasn't fine for Kadar either!"

Gently, he touched her arm again. "Lily, I know it was wrong to deceive you, but I love you. Can you forgive me? I'm still Kadar in many ways."

Lily wasn't sure if she was angry, hurt, or disappointed or a mixture of all three, but she was sure she couldn't forgive him. Roughly, she yanked her arm away from his fingers and wrapped her arms around her body hoping to find some comfort.

"You lied to me. You let me fall in love with you, but it was all a lie."

Mason sat down on the bed and stared up at her, his eyes full of sadness. Nothing he could say would fix what he'd done, but Lily stood still, hoping he'd say that one magic thing that would make everything between them better.

Quietly, he said, "I'll apologize for everything, but not for what I feel or wanting you to love me in return."

She wanted to forgive him, to have him take her in his arms and hold her. But she couldn't.

Lowering her head, she looked into the face of the man she'd imagined a thousand times. "Goodbye, Mason."

He watched her walk away knowing he could do nothing to change her mind. He'd gambled and lost. Disgusted with himself, he wondered how he could have even believed she'd accept his behavior. What a fool he'd been!

Mason slowly dressed and returned to his study, feeling that already the house seemed emptier without her in it. Sitting slouched in his chair, his body clearly telegraphing his emotions, he tried to convince himself that this time was no different than when any other woman had ceased to be in his life, but it was no use.

Lily wasn't just any other woman.

A knock at the door made his heart leap in expectation, but when he opened it, he only saw Akil.

"What do you need?"

"Nothing, Master. I simply wanted to ensure there was nothing you needed."

Mason turned away from the door and sat once again

in his chair as the servant followed. After some time had passed, he noticed Akil still standing in front of him.

"Is there something you need, Akil?"

"No, Master. I haven't been excused and you haven't given me any orders."

"I don't have any to give."

"Master?"

Mason looked up at the man's confused expression but felt no interest in acting like the master of anything at the moment.

"We'll be returning to the city in a short while."

"Yes, Master."

Akil remained standing as still as a statue before Mason. When he met the servant's gaze, he knew he was waiting to comment on the events of the afternoon.

"Akil, you obviously require something, so speak up."

"Master, I noticed Mrs. Norville left in haste today."

Mason bristled at his servant's use of Lily's formal name. "Be careful, Akil. While you may be far more than a typical servant, you're treading on dangerous ground."

Bowing, the servant quickly scrambled to show his respect. "Please forgive me, Master Kadar. I meant no offense."

Mason blew the air out of his lungs in frustration. "I know, I know. You've been a loyal member of my household for long enough for me to be sure you meant no harm."

"Thank you."

"But I sense that you feel you need to tell me

something."

"Master, please forgive me, but you've forgotten who you are. You were given the name Kadar by my people because you were powerful enough to rescue my village. They may call you Mason in this land, but that doesn't change who you are."

Mason considered his servant's words and remembered the event that gave him his name. Caught in the middle between their country's forces and British forces, Akil's family and neighbors had been helpless to protect themselves against both sides' attacks. A little cunning had enabled him to rescue Akil, Nuha, and thirty others before the Afghan forces had overrun their town. His commanding officer had acceded to his requests to help everyone to safety, and Mason had made it his responsibility to watch over the two people who now worked as his servants.

Mason ran his fingers through his hair and closed his eyes. He wore the name Akil and his people had given him with pride, but in England, Kadar had been reduced to showing his power in the tawdry underground world of Victorian sexuality.

"Not all exhibitions of power are equal, Akil."

"Very true, Master, but one who has shown the power to do as you did for my people can surely persuade one woman to return to him."

"It's not power that's needed here."

Akil bowed deeply. "As you say, Master."

Alone, Mason weighed his options concerning Lily. Every choice led back to one ending: he didn't want a

life without her. And if that meant changing the way he thought about power, then so be it.

By the time she arrived home, Lily had cried enough to last a lifetime. Only when she'd lost Jeremy had she cried more. This was different, though. Losing a husband should affect a woman, but what she felt in her heart at losing Kadar seemed wrong to her.

Unless she truly loved him.

The truth of what she felt for him nagged at her with each denial she fabricated. She couldn't be in love with him.

But she was.

She shouldn't feel this emptiness from the loss of him.

But she did.

Lily dried her eyes as the carriage slowed to a stop in front of Richard's Frederick Street home. One deep breath and she readied herself for the outside world. She may be in love with Kadar—Mason—and she may even feel lost now because what they had was over, but she had to be strong because she'd meant what she'd said back in Hertfordshire.

She would not marry Mason.

"Aunty Lily!"

As she stepped out of the carriage, Lily looked up to see William and his governess on their way out of the house. She didn't dread seeing him anymore, but on this occasion found herself truly happy to see her nephew coming toward her.

"Come with us to the park, Aunty Lily. Please?" the boy whined.

Lily looked at the governess, who seemed to instinctively understand now was not the time for a stroll in the park.

"William, your aunt has just returned from her day out and could use some rest. Let's leave her be."

Lily smiled at the younger woman, not even caring that she probably knew more than she should.

"But I never see you anymore," William complained.

In truth, her nephew was right. Lately, if she wasn't traveling to Hertfordshire, she was spending time with Mason. The realization that, in fact, both activities had involved the same person struck her as she stood on the sidewalk and for a moment she became lost in her sadness.

"Pleeease!"

William's wheedling shook her from her thoughts. Lily mussed her nephew's hair and smiled. "I promise tomorrow we can enjoy the park together."

The boy's lips curled into a pout for a second, but just as quickly he returned to the well-mannered child he'd become and smiled up at her. As his governess expertly guided him toward the fun that awaited him at the park, he turned back and yelled, "I can't wait for tomorrow, Aunty Lily!" before he began running down the street.

Climbing the stairs to the front door, Lily reflected on the tremendous change in her nephew. In such a short time, he'd transformed from an insolent terror no one

could tolerate to a loving child she welcomed spending time with.

William wasn't the only member of the house who'd changed. Whether she wanted to accept it or not, she knew in just as brief a time she'd changed from the average Englishwoman she'd always considered herself to be to a woman who felt sensual and beautiful. She knew she had only one person to thank for her awakening.

Kadar.

Mason.

That was the problem, wasn't it? As Kadar, he was the one she thanked for introducing her to a world of sensual delights like she'd never dreamed of before. However, as Mason, he was the person she blamed for deceiving her and dashing her fantasies to pieces. That they were the same person confused and troubled her, throwing her emotions into turmoil.

"Lily, did you see William and Miss Allen? I think they were planning to invite you to join them on their trip to the park."

"I did, Elizabeth," Lily said quietly.

Lily's voice was shaky and she instantly saw the concern on her sister-in-law's face.

"Is everything all right? Did something upset you while you were out shopping?"

The lie she told each time she left to rendezvous with Kadar hung in the air, and she quickly answered, "It's fine. I just feel tired this afternoon. Please excuse me, Elizabeth. I think I'll just go to my room to lie down."

With Elizabeth's blessing, Lily climbed the stairs to

her room and sunk into the bed, exhausted from the day's events.

"Lily, dear. Mason's downstairs. Are you feeling any better?"

Slowly, Lily opened her eyes to see Elizabeth leaning over her, concern written all over her face.

"I'm sorry. Can you please tell Mason I won't be able to see him?"

Elizabeth stroked her hair and pressed her palm to her cheek. "Of course, dear. Can I get you a sleeping draught?"

"That would be wonderful. Thank you."

As Lily listened to Elizabeth rejoin Richard and Mason downstairs, she tried to block out their conversation, but it was impossible.

"Is she ill?" Mason asked, his tone full of worry.

"She is sorry, but she says she can't see you, Mason."

Lily cringed at Elizabeth's characterization of her as sorry. She wasn't sorry, at least not about avoiding him. That her sister-in-law had told him she couldn't see him exactly as she'd said it without the addition of the word "tonight" made her feel a little better, though. She didn't want to see him that night, tomorrow, and if she could help it, ever again.

"Please tell her I send her my best wishes for a rapid recovery."

Lily lay in bed wondering why Mason said things like that. "Kadar would never speak like that," she mumbled as she rolled over to escape the conversation.

As soon as she'd said the words, she silently corrected herself. *Stop that! Mason is Kadar, and Kadar is Mason. You can't keep thinking they're different people.*

Twelve

L ily was relieved to find that she could remain in bed for the better part of the next two days. Richard, like most men, assumed she was suffering from some female malady and never questioned her absence. Elizabeth may have sensed that she was feigning sickness, but to Lily's relief, she said nothing about it. Best of all, Mason didn't return.

Sitting at the breakfast table, she sipped her morning tea and absentmindedly flipped through the newspaper. The warmer weather had settled into Regent's Park, and bees buzzed around the honeysuckle bush below the open window. Inhaling the flowers' sweet fragrance, Lily closed her eyes and concentrated on the beautiful day that lay ahead of her.

"Are you feeling better today, sister?"

Opening her eyes, she saw Richard settling in to his chair to begin breakfast.

"A little."

"Mason was concerned about you. I spoke to him yesterday afternoon, and he asked about you."

"That's nice of him," she murmured as she returned her attention to the newspaper.

"I'm very pleased you two have gotten on so well, Lily. I know you were hesitant at first, but I think you can agree he's a fine man. You'll have a good life together."

Lily forced a weak smile and nodded. There was no point in trying to change Richard's mind this morning. She just wasn't up to it.

While her brother ate, she focused on the Times, hoping her brother would depart to begin his workday and leave her in peace. Her wish was granted just a short time later, but as she skimmed the Agony Column, she was greeted by yet another reminder that she wasn't truly free of Mason quite yet.

"M. misses L. and urgently wishes to reunite with her."

Lily closed the newspaper and sat back in disgust. Mason had posted a notice similar to that one the day before, which had made her nothing but irritated.

"Does he think I need to be reminded every day of his feelings?" she wondered aloud.

For Lily, the idea that Mason would use the Agony Column to relay messages to her — the very place she'd found Kadar — was too much. She'd kept alive the tiniest hope that she'd find a notice from Kadar one of these mornings that would tell her his longing for her was like hers for him. Instead, what she read were the words

Mason would use, at once flowery and almost officious.

But she knew the truth that Mason was part of Kadar and vice versa. She still loved the man, regardless of what she called him. That's why his deceit hurt so much.

Rising from the table, she pushed the paper away from her. She couldn't go on thinking about him, even if her brother wanted her to marry him. Today was the start of a new life for her.

"William, please eat your oatmeal."

Lily looked up from her breakfast to wait for her nephew's reaction. For so long he'd been so difficult, it was a habit to cringe at any request made of him.

"Yes, Mother."

Everyone around the table let out a collective sigh of relief, and Lily winked at him to show how impressed she was at his behavior. As she looked at the relaxed look on Elizabeth's face, Lily smiled at her happiness and congratulated herself for being the architect of William's change. The governess she'd chosen had worked miracles, and the child's transformation had changed everyone around him.

As the rest of the family scattered to begin their day, Lily took the time to consider an idea that had nagged at her since she'd seen Mason's second Agony Column message. Could she truly condemn him for acting one way in public and another in private?

Yes, he'd deceived her, but as both Mason and Kadar, he'd never shown her anything but sweetness and love. And hadn't she intentionally meant to deceive him as she

allowed Mason to court her while secretly sneaking off to meet Kadar in the countryside? That she never truly did deceive him didn't alter the fact that she'd believed she was and had been fine with her own actions.

The truth of the matter was that both had hidden their behavior in Hertfordshire, but it was that time with Kadar that she missed most. Each visit to his home had aroused something deep inside her she didn't want to lose.

For the third day in a row, she read the Times Agony Column hoping today would be the day she saw a message from Kadar. In her heart, she knew she would eventually relent and see Mason again. More than because she had to was because she wanted to. She loved him and could forgive him. But it was Kadar she truly missed.

Like each time before, she read the notices detailing the misery and loss of her fellow Londoners, feeling each writer's suffering with every word. Her heart went out to a woman seeking her long lost love she'd missed for decades and the man desperate to regain the love of a woman who'd left him for another.

And then she saw it.

"K. will see L. at his home in Regent's park at three today."

Excitement raced through her body as she savored the sound of each word as she read his message aloud again and again. It was a command, but its gentleness touched her, arousing her even as she sat alone in the breakfast room.

She would go to him as he ordered. She had no

choice. He was the man she adored, and he'd realized what made her happy. To have the private Kadar, she'd marry the public Mason.

Mason's Regent's Park home was smaller and far less secluded than his Hertfordshire home, but he needed to show Lily that Kadar was a part of him even in their proper London suburb. He'd tried to win her back as Mason and had failed. She didn't want to return to the man who wore the face of a proper English gentleman because society dictated it. She wanted the man who'd introduced her to a different world, a world he knew she craved.

So he'd give her that man.

At three o'clock she arrived, and as he'd instructed Akil to do, he showed her into the study. Kadar waited in an alcove and watched with a full heart as she positioned herself with her back toward the window, just as she'd always done in Hertfordshire.

His heart leaped in joy as he saw her acceptance of him. Quietly, he moved behind her as he always had, and wrapped his hands around her neck. He leaned in next to her ear and kissed her sweetly.

"My Lily. Tell me why you returned to me," he whispered.

She leaned back to feel his body against hers and swallowed hard. "I missed my Kadar."

The need in her voice sent a jolt through his body, and instantly his cock was hard. He'd missed her too.

This time would be different, though.

Slowly, he turned her to face him and looked into those gorgeous green eyes he'd waited so long to see as Kadar. He tipped her head up toward his and bent down to kiss her deeply, loving the feel of her soft lips on his. Drawing her to him, he buried his hand in her hair to release it from its pins. It tumbled over her shoulders, covering his hands, and he pulled back to look at her.

"That's how I love to see my Lily."

Shyly, she smiled up at him. "I love you. I know you must be Mason Danvers to the rest of the world, but can you always be Kadar with me?"

He was sure his heart filled more than it ever had at her request. No more would he be forced to indulge his fantasies with frustrated society women. Finally, he'd found a woman who truly accepted his desires and wanted to share them with him.

"Always."

Lily's wrapped her arms around him and nuzzled his neck. "Please make love to me. I need to feel you again."

Quickly, he drew the curtains and stripped her clothes from her as she worked to unbutton his shirt and trousers. In seconds, he lifted her to him, positioning his cock at her wet entrance and teasing her with the tip.

Kissing him desperately, she wriggled in his arms to force him to bury himself inside her. "Please, Kadar. Don't make me wait!"

Turning to his right, he placed her on the edge of his desk and carefully lowered her to her back. She impatiently wrapped her legs around his waist and pulled him toward her.

"Hurry, please. I need you inside me."

Looking down into those beautiful eyes pleading for him to satisfy her, he couldn't deny her and let his self-control slip away as he buried his cock in her slick channel. Her body welcomed him home with every thrust, and he reveled in the joy of making love to the woman he'd spend the rest of his life with. Bending over, he took her in his arms as they came together, each giving the other the acceptance they sought.

Kadar carried her to the couch and placed her between his legs as he leaned back against the arm. Pressing her body to his, she whispered, "Your fantasy."

"Exactly. And it can't be my fantasy without your favorite treat."

From a table behind the couch, he took a piece of baklava from a plate and placed it in her mouth.

"I love this fantasy, Kadar. It's so delicious to have you hold me as you feed me."

"I'm happy you love it. I want nothing more than your happiness."

Lily moaned her pleasure as he fed her another piece of the dessert. "Kadar, please promise me it will always be like this."

Kadar ran his hands over her breasts, tenderly teasing her nipples, and then to her stomach, stopping just above the juncture of her legs. Every inch of her excited him, and he wanted to spend the rest of his time on Earth exploring every part of her to take her body to heights she'd never thought possible.

"Your submission is a gift I cherish, Lily. I promise to always adore you as I do right now."

He slid one long finger into the dark triangle and teased her swollen clit before plunging into her. With his other hand he gently encircled her neck. One finger led to two, and she writhed in ecstasy under his control.

She was so wet, so open to him. Each dip into her cunt covered his fingers in her juices, and his stiff cock pressed against his belly, wanting what his fingers were enjoying. A few swift movements and she'd be on top of him, his cock buried to the balls in her.

But he wanted something else.

"Let's continue where we left off," he whispered as his fingers trailed over her inner thigh.

"Where we left off?"

Kadar heard the uncertainty in her voice but dismissed it. He wouldn't be much of a Dominant if he couldn't calm his woman.

Guiding her up from the couch, he stood her on her feet. "Stand here."

He slipped into his pants and reached into the desk drawer for the cat o'nine tails. As he did, he saw Lily reach for her dress.

"No. You stay undressed."

Coming out from behind the desk, Kadar saw her eyes grow wide.

"Kadar?"

He heard the fear in her voice but was sure there was curiosity and possibly desire buried underneath. "This will make you feel as wonderful as when I spanked you with my hand, my love. Now hold on to the arm of the couch."

Lily did just as she was ordered and Kadar positioned himself behind her. His eyes traveled over her porcelain white skin as he tenderly stroked her back and hips, slipping his hand over her bottom. Gently, he prepared her for the mixture of pain and pleasure he would soon deliver. Caressing her back and legs, he explained the ways of his world.

"Lily, I'm a Dominant and you're my submissive. That doesn't mean I would ever hurt you or your emotional and physical safety aren't important to me, but it does mean how we make love is different than how you and your husband did."

He stopped talking to kiss her softly on the lips and then continued. "If you ever become frightened, I want you to say the word "sweet" and I'll change what I'm doing. And if you ever need me to stop, I want you to say the word "apple." Do you understand?"

In a tiny voice, she answered, "Yes."

"I would never hurt you, Lily. I told you when we met that force is for brutes and blackguards."

Turning her head to see him, she met his gaze and he saw nothing but love in her eyes. "I trust you, Kadar. I willingly submit to you."

After softly placing a kiss in the middle of her back, he took one last look at her pale skin and flicked his wrist to bring the cat o'nine tails to her back. The buttery leather whips left their mark and instantly her skin began to pinken.

Lily's obvious shock was evident in her sharp intake of breath, but she quickly calmed and just as he had when he'd spanked her, he tenderly smoothed her heated skin with his hand.

"My Lily," he whispered as he readied the toy again.

Once more, he swung the whips toward her back, delivering the sting each inflicted. Lily's hands gripped the arm of the couch tightly, her knuckles whitening, but Kadar knew one or two more swipes would change her fear to desire.

He soothed the skin with his palm, stroking her pain into comfort as he sensed her relax at his touch. "One more, love."

One more became two and then three and as he'd believed, by the last time the leather touched her skin, she was almost consumed by need. Lovingly, he caressed her skin to sweet relief as she begged to touch him.

"Please, I need to kiss you, to feel you. Please, Kadar!"

"Turn around."

He forgave her for not knowing a submissive's proper role and let her take the lead for a moment when she pressed her mouth to his, so desperate to connect with him in her arousal. Her hands slid over his chest and shoulders as her lips and tongue took from his every ounce of pleasure he could offer.

"Tell me what my Lily wants."

"Satisfy my need, Kadar."

In a moment, he was out of his pants and on top of her on the couch, his body melding with hers into one. He entered her in one sharp thrust, their bodies joining in perfect pleasure. Her body clung to his, her cunt sweetly welcoming his cock each time as he sought that spot in her that would make her shatter into a million pieces. Her mouth devoured his, and she moaned her pleasure into him, exciting him more. More than ever before, he needed to satisfy her need to satisfy his own. When she finally cried out to signal her orgasm, he held her close to him as her shaking body dragged his own release from him. They lay for a long time in each other's arms, their heartbeats and breathing the only sounds in the room.

For Kadar, this was everything he'd dreamed of since he'd returned home. There was just one more thing to do.

In her ear, he said, "Time to go, Lily."

The look on her face as she sat upright was full of hurt and confusion. "Why?"

Kadar smiled. "It's time we found the vicar. We've got a honeymoon to begin. How does a week in Hertfordshire sound?"

Lily kissed him and rested her head on his chest. "Perfect. Will there be baklava?"

The End

Masquerade

One

1878

Annelisa concealed herself behind an enormous Oriental vase as she stood outside her father's study spying on the meeting that had just begun inside. She knew exactly who he spoke to. Her future husband.

"My Lord, it is a pleasure to have you in my home."

"Yes, I'm sure. Let's dispense with the pleasantries and get to the situation at hand."

"Yes, of course."

Frustration boiled up inside Annelisa. How could her father be so obsequious and to Thornton, Lord Sutcliffe, no less? Cursing her father's old fashioned ways, she struggled to listen as the two men carefully decided the particulars of her future.

"My daughter will make you a fine wife, my Lord. She's had an excellent governess who has educated her

119

well in many subjects, including French and Latin. Her intelligence is always cited as one of her finest qualities, of which she has many. And she is one of the most beautiful young ladies in all the county."

"Then why does she remain unmarried at such an advanced age?"

Annelisa blanched at Lord Sutcliffe's painfully rude question. To her, twenty-five wasn't an "advanced age" and the disdainful tone of his question offended her. And he had a lot of nerve to refer to anyone's age as advanced. He was twice her age!

"What I need to know, Mr. Fielding, is one very important fact. Is she a virgin?"

"My Lord?"

"You heard me. Is she still intact? It's of the utmost importance that any wife I take be a virgin on our wedding night."

"Yes, yes. I understand, my Lord. I can assure you that my daughter is still as pure as the day she was born."

"Good. Your family will benefit a great deal from this marriage, Fielding."

Frozen in place, Annelisa listened to the indelicate discussion of her virginity, part stunned and part furious. Lord Sutcliffe's claim that her family would profit because of her marriage was only a half-truth, and she knew it. Despite his title as Earl of Swindon, he was nearly penniless. He'd squandered his family fortune in risky business ventures and what some gossiped was a gambling problem. By marrying her, he'd receive the benefit of her father's substantial wealth, thereby solving his financial problems.

It was a situation common in industrialized England. Lord Sutcliffe had a title and some possessions but little wealth. Her father had tremendous wealth from his chemical factories but no real social prestige. The one thing that could remedy both men's deficiencies?

Her becoming Lady Sutcliffe.

But Annelisa didn't want to marry Thornton Sutcliffe. In fact, she didn't want to marry any man. While all her female cousins and friends had long ago found husbands, she'd been content to remain with her books and artwork. Yes, it was true that at one time a few years earlier she'd believed she would marry, just as it seemed every other young English woman did. Now, however, the prospect held no appeal for her, and the idea of marrying a fifty-year-old earl obsessed with her virginity practically disgusted her.

"Then we have a deal, Mr. Fielding?"

"Yes, my Lord."

"Make sure she's ready in a month from now. And I'll expect those payments to begin then also."

Before she could make a hasty escape, her father and Lord Sutcliffe exited the study, and she found herself face-to-face with them.

"Annelisa, you remember Lord Sutcliffe, the Earl of Swindon."

"Yes, Father." Turning to face the man she'd just been promised to, she smiled and feigned politeness. "My Lord. It's lovely to see you again."

Nothing could be further from the truth. As she

examined the man who stood sullenly staring at her, she saw a thoroughly unappealing person. Thornton Sutcliffe was short, pudgy, and appeared almost as old as her father with his salt and pepper hair and overgrown sideburns. That he had the manners of a barnyard animal made him even worse.

With a grunt and a nod, he turned to her father and began walking to the door. Disgusted, Annelisa watched him leave, wishing she'd never have to see him again, and stalked into her father's study.

"I know what you're going to say, but let me remind you that I'm still your father," Andrew Fielding said as he sat in the leather chair opposite Annelisa's.

"Then as my father, how can you marry me off to that...that....cur! Please reconsider, Father."

"You know in the long run this will be a wonderful thing for you. By marrying him, you'll become a Lady. And you'll help this family in ways I never could, even with all my money."

"He's odious! Did you see the way he reacted to me? He only wants this marriage because of your money. He cares nothing for me."

Annelisa watched as her father shifted in his seat and hoped she was getting through to him.

"It's an advantageous match for you, dear. It's not as if there have been many offers of marriage in the past few years. Lord Sutcliffe can provide you with security, social status..."

"What about love, Father? Is there to be no love in my life?"

Andrew Fielding grimaced at the truth his daughter refused to ignore. Annelisa knew she was being difficult, but if it took that to change her father's mind, she would happily cause him discomfort.

"It's not always possible for one to have love in a marriage, my dear Annelisa."

"Then am I to be sacrificed on the altar of expediency and usefulness?"

Annelisa saw she wouldn't win this fight. Frustrated and frightened by the life that lay before her, she struggled to hold back the tears. Unless she could change either her father's mind or Lord Sutcliffe's, she would be married in a month and her life of misery without love would begin.

"Please understand, dear. We can talk about this later, but now I have an appointment with the Russian minister."

Knowing this was her cue to leave, she rose and made her way out to the hallway where her father's appointment waited. Annelisa forced a smile onto her face in respect for Nikolai Shetkolov, the Russian minister who'd become close to her father in the months since he'd arrived on assignment in Britain.

"Good afternoon, Count Shetkolov."

"Good afternoon, miss. How are you today?"

"I am traded, sir."

Nikolai's face registered his confusion at her remark. "I'm afraid I don't understand, miss. I find sometimes my English is woefully lacking."

"No sir. I apologize. I was being intentionally confusing. I am fine, thank you. My father waits for you."

"Thank you. Enjoy your afternoon, miss."

Nikolai bowed in respect, and she returned the courtesy. He left her alone in the hallway with her misery, but she wasn't ready to give in just yet. If she couldn't find a way around marrying the distasteful Earl of Swindon, then she didn't deserve to be considered intelligent.

And if there was one thing she prided herself on, it was her intelligence. There was a way out of this. She was sure of it.

"Nikolai, you're a welcome visitor today—a respite from my troubles. Sit. May I pour you a drink?"

"Thank you, yes."

As he took a seat in the chair in front of Andrew Fielding's desk, he saw that his friend indeed did look beset by problems. His normally genial grin was absent, replaced by a furrowed brow and frown, and the tone of his voice had an air of melancholy.

Nikolai took a sip of his drink, letting the alcohol slide down his throat before he spoke. "What bothers you today, my friend?"

Andrew groaned. "Do you have a daughter, Nikolai?"

"No, I have no children," he answered with a chuckle.

"Be happy. And when you do, if you have daughters, don't indulge them as I have mine. You'll regret it for the rest of your days."

Sighing heavily, Andrew Fielding leaned back in his chair. "You've met my older child, Annelisa. She's a lovely girl, the apple of my eye. Maybe that's why I spoiled her. She's had the best governesses money could buy, but they did their job too well."

While his friend stopped to take a drink, Nikolai wondered how there could be a problem with Annelisa Fielding. Beautiful, charming, intelligent—she was exactly what any man could want in a wife.

"She's twenty-five now, although I wouldn't say that's an advanced age. But it's not even that she's still on the shelf at twenty-five. The problem is she's not what young men want."

"If I may say so, then they are blind."

"Oh, it's not an issue of beauty or grace. It's her intelligence. She's just too smart. I always thought she should have been a man.. As a man, she'd have the world by the tail. But as a woman...that's a different story."

Nikolai saw the frown deepen on his friend's face and knew his problems were more than a daughter with above average intelligence. Something more was bothering him.

"It's a father's job to see that his children are taken care of. You want them to have good lives, secure lives. Sometimes that means making difficult choices, but that's how it must be. So I've arranged a marriage that will ensure Annelisa is secure for the rest of her life. In one month, she's to marry the Earl of Swindon."

That explained why Nikolai had seen the earl walking from the house, his face in its typical full scowl. Always a surly man, Thornton Sutcliffe seemed an unlikely husband for a woman blessed with so many gifts.

"Needless to say, my daughter is less than thrilled

about the arrangement. She doesn't understand what this marriage can do, Nikolai. She'll be Lady Annelisa Sutcliffe. For all my success and money, I could never give that to her."

Nikolai sympathized with his friend. Many British industrialists felt trapped in a bourgeoisie status, millionaires with tremendous influence but never as high on the social ladder as those of the peerage. However, the idea of Annelisa bound to that bore for the rest of her life seemed a poor trade for a step up in society.

"And I have no answer for her when she asks me if it matters that this isn't about love. Young women today seem to think love is paramount in marriage. Silly romantics!"

"I feel certain she'll understand soon enough. As you say, she's a wonderful daughter and a smart young woman."

"I hope you're right, my friend."

Andrew sighed and Nikolai considered the marriage he believed was made just a few feet below heaven.

Annelisa lay across her bed, her arm covering her eyes. "Cecile, think. There has to be a way."

"You don't think father will do this to me, do you? I couldn't bear being stuck with an old man!"

"Cecile!" Annelisa sat up and glared at her younger sister.

"I'm sorry! It's just so awful."

"That's exactly why we need to figure out a way to

make the honorable earl not want me."

Cecile sat down beside her sister, puffed her cheeks, and blew the air out in frustration. "What if you became big and fat? Men never like that."

"In one month? I don't think even Pippa could make enough pies to achieve that."

"Could we make you uglier?"

Annelisa leveled her gaze at her sister and squinted her eyes.

"I didn't mean that you're already ugly! Don't look at me like that. You know what I meant!"

"I know, but this isn't helping. I don't think Thornton Sutcliffe would care if I got fat or ugly. As far as I can tell, he barely noticed I'm even human."

Annelisa fell back onto the bed in disgust. Cecile meant well, but they were getting nowhere. She was missing something right under her nose.

"Do you know anything about him? Oh, Anne! How could father do this?"

"I know very little of him, and what I do know, I don't like a bit."

"Other than his shortness, stoutness, and surliness, what else do you know that could help you?"

Annelisa buried her face in a pillow. "Cecile, there's nothing else to know. He's odious."

"Oh, don't cry! There's got to be something that will make him call off the marriage."

The two sisters remained silent until Annelisa sat bolt upright. "I've got it! I know what I have to do!"

"What? Tell me!"

"You must promise you'll tell no one, Cecile. No one can know what I'm going to do."

"I promise! Now tell me!"

"The earl seems to think it's of vital importance that I'm a virgin. So all I have to do is not be one."

Cecile leapt to her feet in shock at her sister's implication. "Annelisa Fielding, you can't! It's improper!"

"What's improper is that in this day and age a woman is still traded like cattle. Relinquishing my maidenhead is a small price to pay for my freedom."

"I don't know about this," Cecile said as she began to wring her hands.

Annelisa rose to face her sister. "I need to know you'll keep my secret, Cecile."

Her sister hesitated a moment but then nodded. "I promise I won't tell another soul as long as I live."

"Good. Now I just need to decide who will be my comrade in arms. Any suggestions?"

"You can't do that with any of the men we know. It would be a scandal."

Pacing, Annelisa nodded in agreement. "I know. There must be someone who would be willing to keep our coupling a secret."

"Perhaps you can find someone at the Stewarts' masquerade ball tomorrow night. There are sure to be many possible men attending."

Annelisa stopped and considered her sister's idea. The season's first masquerade ball would be perfect. Everyone would be wearing masks, and if she wore her hair differently, her choice wouldn't know it was her.

"But most of the guests are from our social circle."

"Not everyone."

"Annelisa, who do you have in mind?"

"Someone who is respectable, honorable, and best of all, soon to be leaving Britain."

Cecile grabbed her sister's arm to stop her from pacing. "Who?"

A broad smile lit up Annelisa's face. "He's perfect. I just hope he's not too honorable."

"Annelisa! Who?"

"Count Nikolai Shetkolov."

"Father's friend?"

"Yes." Annelisa saw the shock registered on Cecile's face. "What's the problem?"

"Do you even know him?"

"What do I need to know? He's an appealing man, always charming, obviously intelligent as he's a diplomat for the Russian Tsar, and if I'm not mistaken, he told Father he would be returning home soon."

"But isn't he a bit older than you?"

"Cecile, I'm not choosing a husband. I'm choosing a lover for one night to eliminate the one thing the Earl of Swindon believes is worthwhile about me."

"I'm worried. What if something goes wrong? What if you become pregnant?"

Annelisa cradled her sister's face in her hands. "Don't worry, dear sister. I'm an intelligent woman. I'll find a way to prevent that from occurring and secure my freedom all while keeping my identity from the good Count Shetkolov."

"I hope so."

Annelisa laid out her plan to her sister and secretly prayed she'd be able to pull it off. She had to.

Two

Nikolai Shetkolov arrived to the Stewart mansion punctually at seven o'clock. He found a scene as festive as any he'd seen in his months in Britain. Champagne flowed freely from twin fountains shaped like swans in the enormous dining room, and tables of fine dishes and desserts from around the world ringed the room. The Stewart family had made its fortune in the railroad boom, and with their considerable wealth, John Stewart and his wife Alice had traveled the world. Evidence of their globetrotting could be found on each overflowing food table. Nikolai recognized the dish of caviar on a far table and slowly made his way toward it as he kept an eye out for his host.

Everything about the Stewarts was big, from the mansion they lived in, to the superb chandeliers that hung in the middle of the dining room ceiling, and even to the man himself. Nikolai spied him making his way through the throngs of people who milled between the dining and ball rooms. As the portly man reached him, he extended his hand to greet the Russian.

"Nikolai! It's wonderful to see you! But Alice will be disappointed you aren't in costume."

As he shook John Stewart's hand, Nikolai searched the room for his wife. Equally as corpulent, Alice Stewart possessed a personality that many found difficult to disappoint. He, however, had to draw the line at dressing up in costume and parading around in a wig and mask as most around him did.

"I will do my best to make amends, John. A diplomat on assignment from the Tsar himself shouldn't be found dressed as a famous actor or a long dead king."

John slapped him on the back and let out his trademark deep belly laugh. "So serious, my friend. Come, let us find Jacobs and Josephson so we may talk business. We'll leave the partying to the rest."

After a half hour of performing his diplomatic duties in the service of Russia, Nikolai was ready to enjoy some champagne and the company of the revelers. As he stood filling his glass at one of the fountains, he recognized Andrew Fielding and his family entering the ball.

"Nikolai, how are you tonight? And no costume! Oh, the joys of being a bachelor," his friend joked as he shook his hand.

"It looks like you escaped the fate of others here, Andrew. You're still recognizable. Josephson is dressed as a sheik, and I swear you wouldn't know it was him if he didn't speak first. Your military costume hides little of you."

"It's very nice to see you again, Count Shetkolov."

Bowing to Eleanor Fielding, Nikolai said, "Pardon my manners, Mrs. Fielding. You look lovely tonight. As do you, Miss Fielding. But where is the other Miss Fielding tonight?"

"She's home, sick to death about her impending marriage to the Earl of Swindon, Count."

Nikolai struggled to stifle a smile at Cecile Fielding's candor and instantly saw the look of shock and displeasure come over her father's face. It was obvious Andrew's home life hadn't improved yet.

An awkward silence hung between the four until his wife graciously excused her daughter and herself, leaving the men to talk candidly.

"I'm sorry to hear Annelisa is still unhappy, but as I said yesterday, I truly believe she'll come around."

His friend rolled his eyes. "I do hope so, Nikolai. I hate to see her so miserable. When we left, she was in her room crying."

Nikolai sympathized with him, even if he disagreed with his choice of husband for his daughter. He'd seen firsthand the politics of marriage back home and secretly dreaded the day he might be forced to marry a woman merely because her lineage improved his own family's position. He should count himself a lucky man if he were to be married to someone like Annelisa Fielding.

"Excuse me, my friend. Let me rejoin my wife and Cecile. We'll speak later."

"Of course. Enjoy your night."

As he watched the room fill, Nikolai looked around at the women, finding none particularly appealing. Too many seemed the copy of every other woman in Britain.

How wonderful it would be to meet someone new tonight.

Annelisa's plan had been successful so far. It had been nothing to convince her parents of her inability to attend the ball because of her devastation over her impending nuptials. The distress on her father's face had tugged at her heart for a moment, but just the memory of his conversation with the earl cured her of any sympathy for his sadness.

Now, as she walked up the steps to the Stewart mansion, she scanned the entrance to see if she needed to overcome one last possible obstacle. She'd intentionally arrived late, hoping to slip in unnoticed as the rest of the guests enjoyed themselves, but if the hosts were still greeting people at the door, her plan might be dashed before it had a chance to succeed.

Luck was on her side this night, and she simply walked through the unguarded front door without a question asked. Now it would begin.

She saw him the moment she entered the main hallway. Much taller than most of the guests, Count Nikolai Shetkolov stood out with his light blond hair and chiseled features. Annelisa thanked God he'd chosen to attend the ball out of costume, solving yet another potential problem. Despite his stature, he wasn't the only tall man in attendance and if he'd been masked, she may have had to suffer through a number of conversations before she found him.

A quick glance in the antique carved and gilded mirror in the entryway ensured her that her white gown showed just enough skin as it sat off her shoulders while her shimmering white and silver mask covered the top half of her face perfectly. One deep breath and she was ready.

Casually, she approached him, confident her wig and mask concealed her true identity. However, just in case, she'd decided to add another layer of deception: she would affect a French accent, thankfully perfected through years of study of the language.

Perhaps I'll even speak some French if the situation calls for it, she thought, smiling.

He stood alone near the entrance to the ballroom, almost as if he were waiting for someone. All she had to do was make him interested in her and seduce him into joining her in some secluded spot nearby. Taking another deep breath, Annelisa willed away the butterflies in her stomach and reminded herself she had to succeed if she wanted to keep her freedom.

In her most alluring voice, she began. "Monsieur?"

He turned toward her and immediately she registered that he appeared different this night.

«Madame?»

«Mademoiselle, monsieur.»

«Pardon moi, mademoiselle.»

Annelisa was impressed by his accent. While his harsher Russian accent tinged his speech when he spoke

English, it was absent as he spoke French.

"No need to apologize, sir," she answered in a heavy French accent.

"You speak English?" he asked, his Russian accent obvious once again.

"Of course! We are in England."

As they spoke, she studied his face for any sign he was interested. In just a short time, she saw she'd piqued his interest.

"Allow me to introduce myself. I am Count Nikolai Shetkolov, diplomat for Tsar Alexander II."

Annelisa extended her gloved hand, and he bowed to place a kiss on the back of it.

"And who are you, mademoiselle?"

"I am the goddess Aphrodite, of course!" she teased.

Nikolai smiled. "No, I meant what is your name."

Annelisa had decided to use the name of a woman her governess had told her about—a French woman she'd known when she was a child.

"Violet Moceanu."

"It's a pleasure to meet you, Miss Moceanu."

"Are you enjoying yourself, Count? You don't dance?"

Annelisa watched him change as a stiffness overcame him.

"Not particularly well, my lady, but I will make an exception for you."

Behind her mask, Annelisa beamed. This was going to be even easier than she'd hoped.

"Perhaps later. For now, I prefer to enjoy your

company this way."

She watched as relief washed over him and his body relaxed. "I think I'd like to take a walk outside for some fresh air. Would you care to join me?"

"Absolutely, Miss Moceanu."

Taking her arm in his, he guided her through the library to the outside. As they strolled around the well-manicured Italian gardens famous to the Stewart mansion, they made conversation while Annelisa's eyes scanned the area for the place she'd bring her plan to fruition.

Just the way he spoke to her as if she were an intelligent being impressed her. She'd made a good choice in Nikolai, but as they continued to walk the mansion's grounds, she worried he might be a little too respectful to do what she needed him to do.

Subtly, she began stroking his arm with her free hand and then slid her gloved fingers inside his sleeve to touch his wrist. Even through the fabric, she felt the heat of his skin and sensed his pulse quicken as they continued their conversation.

She was sure he was interested. Now if she could induce him to make a move, she'd willingly oblige him and achieve her goal.

Stopping behind a large hedge out of the view of the other partygoers, she looked up at him and moistened her lips. Fear thrummed in her veins as she waited for him to act on her signals. What if he was too honorable to help her complete her plan? For a long moment, she wondered if she would fail as the thought of marrying

Thornton Sutcliffe made her heart sink.

Nikolai touched her mask and she quickly grabbed his hand to stop him.

"No."

"How am I to give you what you've been telling me you want if I can't see your face?"

"The mask must stay."

Despite his obvious confusion, her requirement didn't deter him. Gently, he pressed his lips to hers and kissed her. Annelisa's heart pounded against her chest at the thought that this was her first real kiss. Suddenly, fear raced through her. Was she doing it correctly? Would he know she was inexperienced in this, and therefore, in what she hoped would follow and end their tryst prematurely?

As she worried about these things, Nikolai dropped his head to her neck and softly planted kisses near her collarbone. In a hoarse voice, he whispered, "Moya milaya" against her skin.

The effect of his kisses surprised her, and an unfamiliar ache began to throb inside her. She pulled his head closer to her, weaving her fingers in his thick hair, and pushed her body to his, only intensifying the ache inside.

Each touch of his lips, each dart of his tongue against her skin excited her more. Her effect on him seemed equally arousing, if she was judging correctly the hardness that pressed against her body.

Sure she couldn't withstand much more, she pulled him back up to kiss him and timidly, out of curiosity, stroked her hand over his pants where her fingers felt his hardened cock. Suddenly, fear paralyzed her. What waited for her beneath his trousers—what would soon take her all-too-important virginity—felt enormous under her fingertips.

He whispered "Moya milaya" again, this time in a voice edged with need.

"Yes."

Annelisa wasn't sure what to say. It seemed that every bit of intelligence she so prided herself on had evaporated from her mind, leaving only a strange mixture of fear and desire to guide her.

His hands moved quickly to lift her dress, and at the first touch of his fingers on her thighs, the breath caught in her throat. His kisses stole the air from her, and she felt lightheaded. In seconds, he moved his hand to between her legs, cupped her sex with his palm, and groaned.

"Unfasten my trousers and use your hand on me."

Annelisa followed his order without a thought and soon had her fingers around him. Just touching his erection, with its hardness of steel but the softness of silk, took her breath away once again. Unsure, she slid her fingers over its top and felt a dampness.

As she reveled in the experience of his stiff cock in her hand and the effect her movements had on him, he slid a finger through her sex past a place she would have begged him to touch again if she could speak or even think clearly.

"Oh," she moaned against his lips.

"You like that? Do you like this?"

As the last word left his lips, he slid his finger into

her and began gently stroking its tip against her virginal walls. The invasion, coupled with the gentle circling of his thumb on the spot he'd touched before, sent waves of pleasure through her.

Frantically, she tugged at his hair near his nape as he continued his sweet assault. Nothing she'd experienced before in her life had ever made her feel like this. Her legs felt like they hadn't the strength to keep her standing if his strong arms released her. Every stroke of his finger made her want more—more of him, more of this.

She wanted to make him feel as good, so she became bolder in her touch, running her hand the full length of him from base to tip. With each stroke, his kisses became more passionate, more desperate for her.

Finally, he slid his finger out of her and tore her hand from him. "Violet..." he groaned and lifted her onto his cock. Holding her to him, he slowly pushed into her tight body, taking what another man prized above all else about her.

He filled her completely and stilled to allow her body to stretch as it took him all in. When her body relaxed around him, he retreated from her only to plunge into her again and again. Each thrust was accompanied by a grunt that seemed to come from deep inside him.

Annelisa held him tightly, her hands pressed against the back of his neck, as he rode her for what seemed like forever. She'd prepared herself for this—she'd read as much as she could find about sex, memorizing names and positions along with every physical detail and description books had offered.

But nothing had made her ready for what her body was experiencing.

Nikolai panted next to her ear as every thrust into her inched him closer to release. Frantically, Annelisa remembered she hadn't taken any precautions against pregnancy. She squirmed and bucked against him to release herself from his hold, but this only seemed to increase his passion.

"No!" She couldn't let him finish inside her!

"Yes," he groaned as he pulled her tightly to him. "Yes, yes..." he said as he plunged into her for the last time before he stopped and buried his face in the crook of her neck.

Annelisa felt the hot liquid flood her insides as his cock pulsated inside her. She'd done it. She'd lost her virginity and ensured her freedom from a loveless marriage to the dreadful Earl of Swindon.

But now she had to accept the very real fact that she may have just allowed Nikolai to impregnate her, sealing her fate once again. For if she were with child, she would be forced to reveal her deceit and marry him.

For all her intelligence, she hadn't planned on this.

Tenderly, he kissed her while he pulled out of her. Placing her on the ground, he covered himself and then reached for her mask.

"Now I must see my love's face after what we've just done."

"No!" she cried as she turned to run away.

Nikolai caught her by the hand to hold her, but as he grabbed her, she slid her fingers out of her glove and fled. She turned back once to see him still watching her, stunned that the woman he'd just made love to was running away.

By the time Annelisa arrived at her carriage, she was out of breath, her head spinning. She'd accomplished what she'd set out to do, but she feared she may have gotten more than what she'd bargained for.

Three

"Tell me everything!" Cecile whined as she climbed into bed across from her sister. "I've wondered all night."

"First, tell me if Father or Mother suspected anything."

"Nothing. Father is upset that you're not happy, but I heard neither of them say a thing about you all night, even when Count Shetkolov asked about your absence. I made sure to mention how devastated you were about the marriage, just as you said to."

Annelisa smiled. At least that part of her plan had succeeded.

"Now tell me!"

"Everything went just as I planned," she lied. "I arrived and immediately saw him standing alone. It was like fate was smiling her favor on me."

"You know, Annelisa. I studied him carefully tonight. He's quite attractive with those pale blue eyes of his."

"Cecile, we're not engaged. Stop talking like he's taken the earl's place."

"Did I say that? I just noticed he's very handsome."

Annelisa shrugged. "Be that as it may, it matters none to me."

"Fine. Then tell me what happened next."

"I began speaking to him in French, and he responded in French but with no Russian accent. It's strange, but he sounds entirely different when he's not speaking English. There was no hint of his accent at all."

"Really?"

"Yes. Then I got him to join me outside in the garden where we walked and talked."

"What did you talk about?"

"Many things. He's quite intelligent, and I think he found me to be the same. We discussed the Stewarts' Italian garden. He told me about some real Italian gardens he saw when he lived in Rome as the Russian attaché to Italy a few years ago. He says the Stewarts' garden is very authentic looking."

Realizing how dreamily she sounded as she recalled their talk, Annelisa quickly changed the subject. "Then I gave him the signal that I was interested in more than simple talking."

Cecile's face expressed a combination of fear and curiosity. "What did you do?"

"I slid my hand underneath his coat and shirt cuff and caressed his arm."

"Oh, Anne! I can't believe what you're telling me! You're so brazen!"

"Not brazen. Brave. Father and the earl gave me no choice. I had to be fearless if I were to keep my freedom."

"So then what happened? I can barely wait to hear!"

Annelisa frowned and put her finger to her mouth. "Shhh. Lower your voice. I don't need Father or Mother hearing this."

Cecile took her sister's hands in hers and squeezed. "I'm sorry. You're right. It's just that I can't help myself. This is more exciting than anything I've ever heard."

"So after I let him know I was interested in more from him, we did it."

Annelisa sat back on her elbows and watched her sister's face change from curious to shocked.

"Did it? Tell me! There has to be more to sex than simply calling it IT."

As she listened to her younger sister's plea, she wondered how much she should tell her. Their mother had never told either of her daughters anything about sex. Prim and proper, Eleanor Fielding was the definition of old-fashioned. Annelisa couldn't imagine her even thinking of doing what she and Nikolai had done just hours earlier.

Everything she and Cecile knew about what a man and woman did in bed—or in the garden—together had been gleaned from books she kept carefully hidden away. Cecile had always been a less interested student of their knowledge, Annelisa suspected out of fear, so she knew even less.

How much should she tell her? Should she go into detail about how painful the experience had been while at the same time creating the most delicious sensations in her?

"Annelisa, you promised. How am I to know about these things if you don't tell me? Father's certain to see me married any day since I'm nineteen now. I need to know what to do."

"Okay, but don't get frightened. I'm sure it's much better between a man and woman who are in love...and in a bed. He touched me down there with his fingers, and it felt wonderful."

Annelisa felt foolish calling it "down there," but something told her it had been the graphic terms pussy and cunt found in her books that had caused Cecile to turn away from them.

Her sister's eyes grew as wide as saucers. She stammered, "Down there? With his fingers? Wonderful? Really?"

"Yes. It was wonderful."

"What about when he put his thing in you?"

Annelisa chuckled. She'd call female parts "down there," but she drew the line at calling his a thing. "Cecile, it's a cock. Or a prick, if you prefer."

Cecile waved her hands as if to make the two words her sister had said go away. "Whatever. How did that feel? Was it wonderful too?"

Annelisa sat up. "Not exactly. It was a bit painful, just as I read it would be."

She'd also read an average man was around five to six inches in length and easily encircled by a woman's hand. Obviously, Nikolai was an above average man, she concluded.

"But you feel fine now?"

Quickly, Annelisa sought to allay her fears. "Yes, I'm fine now. Best of all, Cecile, I'll be released from the dread of a marriage to Thornton Sutcliffe, the Earl of Swindon, and remain a free woman—a woman who can choose if and when she'll be married and to whom."

"How will you face the count when he comes to the house again knowing what the two of you did?"

Annelisa lay back on the bed. Facing him would be easy. He had no idea the woman he'd made love to was anyone other than a Frenchwoman named Violet Moceanu.

"Only I know. He doesn't even know what the woman looked like. I never took my mask off, so it won't be a problem."

Cecile fell onto the bed and hugged her sister tightly. "Oh, Annelisa! You're so brave. I don't know how you did it. I could never be like that."

"Yes, you could. And if father tries to marry you off to some old man you don't love, we'll just have to do the same for you. I won't let him do that to you."

Cecile sat up, her face full of terror. "Oh, no! What if he tries to marry me to that awful Earl of Swindon now?"

Annelisa patted her on the knee. "The earl won't want to have anything to do with either of us when he realizes my precious virginity has been taken. Even if he did, we'd just find you your own Nikolai to solve that problem."

Cecile calmed down and kissed her goodnight. "I

love you, Annelisa. If only I could be as clever as you."

Smiling, Annelisa hoped she had been as clever as her sister believed. For now, though, she'd revel in her victory over old fashioned paternalism and worry about everything else later.

By noon the next day, Annelisa was eager to give her father the news of her deflowering. She'd accepted that he would be furious, but the prospect of a loveless marriage to a man twice her age was much worse than the temporary anger of a father.

Business kept Andrew Fielding out of the house until mid-afternoon, but soon he was back in his study and she had to wait no longer.

Peeking her head into the room, she smiled at him as he sat behind his desk. "May I speak to you, Father?"

Andrew Fielding's face lit up in happiness. "Of course, Annelisa. Please come in."

She took a seat across from him and smiled in return. "Thank you, Father."

As he began to speak, he reached over the desk and took her hands in his. "Annelisa, I know you've been very cross with me, but I'd like to explain why your marriage to the earl is so important."

"That's what..."

Her father cut her off and continued. "Dear, I've worked very hard in my life and in many ways I've achieved great success. I can provide for your mother, sister, and you in ways most of my countrymen can only dream of."

"Yes, I know, but..."

"I can ensure we have a beautiful home, the best carriages, and the finest clothes. My success has allowed me to hire the best governesses for you and Cecile, and you've received the finest education money can buy. Do you realize there are many young men who can't say they've received the education you girls have?"

"Yes, Father. But I..."

"But there are things that will always be out of my reach, no matter how wealthy or successful I am. I want to see you and your sister securely married. Cecile I worry less about, but you're twenty-five now, and your choices are fewer. I don't agree with that, but this is the way of the world."

Annelisa saw there was no point in interrupting her father again. He needed to explain his reasons for wanting her to tolerate a life without love married to a man who couldn't even be bothered to feign kindness toward her in front of her own father. What she needed to say would have to wait.

"I know the Earl of Swindon is a bit mature, but he can give you something—give this family something—I never can. You will be Lady Annelisa Sutcliffe. You may not see the importance of this now, but when the earl's titles pass to your sons, you will see how my choices today made life better for this family for generations to come."

The thought of doing what she'd done with Nikolai with Thornton Sutcliffe made her stomach turn. She could only imagine how terrible it would be to have that callous oaf on top of her as she closed her eyes to block out the sight of his old face and body. There would be no French, no gentle kissing of her neck, no gazing into pale blue eyes the color of the sky.

"I understand some of this is my fault, Annelisa. I've spoiled both you girls, but you even more. Maybe if I hadn't been so successful you'd understand the value of what a marriage to a man like the earl offers."

Annelisa felt any guilt she'd had about what she'd tell her father quickly evaporate now. So she had no right to expect love or respect from the man she'd marry and because she did expect these things she was spoiled? She knew exactly what the value of her marriage to the Earl of Swindon was. He would receive a great deal of her father's money to stave off his near bankruptcy, and her father would gain from the earl what he'd never been able to obtain on his own—a much higher social position.

That she'd gain nothing and lose everything she held dear meant nothing to either of them, it appeared.

"So I'm very pleased to see your mood has improved from last night, my dear. What did you want to discuss with me?"

Annelisa forgot about everything she'd practiced that morning to say to her father. The words "spoiled" and "value" rang in her ears, infuriating her.

"Well, Father, I am in a much better mood today, but not because I've accepted marriage to Thornton Sutcliffe. I still have no interest in marrying some old man who shows no interest in my current or future happiness. I don't care if he's an earl, or a duke, or Queen Victoria's brother! I don't want to marry anyone, but especially the wretched Earl of Swindon. And if I do ever marry someone, it will be because I love him and he loves me."

Andrew Fielding grimaced as he sat back in his chair. "I had hoped you'd had a change of heart when I saw your smiling face in the doorway, but I see now that is not the case. Well, nothing has changed. You'll still marry the earl in a month's time, so you'd better get used to it."

Annelisa rose to her feet and steadied herself with her hands on the desk. Adrenaline pumped through her body as she prepared to announce her news.

"Everything has changed, Father. I will not be marrying the earl because I no longer possess the one thing of value he seems to believe I, or any other woman, should own."

"What do you mean?" her father said nervously.

"Thornton Sutcliffe wants two things from this family: your money and my virginity. As of last night, only one of those things is available to him."

Her father sat in his chair dumbfounded. Her words hung in the air like the heavy smoke that poured from the Fielding factories' smokestacks, and just like the smoke, they cast a pall over everything.

Annelisa waited for him to reply, to say anything, but he simply stared up at her as if she were a stranger. She steeled herself for his eventual reaction, which she was sure would be full of pure rage.

His first movement was to stand and just as she had, he braced himself with his hands on the desk. The effect was one of two adversaries facing off against one another.

For a long time they stood like that until he finally spoke, his voice full more of concern than anger.

"How could you do this? Do you realize what you've done?"

"I know exactly what I did. I saved myself from being trapped in a loveless marriage that benefited everyone but me."

"You don't know the half of it, Annelisa. I will have to pay the earl to keep him from disgracing you. If I don't, he'll let everyone know what you've done."

"Is that all that matters to you? Does my happiness mean nothing to you?"

The tears began to well up in her eyes, and Annelisa stepped away from the desk, shaken by her father's words. His silence gave her his answer and his stony stare showed her how little he thought of her happiness.

"Jane!" he bellowed for the maid.

A young woman in a telltale black and white maid's uniform appeared almost instantly, a look of terror on her face. "Yes, Mr. Fielding."

"Where's Mrs. Fielding?"

"In the garden, sir."

"Tell her I need her here now."

The maid skittered away to find Annelisa's mother, leaving her alone with her father once again.

"I want you to tell your mother what you told me. Watch how she takes your news."

"I will tell whomever you'd like that I willingly did what I had to do to save myself from what you would force me to do."

"I always knew you were willful..." Andrew Fielding broke off his sentence and stormed over to join his wife in the doorway.

"Eleanor, close the door. Annelisa has something she needs to tell you. Go ahead. Tell her."

In a far less combative tone, she said to her mother, "I won't be marrying the Earl of Swindon because I am no longer a virgin, which was part of the deal to marry me."

Annelisa saw the blood drain from her mother's face and then Eleanor Fielding staggered toward a chair, as if her words had sapped all her mother's strength. Her father moved to support her and remained standing behind her.

"Why would you do this?" her mother asked in a sad voice.

Could her mother ever understand even if she explained her reasons? She'd always seemed confused by her daughter's behavior, often calling her "modern" as if the description were an insult. Would she relate to the idea of wanting to be more to a man than a breeder?

Before she could begin to explain, her father spoke up. "I don't care why anymore. What I want to know is who the man is. He will do right by her and marry her, or I'll see him shot. Tell me his name."

"I will not reveal his name, Father."

Shock registered on Andrew Fielding's face. "Why? Is he not an honorable gentleman who would do the right thing?"

"He is very honorable, but I don't want to marry him or anyone else. I will not be forced into marriage, regardless of the man."

Annelisa stormed out of her father's study, leaving her stunned parents to figure out her meaning. Locking herself in her room, she congratulated herself for standing up to her father's antiquated attitude. Now all she could do was pray she wasn't pregnant with Nikolai's child.

Four

Nikolai settled in to his bed after a long day of negotiating diplomatic efforts. Often his days were filled with events that appeared more social than work, but the past few days had been some of the most taxing since his arrival in Britain. With events in Eastern Europe continually changing, mostly for the worst, and the new German state disrupting the whole of Europe since its birth just seven years earlier, he saw more work and less drinking with the English in his future.

As he let his muscles relax, he thought about his rendezvous with Violet in the Stewarts' garden. Never before had he been so careless. As a diplomat, he was expected to behave with the utmost discretion, and as a rule, he did. Normally, the thought of fucking a strange woman at a ball just yards from hundreds of party guests would be dismissed in disgust as something far too dangerous.

But something about Violet Moceanu had made him disregard everything he held dear.

He raised her glove to his nose to inhale the scent of her perfume that lingered on the fabric. Its spicy sweetness seemed so familiar, yet he continued to draw a blank as to where he'd smelled it before and on whom. He'd recognized it as soon as they'd begun speaking, its unique fragrance softly wafting up from Violet's neck and wrists to his nostrils. The perfume had been intoxicating later as he'd nuzzled near her ear.

The memory of their time together thrilled him even now days later, and as he lay in bed replaying the events of that night, his cock began to harden. She'd been so tight when he'd entered her, he'd wondered if she was a virgin. He dispelled that thought almost as quickly as it came, however. Virgins didn't seduce men as Violet had him.

He'd wanted her the moment they began talking in the garden. Rarely had he been so fortunate as to meet such an intelligent woman. Most women seemed content to be told things—what to say, how to act, how to dress— but it was a rare woman who possessed a mind of her own. He admired a woman who could think for herself.

They'd had a genuine conversation with both of them contributing. How long had it been since he'd gotten to enjoy that? When she'd touched his arm, a clear signal she desired more than just stimulating conversation with him, he'd felt a twinge of disappointment. How refreshing it had been to enjoy another's company simply through the exchange of ideas!

Not that the opportunity to make love to her had been a disappointment or something he dreaded. Even without seeing her entire face because of the mask, he'd found her stunning. Blessed with a body that would please any man, she captivated him physically with little more than a touch.

Rarely before had he been so attracted to a woman, not to mention one he'd just met. It seemed unlikely he would see her again, however. Something had happened to make her flee from their coupling, but he couldn't place what it could be still days later.

Dozens of possibilities ran through his mind, threatening to tarnish his memories. There was no point in recriminations now. Whatever it had been, it was over. All he had was her glove and the memory of an enchanting woman who'd given him a night of pure pleasure. Anything else he wished it could be was just that—a wish.

The Fielding household appeared to be in a state of excitement, and Nikolai doubted his arrival was the cause. As he waited in the hallway for Andrew to finish his meeting, he sensed the household staff nearby whispering and tittering about something.

The door of the study opened and out marched the Earl of Swindon, Andrew's soon-to-be son-in-law. Nikolai had to step out of his way to avoid getting run over as the earl left, slamming the door behind him.

"Nikolai, please join me," Andrew said as he turned

back into his study.

As he made his way toward the door, bits and pieces of a conversation reached Nikolai's ears.

"She's lost yet another one. That girl loses them more often than anyone I've ever met."

"You better tell her mother, but I'd wait. The poor lady has had a difficult week."

Confused but curious if this had something to do with the furious exit of the earl, Nikolai entered Andrew's study and sat beside him in front of the fireplace. The pained look on his friend's face told him something serious had occurred since he'd last visited three days ago.

"I'm afraid I'm not prepared for our meeting today, my friend. Please don't think this is any reflection on your interests. I'm still as much a supporter of enhanced British-Russian relations as I've ever been, and I hope I can still count on your support for my business interests in your country."

"Of course. If you'd prefer, we can reschedule."

Andrew Fielding looked up toward the ceiling. "Yes, yes. We can certainly reschedule. It's been a very trying day."

"Andrew, may I help with anything?"

After a deep sigh, he replied, "I wish you could."

Nikolai remained silent as his friend sat pinching the bridge of his nose, his eyes closed. More than once, he sighed and looked up. Nikolai thought he might speak, but then he simply returned to pinching his nose again. While he waited, Nikolai's mind wandered back to the masquerade ball and Violet.

He slid his hand into his coat pocket and fingered her glove. As foolish as he knew it was, he enjoyed the idea that part of her still remained with him. His fingers toyed with the soft fabric as he remembered her soft lips on his, almost unsure in their exploration of him.

She'd been bold yet tentative in her seduction, a strange contradiction that wouldn't leave his memory. Would he see her again? The idea brought a smile to his face and for a moment, he enjoyed the fantasy.

"The marriage has been called off."

Nikolai was yanked out of his daydream back into the present by his friend's somber announcement. "Pardon?"

"My daughter won't be marrying the Earl of Swindon at the end of the month."

That explained Sutcliffe's leaving earlier, but Nikolai felt no regret for Andrew's dashed hopes. The earl's boorish behavior was nothing Annelisa Fielding should be forced to tolerate. But it was obvious that his friend was disappointed.

"I'm sorry your plans haven't worked out, Andrew."

"And she's going to be ruined if I don't pay him the money I promised would accompany the marriage."

Nikolai's hands balled into fists. That villain Sutcliffe was just the type to use some slight or tiny imperfection in her to take her father for all he could.

"Thornton Sutcliffe is a cad. Be happy he's shown his colors now before you presented him one of your children."

Andrew hung his head and in a defeated voice said,

"It wasn't the earl who misused Annelisa. She misused him...and me."

"My friend, whatever that sorry excuse for a man claims she did is a lie. I simply cannot believe your lovely daughter could misuse anyone."

Never looking up, Andrew explained, "She allowed a man to take her maidenhead just nights ago knowing the earl sought a virgin for his bride. And now she refuses to identify the man who deflowered her. The earl doesn't know, but he has to assume that this can be the only reason I'd withdraw my approval of the marriage. If he talks, she'll be ruined."

Nikolai sat stunned by Andrew's words. Was it possible?

"Are you sure? When did it happen?"

"The night of the Stewarts' masquerade. She deceived her mother and me and snuck off while we were away."

Sure his friend could see the guilty expression written all over his face, Nikolai turned away to face the window. The room seemed to shrink and close in on him, and his chest tightened as his breath caught in his lungs.

He'd made love to Annelisa Fielding. And he'd taken her virginity. He was the man guilty of ruining Andrew's dreams.

Nikolai's stomach turned, and he struggled for air. It was his duty, as a gentleman and Andrew Fielding's friend, to confess what he'd done and make every effort to right the situation. While he fought to keep his composure, he watched as his mystery woman strolled in the garden just outside the window.

Had she harbored feelings for him or was their time together part of a plan to rid herself of the loathsome earl? Nikolai's mind leapt from one possibility to the next, settling on nothing definitive. But one thing he knew for sure.

He had to find a way to be alone with Annelisa and soon.

Turning back to face her father, he asked, "Do you believe she will relent and give up the man's name?"

Andrew shook his head. "I doubt it. My guess is that the man meant little to her. She simply wanted to ensure she wouldn't have to marry the earl."

His friend's words stung, and the last of Nikolai's fantasy about Violet—Annelisa—disappeared. He had to speak to her!

Jumping to his feet, he abruptly announced, "I must go, Andrew. We'll continue this another time, I promise."

His head hung, Andrew said, "Of course. I understand."

Nikolai knew that his friend believed he was passing judgment on him and he regretted that, but he'd make it up to him later. Now, he had to find Annelisa.

With a quick pat on his friend's shoulder, Nikolai left hoping to find her still in the garden. Impulsively, he charged out the front door and made his way toward where he'd seen her, never considering she may not be alone.

He spied her near the gazebo at the far end of the garden. She appeared to be upset—or was it sadness her face conveyed? No matter. He would make things right

161

and from this day forward strive to ensure all her days were happy ones.

"Miss Fielding?"

Annelisa turned slowly toward him and smiled. "Yes, Count Shetkolov?"

Nikolai approached her cautiously as to not frighten her. When he reached her, he whispered, "I think it may be permissible for us to use our first names considering our recent history."

The smile disappeared from her face, replaced by a look of surprise. Her voice, however, betrayed nothing more than its usual politeness.

"Recent history, sir?"

"There's no need for any more lies, Annelisa. I know it was you at the ball. And I intend on doing the honorable thing, I assure you."

"The honorable thing?"

"Why, of course. I'll confess to your father my part in our rendezvous and properly ask for your hand in marriage. While what we feel may not be love now, I believe it will grow in time and we can be quite happy."

Bending down on one knee, Nikolai took her hand in his and gazed up into her eyes. "I pledge to make you happy and take care of you, as I know you will me."

While he'd never proposed marriage before, he was sure her stunned reaction wasn't common. But perhaps she'd underestimated his honor.

"Did you think I'd abandon you when you need me most?"

"Count Shetkolov, please get up."

Nikolai rose and stared down at her, liking what he saw.

"Sir, please forgive me, but I no more want to marry you than the Earl of Swindon. While I'm positive you are an honorable man, I simply don't want to marry anyone at all."

Nikolai stood stunned. "Pardon?"

"I see by your expression that I've offended you. I am sorry. But I'm not in need of a husband."

"But what we did in the Stewarts' garden..."

"Was what I had to do to be free of the earl. Nothing more, Count."

"Please call me Nikolai. And it was far more than what you say. I took your virginity, and for that we must marry. I would be a scoundrel if I allowed you to face this alone."

Annelisa smiled and touched his hand. "Nikolai, for that I must thank you for you helped me retain my freedom. I am sorry I had to resort to tricking you, but if I remember correctly, you enjoyed yourself. Let's leave it at that—an enjoyable experience each of us will remember."

Nikolai glared down into the face of this obstinate woman.

"Uprymaya!"

"What does that mean?"

"Perhaps French would be better, mademoiselle. Fille tetue."

Annelisa dropped his hand and stepped back. "Stubborn girl?"

"Yes, and if you won't agree to marriage, I'm sure your father will when I confess to him that I'm the man he seeks."

"You wouldn't! He'd be furious. He'd never forgive you."

"Oh, I'm sure he'd be angry, but he likes me. In time, he'd forgive me."

Nikolai held out his hand and waited for Annelisa to take it. "Shall we?"

All confidence drained from her face. "Don't do this, please! You don't love me, and I don't love you. Why would you want to marry me?"

"Because it's the right thing to do."

"Why is everyone always telling me what they want to do is the right thing?"

Ignoring her question, he repeated his question and added, "Or perhaps you'd prefer I approach him myself?"

Nikolai began to walk back toward the house. In truth, his stomach was in knots over telling her father what he'd done, but he had to show her he meant business. If she even thought he might be anything less than strong now, she'd never respect him as a husband.

Annelisa ran in front of him and stopped him with her hands on his chest. "Please, Nikolai! Don't do this. I'll do anything you require. Just not marriage."

Every word from her mouth insulted. Did she believe him to be unworthy of her hand?

"Anything I require?"

"Anything!"

So now she was willing to submit to anything he

required as long as it wasn't marriage to him? What about everything? That would be better yet.

"Then anything it shall be, Annelisa. The cost of your freedom will be the continuation of what we began at the Stewarts' ball. Unless you're willing to do this, I will leave to speak to your father now."

"The continuation of..." she stammered.

Nikolai watched as her face grew red. "There's no reason to be bashful now, Miss Fielding."

"So I am to be your sex slave?"

Finally, something had left her mouth that didn't offend him. "Sex slave? No, not exactly. I'm looking forward to your efforts showing the eagerness of our first time together."

"I thought you were an honorable man, Count Shetkolov."

Nikolai chuckled at her attempt to sway him through his honor. "I'm not the one who began this, my dear, but I see nothing dishonorable in what we are to do."

Annelisa stood looking up at him, a look of exasperation on her face. Nikolai enjoyed her irritation and hoped his words had bothered her as much as hers had him.

"You leave me with no choice then. Either I am to be your unwilling wife or your willing concubine, but I must be one."

Ordinarily, he would agree with her assessment of his behavior as lacking honor, but the combination of wanting her again and wishing to retaliate for her insults blinded him to the impropriety of his demands. At the moment, though, the pleasure of watching her chafe under his power over her was perfect.

"I will expect you at my home tomorrow at three."

"And if I refuse?"

"Then we speak to your father and at the end of the month, we will be married."

Annelisa turned on her heels and stormed away ahead of him before spinning back toward him, as if she'd suddenly remembered something important.

"Is it true you are soon to be recalled to St. Petersburg?"

Grinning, Nikolai took his time answering as he walked toward her. When he stood in front of her, he leaned down to inhale her sweet perfume and whisper in her ear, "You won't get rid of me that easily, my dear Annelisa."

Five

Nikolai's home loomed at the end of a long stone pathway that connected the house to the road. Annelisa stood hesitant to take that final step toward what would happen that afternoon. Was she truly going to go through with it? Was she going to make love with Nikolai Shetkolov? Was there no way out of the arrangement?

She tried to convince herself that this would be no different than what they'd done at the masquerade ball, but to no avail. This would be nothing like that. Then she'd had a mask and had acted like a worldly French woman. Now she'd be laid bare, seen by him, and her inexperience would be obvious.

Cursing her foolishness for ever thinking her plan would be successful, she furtively looked around to ensure no one saw her and stepped onto the first stone on the path to his front door.

If this is what I must do to keep my freedom, then this is what I'll do. At least he's not the Earl of Swindon.

Each step was accompanied by an increase of butterflies in her stomach. In minutes, he'd know she had only the knowledge of books when it came to lovemaking.

Annelisa mumbled to herself, "Oh, what does it matter? If he doesn't like me, perhaps he'll free me from this deal with the Devil. If not, then I only have to withstand this until he's called home, unless I can devise a way out."

Her pep talk buoyed her spirits, and with a deep breath, she stepped onto his front porch and knocked at the door. She was surprised when he answered only in his shirt and trousers.

"Come in."

As she walked over the threshold, she knew there could be no turning back. Once inside the entrance hall, she quickly looked around for any signs of the household staff but saw none.

"Where is your help?"

Nikolai closed the door and walked past her into the parlor. "There's only a manservant who attends me, the maid, and a cook. I gave them the afternoon off so there could be no chance of gossip. No one knows you're here, unless you told them."

"No, I told no one."

She hadn't even told Cecile, mainly because there would be no way she'd keep this secret. Plus, her sister had already taken a liking to him, so she'd never understand why she wouldn't love to be his wife. But worst of all, if Cecile knew she was here and the reason why, she'd know her plan had failed.

No, it was better no one knew what she was about to do.

Nikolai had already sat down on the settee, and Annelisa looked around the room for somewhere else to sit other than next to him, but there was no other piece of furniture available. Not a chair. Not even a stool!

"What kind of house has only one place for guests to sit down? Where is the rest of your furniture?"

As Annelisa faced him, she saw that he was enjoying her discomfort. He sat with his legs opened, his head leaning against the back of the settee, and slyly grinned at her.

"I removed them."

"You removed them? What on Earth for?"

"I didn't see any reason to give you the chance to drag this out. So come sit down next to me and we can at least talk a bit."

Annelisa couldn't contain her nervousness and fear, and before she knew it, evidence of them both came out for Nikolai to see.

"Why are you doing this? Have I offended you in the past and this is my payback?"

Never letting the grin leave his face, he answered, "I haven't done anything yet, and other than your refusal to marry me, I don't think we've ever had a full conversation before yesterday...well, not counting the night at the ball. So, no, you aren't being paid back for any offense."

Annelisa turned away to conceal the tears that began

to well up in her eyes from her frustration. There was no way out of this.

"Come, sit with me."

When she didn't move, he said in a softer voice, "Annelisa, please come sit next to me. I enjoyed our talk the other night and hoped we could continue it here before we do anything else."

Resigned to her fate, she turned around slowly to see the taunting grin gone and a look of genuine happiness on his face. Cecile's comment about his eyes flashed through her mind as she looked into them. There was something beautiful about their pale blue color next to his sandy colored hair.

As she sat down on the sofa, careful to keep as much distance between them as possible, she avoided looking at him. "What would you like to talk about? I enjoyed our discussion of Italian gardens."

"While I enjoyed that myself, I'd like some answers first."

Nikolai took her chin between his thumb and forefinger and gently turned her face toward him. "Look at me, Annelisa. I'd like some answers."

She closed her eyes, afraid of what he'd ask. He seemed so close...too close.

"Did you pick me simply because you thought I'd never figure out who you really were?"

Annelisa's eyes flew open and she swore she saw an expression of hurt on his face.

"No, it wasn't like that at all."

"Then why me?"

Looking down at her hands in her lap, she said quietly, "Because you're honorable and respectable. And I wouldn't choose anyone in my social circle."

She didn't have the heart to add that she'd heard he'd be soon returning to Russia.

"Your actions were rash. What if you're with child now?"

"I know. I remembered too late that I hadn't taken any precautions."

"You understand if you are, you'll have no choice but to marry me. I won't allow my child to be a bastard."

"Oh, I've made such a mess of things! All I wanted was to ensure I didn't have to marry the Earl of Swindon. Now I may be pregnant and forced to marry anyway."

Nikolai remained silent, and Annelisa feared she'd insulted him. "I'm sorry. I didn't mean to offend you."

"Why are you so against marriage? Or is it just to me or Thornton Sutcliffe?"

This was a topic she was passionate about, and she rose to her feet as she answered. "I'm against the idea that I, or any woman, should be traded like cattle to simply improve a man's life. I never wanted to be Lady anyone, but my father wants that for me, so my marriage was arranged. I never loved the earl, but he needs my father's money, so my marriage was set. But what about me? What about what I want and need?"

Before she realized it, she'd paced back and forth in front of him lecturing on her ideas of marriage. When she was finished, she saw him grinning up at her again.

"What's so funny?"

"Nothing's funny. However, I definitely know your mind on marriage now."

Annelisa returned to the settee and turned toward him. "I'm sorry. That was a bit much. It's not that I have any inherent problem with marriage. I just believe I should be more involved in who I marry and why. Do you know there are some who believe just as I do? They also believe women should get the right to vote and some measure of equality with men."

"I had no idea Andrew Fielding's daughter was such a radical."

"Is it radical to believe women are capable human beings? Is it radical to believe marriage should be based on love instead of money or status or worst of all, convenience?"

Shaking his head, Nikolai smiled. "No."

Annelisa sat quietly as the butterflies returned to her stomach. Their discussion of marriage had ended, and as he sat silently next to her, she was sure the reason for her visit would begin at any moment.

Nikolai liked the fiery look she got in her eyes when she talked about subjects she was passionate about. Even though he was sure she was frightened of what was to come, he saw a strength in her she may not even have known existed.

Bringing her hand to his lips, he softly kissed it. "No more talk of marriage. Agreed?"

Annelisa nodded. "Then what should we speak of?"

"No more talking," he whispered as he leaned in and placed a single soft kiss just below her ear.

The scent of her perfume—that fragrance that had haunted him—drifted into his nose, enchanting him. So delicate yet so desirable.

"Nikolai, I..."

Annelisa's voice trailed off as he continued to caress the tender skin of her neck with his lips. When he moved up to her mouth, he took her face in his hands.

"Annelisa, there's no reason to be afraid. We know each other this way already. Let yourself enjoy this, and let me give you what you gave me."

Before she could answer, he covered her mouth with his and slipped his hand behind her head, pulling her to him. Her mouth opened under his, and he slid his tongue over hers. Slowly, he flicked the tip over her lips and back into her mouth.

Despite her actions at the ball and what he'd believed, he sensed her inexperience now. The confident and seductive Violet was gone, but in her place he found a woman whose near innocence charmed him. As he kissed her, more and more he found himself falling for her.

"Nikolai...I..."

"What's wrong?"

Annelisa hesitated. "The first time we were together...I was...I mean..."

Nikolai kissed her on the lips. "I know. I suspected that night, but I know."

"No, I don't mean about being a virgin. I mean it was different. I had a mask on. I didn't feel so...so exposed."

Annelisa looked away, but he pulled her back to meet his gaze. "This shouldn't be something you fear. Pleasure should make you happy. I promise you'll like it."

Trailing kisses up her neck, he heard her say quietly, "I guess I don't have much choice, do I?"

Nikolai didn't answer her and returned to kissing her neck. He didn't like blackmailing her. When he'd first demanded she continue what they'd begun at the ball, it had been a reaction to her rebuff. It hadn't taken long for that to wear off, leaving a desire for her in its place. He'd rather her come to him willingly, but if he couldn't have that, he'd take this.

Never had a woman had such an effect on him! Whether as the seductress Violet or the innocent Annelisa, she made his body come alive like never before. Just kissing her made his cock stiffen, and in no time he was wishing to be inside her like just nights before.

But today wasn't about him. Today was the first step in her desiring him.

Gently, he lowered her onto her back and positioned himself over her. How beautiful she looked as she stared up at him!

When he began inching his hand up her leg, she flinched and he waited for her rejection, but none came. Never taking his eyes from hers, he watched excitedly for her response as his hand caressed her thigh. He wasn't disappointed.

As his hand slowly slid to her inner thigh, Annelisa closed her eyes and sighed. But would she allow him to reach his goal?

Carefully, he eased his hand toward the V between her legs. Her dress concealed what he'd soon touch, but as his fingertips first grazed her downy hair, he instantly knew she hadn't closed her eyes in fear.

With one finger, he stroked between her damp curls, feeling her soft folds as he watched her expression change to pure desire. Opening her eyes, she looked up at him with a pleading look. Over and over, his fingertip slid through her moisture, grazing her excited clitoris.

It would be so easy to bury himself in her. She was wet and willing. Putting these ideas out of his mind, he eased back his hand to pull up her dress.

"Nikolai?"

He heard how unsure she was as her voice broke and wanted to reassure her. Dipping down, he kissed her lips and stroked her cheek.

"Trust me."

Raising her dress, he piled it above her waist and slid down to see what his lips and tongue eagerly desired. Within her glistening brown fleece sat a swollen, pink nub begging for his mouth's attention.

Licking his lips, he whispered, "Yes," just as he touched it. Gently at first, he planted soft kisses on her, as she whimpered above him.

As his mouth began to pleasure her, he slid a finger down her slick seam and carefully entered her. She was so tight around his finger!

"Oh, Nikolai! I...it feels so..."

Spurred on by her words, he worked to bring her to orgasm. Every drag of his tongue over her cunt sent pleasure through her and with every sensation, she moaned and pleaded for him to continue.

She tasted so good on his tongue, and he greedily lapped her, wanting more. Musky sweet, her flavor excited him. Slowly, he became conscious of her leg pushing against his cock — no rubbing, like she was trying to pleasure him.

The feeling was exquisite. Every touch of her leg on his swollen cock brought him closer to coming. As his body careened toward its own release, his mouth sensually devoured her cunt and his finger fucked her.

Sure he would come before she did, he maneuvered his body away from her leg, instantly missing the feel of her on him. But he wanted her to have today what she'd given him.

She buried her hands in his hair, pulling him tightly to her and he knew she was close. A few more licks and thrusts and she'd come apart. Taking her clit in his mouth, he sucked her just to the point of no return and when her body clenched around his finger, he gently began nibbling her swollen nub, sending her over the edge.

"Oh, God! Please don't stop. Don't ever stop!"

Her body shook under his touch, and he rode her orgasm until all that was left were minor shocks and quivering that continued to wrack her spent body. Eager to see her face, he rose to his knees but saw nothing he expected.

Why was she crying? He knew she'd enjoyed everything he'd done, so why the crying?

"Annelisa, what's wrong?"

She scrambled to cover herself as she sat up, tears beginning to stream down her face. "Nothing. Nothing's wrong."

Nikolai sat back unsure of what to do. His plan had backfired, and it was only their first time together. Where had the strong, fiery woman from earlier gone to?

Annelisa jumped to her feet. "I have to go. Please don't tell my father about the ball. I know I have to abide by our agreement, but I really must go."

Before he could answer and console her about whatever was upsetting her, she ran out the door. At the window, he watched as she ran to the road and stopped.

Had she had a change of heart?

As he waited to see if he should go to her, Annelisa suddenly swayed and crumpled to the ground. Nikolai bolted out the door and ran to her, finding her passed out on the side of the road. Carefully, he picked her up in his arms and carried her back into the house to one of the bedrooms.

After only a short time, she came to. "What happened? Where am I?"

"You fainted and I brought you here to ensure your safety."

"Fainted?"

Nikolai nodded and sat down on the bed next to her. "Are you feeling better?"

"I think so." Sitting up, she righted herself, smoothing her dress. "I'm fine now. Perhaps I should consult a physician. I do hope I'm not suffering from hysteria."

Nikolai grinned. "Hysteria?"

"Oh yes. And if that's the case, there's no telling how long I'd be bedridden. It could take weeks before I'm up and around again."

He took her hand in his and said, "I do hope it isn't that, my dear Annelisa, but you do know what the prescribed treatment for hysteria is, don't you?"

Her silence told him she knew exactly what he meant.

Nikolai pushed the hair from her face and leaned in toward her. "I wouldn't worry about hysteria considering our arrangement. I can assure you I plan to do everything in my power to ensure you never suffer from that particular ailment."

Six

After she agreed to return in two days, Annelisa left and Nikolai set off toward London to return to his work. As his carriage rambled along the uneven country roads toward town, he thought about Annelisa and her failed attempt at reneging on their deal.

Chuckling, he mumbled, "She's a minx, that one."

She'd almost convinced him something was wrong until she'd mentioned hysteria. With that, she'd tipped her hand. A catch-all diagnosis, hysteria was invoked by English doctors for everything from weight gain and tiredness in women to the recalcitrant wife no man knew how to handle. And fainting was a primary symptom of hysteria, as Nikolai was sure she knew.

He smiled as he thought of her beautiful face as she pretended to be sick. *She probably faked the fainting too*, he thought to himself.

He'd have to stay on his toes with Annelisa Fielding.

Her father had been right when he'd described her as intelligent. He'd also been right when he'd said she could control the world if she were a man. Rarely had Nikolai encountered a craftier politician in Britain or elsewhere he'd served who could best her wiles and cunning.

The Earl of Swindon should be thankful she did get away. She'd have taken his titles and truly left him with nothing. Would serve him right.

Nikolai stretched his legs out in front of him as the carriage continued on its way. Her tendency to manipulate didn't bother him. If anything, he enjoyed it. Nothing like a challenge to keep a man alert. And her creative way of using her intelligence meshed well with her womanly charm, which affected him considerably. In fact, it was that charm that he found far more dangerous. She had already ensnared him a bit too quickly for his taste.

The truth was he'd already fallen for her as Violet, and the change to Annelisa hadn't dampened his interest any. Closing his eyes, he licked his lips, savoring the taste of her that still lingered on them.

He preferred to remember the moments when her body had come alive under his touch—how she'd begged him to never stop tasting her, worshipping her with his lips and tongue. In those moments, she wasn't scheming her way out of marriage or their arrangement. She was just a woman who loved the pleasure he could provide.

Just thinking about the way her silky folds had felt under his tongue, the slick dampness helping it glide from her tight entrance to her quivering pink clit, made his cock strain against his pants. He looked forward to their next rendezvous, two days away.

Until then, there was the business of diplomacy to attend to.

Nikolai's carriage jerked to a halt in front of his London residence. As he stepped out onto the cobblestones, he was confronted by the troubles of the day in the person of his fellow diplomat, Maksim Androsky.

"Nikolai, where have you been? I've heard from four members of Parliament in the last hour!"

Maksim seemed even more nervous than he was by nature this night. His small stature was all-a-quiver, and his small eyes widened in excitement. Nikolai waited for him to calm down before he asked about what had obviously upset his subordinate, but his state of distress only seemed to grow with the silence.

"The British government has learned of the Treaty of San Stefano. They reject the autonomy of Bulgaria and have made it known they won't allow it."

As Nikolai headed up the steps to his front door, he attempted to allay the man's fears. "Maksim, before we move on this, let me explain something. The British government prefers to remain friends with our country. This is one treaty. Remember that."

Trailing behind him, Maksim complained, "Nikolai, I don't think you appreciate the British feeling on this treaty. The men I spoke to already want assurances that the Tsar doesn't plan on using it to expand his empire."

Maksim closed the door and hurried to catch up to Nikolai, who was already seated behind his desk composing a letter. Throwing himself into a chair, he wrung his hands while he waited for Nikolai to finish.

"Calm yourself, friend. I'm requesting a meeting with the Foreign Secretary. That will show us where the official position of this government lies."

Sitting back in his chair, he considered what he knew of the British Foreign Secretary. The Marquess of Salisbury, Robert Cecil, was by and large an unknown factor, only in the position less than a month, but Nikolai had sensed in their few meetings that he favored the Russian position in the east.

"But Nikolai, Robert Cecil may be like Prime Minister Disraeli..."

Nikolai raised his hand to stop Maksim's train of thought. The Prime Minister had been far clearer in his opinion of Tsar Alexander's actions in the recent war with the Ottomans, and Maksim's concern that the Foreign Secretary's ideas may match Disraeli's were valid. But Nikolai believed Cecil to be sympathetic to his country, so he would begin with him instead of the Prime Minister. Better to start with friends first.

"Time will tell, my friend. For now, we begin with the Foreign Secretary and go from there."

Maksim appeared to want to argue more, but Nikolai closed his eyes in what he hoped was a clear sign he didn't intend to discuss the issue further.

"How is your family, Maksim?"

Nikolai let the man talk about the various goings on of his family, thankful he could be so easily distracted. Years younger, Maksim was a novice diplomat who still had a great deal to learn about the service, but Nikolai appreciated the care he took with their assignment. He could be quite taxing when his feathers were ruffled, something he'd learn to control as he grew in the job, but in general, the young diplomat was a helpful addition to the Russian contingent in Britain.

When he'd finished providing far more personal details than Nikolai preferred to know, Maksim sat silently. Nikolai wished the two of them could remain like this — quietly in thought — but he knew him too well. A further distraction was required.

"Have you had any success in acquiring Karentin's approval for your marriage to his youngest daughter?"

Nikolai knew this would elicit a near dissertation length response from Maksim, but that was the point. He'd listened to his lamentations concerning the father of his intended as an older brother would, agreeing with his unhappiness and counseling him to remain steadfast if he truly loved the young woman. Personally, Nikolai believed it was only a matter of time before Irina Karentin's father gave his blessing to Maksim's suit, primarily due to his potential son-in-law's position in service to the Tsar.

"I am still denied, but I continue to press my case. Thankfully, I can be sure of my dear Irina's love for me. Perhaps upon my return, her father will finally agree to our marriage."

Nikolai tuned out Maksim as he explained in detail exactly what he thought of his future relative's refusal. Quickly, he slipped into the memory of his time with

Annelisa, mentally reliving each caress of her tender flesh as her body opened up to his touch.

Suddenly, what had always been enough—serving his Tsar wherever and however necessary—wasn't enough anymore. Like Maksim, he wished for the settled life of marriage, a wife, and children.

With Annelisa.

"And you, Nikolai? What fine lady will make you leave your life of bachelorhood? As a count, you must have far better opportunities than I. A countess? Or a duchess?"

"I leave the matrimonial drama up to you, Maksim," he said with a chuckle.

"Life should not be all work. Man needs a home, Nikolai. A family."

"So true, Maksim. And how do you plan to attain yours?"

Maksim sighed. "I hope to wear him down through sheer persistence. Irina believes he will say yes eventually. I must simply be patient."

A courier interrupted the men, and Nikolai rose to meet him. Handing him the letter, he instructed him, "Deliver this to the Foreign Secretary with all speed. If you are given any reply, return immediately."

"This will give us the information we need, Maksim. For now, we wait. Go home and relax. I'll contact you when Robert Cecil replies."

Nikolai patted the younger man on the back as he made his way to the door. "Enjoy a nice dinner. I'll be in touch."

Nikolai returned to his desk feeling more confident than Maksim concerning the Foreign Secretary's response. What the junior diplomat had missed because of inexperience was the subtle but important fact that Robert Cecil hadn't approached him. If he'd been truly concerned, he'd have been quick to contact Nikolai. While members of Parliament may be upset, he gauged that the situation hadn't grown to a level that was of concern yet.

Pouring himself a drink, he relaxed, letting the taste of the finest Russian vodka settle into his mouth before the liquid slid down his throat. Loosening his tie and shirt, he willed the tension of the day to drift away. Unconsciously, he stroked his goateed chin and returned to the thoughts of his journey into London.

Maksim's words upset his reverie, however. "A countess or a duchess?" These were the very real possibilities Nikolai faced in his marriage bed because of his birth. As with all Russian nobility, it was expected that he would marry in such a way as to benefit his family. What he'd want and whom he'd prefer were of no consequence.

Nikolai catalogued his potential mates in his mind, eliminating each woman as he compared her to Annelisa.

Too short. Too tall. Too old. Too uneducated. Too unappealing.

Dozens of countesses and duchesses later, he was disgusted by his personal future. Preferring not to think any more on it, he let the thought of Annelisa's face push every other thought from his mind. How beautiful she'd looked that afternoon—no, every time he'd seen her.

Devoid of an all-important title, she possessed qualities none of the nobility he'd encountered in either Russia or Britain even knew to want.

What was the outer appearance if what resided on the inside was lackluster, or worse, ugly? How many ladies, countesses, duchesses, and even princesses had he met who the world deemed worthy of admiration simply because of their physical appeal? Far too often, those same women lacked the merest hint of wit. And intelligence? It was a rare woman who possessed a level of intelligence he admired, noble or not.

But Annelisa, for all her middle class, commoner blood, had all of the traits he wished for in a woman. Her intelligence, despite her tendency to misuse it, intrigued him, and even now as he sat in the dim light of dusk drinking alone, his mind traveled back to their conversation in the Stewarts' garden.

"Does your Tsar favor this country's current moves into African regions, Count?"

Nikolai looked at the woman who walked beside him with an expression of surprise. "My lady, your interest in world affairs is remarkable, to say the least."

Violet turned her body to face him, and she tilted her face toward him almost defiantly. "Why is that, sir? Because I am a woman?"

Before he could respond, she continued. "Am I not to have a mind to think with to go along with a body to bear children with? Is a woman to be nothing more than lips to kiss, breasts to suckle, and a womb for a man's seed?"

Nikolai stood still as a statue as she spoke, stunned by her forthright language. Never had he encountered a female who exuded such strength of mind and spirit.

"What would you believe a woman to be?" he asked, more interested in her answer than he may have ever been in anyone else's.

With her masked face looking up toward his, she said, "A woman is many things, Count. She is one to love and cherish who can nourish your very soul if she's treated with respect. Just as a man can be the center of a woman's existence, so too can a woman be that for a man. But make no mistake about it, sir. Another may be central to one's happiness, but that doesn't mean happiness comes exclusively from one person."

"And what kind of man would accept this woman you describe?"

"Why, of course, the only kind of man deserving of my respect. One who is strong and confident with the desire for a true mate instead of a mere plaything at night and a glorified scullery maid the rest of the time."

Violet turned and began walking again. Nikolai hastened to catch up to her, eager to hear more of her ideas. Far more modern than he typically preferred in a woman, they were intoxicating, nonetheless. She was intoxicating, and he yearned to hear more from her.

Beside her once again, he brushed against her arm and a jolt of arousal spiked in him. He wanted her, wanted to make this strong woman cry out for him.

"You must think me excessively proud, Count," she said, teasing him as she took his arm once again.

"No, my lady. I simply wonder where such a man as you describe exists. Are French men such men?"

Squeezing his arm, she giggled. "Some, I dare say, are such men. I find Englishmen are infrequently like the men I describe. But Russian men...I'm afraid I lack the required expertise to make a judgment on them. What is your verdict on that question?"

As he explained the Russian male character, she slid her hand under his coat and slowly stroked his wrist. Her touch excited him, making his explanation trail off. When she ducked behind a hedge, he followed, wanting to feel her lips on his.

She insisted on keeping her mask, but his desire to see her lovely face was overpowered by his need for her. Her mouth met his, opening to take his tongue in, her lips sucking gently on it. Her hands skimmed down his sides and brushed over the front of his pants. The feel of her touch on his throbbing cock, even through fabric, was more erotic than he could stand.

He needed to feel her touch on him. "Use your hand on me."

Each slow drag of her hand over his cock took his breath away. Her breasts pressed against his chest still covered by a shirt, but he felt her hardened nipples pushing against her dress and scraping against him. While his left hand slid through her wet sex, he used his right hand to squeeze one excited nipple. His reward was a needy moan he wanted to hear every night for the rest of his life as he buried himself deep inside her.

"Violet..." he groaned in return before he lifted her up and slowly slid into her tight passage.

Nikolai leaned back in his chair and stretched his legs out in front of him, hoping to ease the tension his excited cock and memories of making love to Annelisa had created. Drinking the remnants of his vodka, he enjoyed the knowledge that at least he would see her soon.

Perhaps another masquerade, he thought to himself.

Seven

"Annelisa, where are you going?" Cecile called across the garden to her sister.

She'd hoped to sneak out without being noticed, but with that plan in shambles, Annelisa scrambled to concoct a believable story to explain her leaving secretly.

"To visit Mrs. Jenkins."

The oldest women in the neighborhood and disliked by most who lived near her, Mrs. Jenkins had taken a shine to Annelisa because as a child she'd never scared like the rest of the children in the neighborhood. Now as a grown woman, Annelisa was one of the few people she permitted to visit her, claiming most of her family and neighbors were "thoroughly idiotic." She had no love for Cecile either, who seemed to irritate her with her naiveté, and she made no secret of the fact that she considered her a "ninny."

"Oh." The news of her visit to the cantankerous, old Mrs. Jenkins stopped Cecile in her tracks.

"I'll be back in a few hours. Tell Mother, would you?"

"I will. But is everything all right, Annelisa?"

Was her fear of returning to Nikolai's home that clearly written on her face? Annelisa forced a smile and quickly answered, "Of course. Why do you ask?"

"You've seemed more secretive since everything that happened with the earl. Has something gone wrong with Count Shetkolov?"

Gone wrong? Like I now must continue our relationship or he'll tell Father and I'll be forced to marry him?

Annelisa leveled her gaze on her sister. "Everything is fine, Cecile. No one knows a thing, except for you, and I need to know you'll keep my secret."

"Of course I'll keep your secret! I would never betray you, Annelisa. Never!"

Taking her sister's hands in hers, Annelisa squeezed them. "Thank you, Cecile. You are my one true confidante."

Cecile looked into her eyes, her own wide with concern. "And I will forever be. You can trust me with anything. You do know that, don't you?"

"I do. Now let me be off to visit Mrs. Jenkins. You're welcome to tag along, if you'd like."

Her sister's face twisted into an expression of distaste. "No, thank you. She's never liked me as she does you."

Annelisa nodded and smiled. "I'm sure it's only because I'm more like her."

"Don't say that! You're a thousand times nicer than

191

that old woman."

Turning to be on her way, Annelisa waved goodbye. "Maybe you're right," she called back.

Half a mile down the road, Annelisa reached Mrs. Jenkins' home, a stately residence that seemed appropriate for a woman of her age. As she knocked on the front door, she hoped this wasn't the day the woman had chosen to leave her house. She needed her too much today.

The door opened and the old woman's butler recognized Annelisa and let her in to wait until he'd announced her. Standing in her great foyer, she prayed Mrs. Jenkins could help her while at the same time wishing she didn't need her help at all.

But Nikolai's letter had been quite clear. She was to dress in men's clothes for their rendezvous today.

Annelisa turned his demand over and over in her mind until she'd come to the conclusion that she had no clue as to why he required her to dress as a man this day or any other day, for that matter. Was this some trick to make her look foolish?

"Annelisa, what a wonderful surprise! My child, come here."

Turning toward the elderly woman, Annelisa smiled and began to make her way toward her. Short and stout, Mrs. Jenkins barely reached Annelisa's shoulders, and she bent down to hug the woman.

"Mrs. Jenkins, thank you for seeing me with no notice."

The woman looked up at Annelisa and took her hand

in hers as she made her way toward the nearby sitting room. "You know for you, dear, anytime. You're not one of those ninnies I'm related to, thank God."

She sat down on a large, well-worn chair and folded her hands on her stomach ready to discuss the world with one of the few people she genuinely liked. Annelisa took a seat on a chair that seemed as new as the day it had been made and adjusted herself to the stiffness.

"It's been too long, my dear. How are you? Please tell me I heard incorrectly and you aren't marrying some stuffed bird...what was it I heard?"

As the older woman squinted her eyes to remember, Annelisa grumbled, "The Earl of Swindon."

"Oh, yes. Oh...please tell me he's better than his father. What a dreadful man!"

"No, he's just as dreadful, but I found a way out of that, thankfully."

Reaching over, the older woman grabbed Annelisa's hand and squeezed. "That's my girl! You didn't need to be the wife of such a revolting man."

"But I've gotten myself into something else I need your help with. Do you still have any costumes from your days on the stage?" Then after a long pause, she added, "And Mr. Jenkins' days?"

Annelisa shifted uneasily in her chair. She loved Mrs. Jenkins and in some ways, she was more a maternal figure than her own mother, but somehow she couldn't imagine telling her that she needed to dress as a man because her secret Russian lover demanded it.

Seeing the confused look on her friend's face, Annelisa

moved to reassure her. "Trust me when I tell you that it isn't for anything bad."

Well, depending on whether or not you consider having a sexual rendezvous with a man who's blackmailing you bad.

Mrs. Jenkins looked intently at Annelisa's face for a long moment, as if she were studying it or looking for the truth, and then said, "Of all the people in this world, Annelisa, I trust you to be levelheaded the most. If you need something, I'm sure it's for a good cause."

Annelisa hoped she didn't look as sheepish as she felt, but she could think of no one else to turn to. Damn Nikolai! Yet another person she was forced to lie to because of him.

"What do you need?"

One deep breath and then she said the words. "I need to dress as a man."

Annelisa was sure she'd never felt more awkward in her entire life. The pregnant pause that followed her statement seemed to go on forever until she began to wonder if she'd made a mistake. But there was no turning back now.

Thankfully, Mrs. Jenkins' brain shifted into stage mode, and she began listing the various pieces of the costume needed to change a young woman into a young man.

"Trousers, yes. Shirt, yes. Hat, of course. Boots, we should be fine with."

With the basics settled in her mind, she rocked herself out of her chair and onto her feet and took Annelisa by the hand. "Come child. It's show time!"

Upstairs in a bedroom that hadn't been used in years, the old woman rifled through a trunk filled with clothes of all kinds. Gaily colored dresses unlike any Annelisa had ever seen, fine silk scarves, corsets that looked far sexier than usual undergarments—had Mrs. Jenkins worn these all those years ago? The idea of her friend as a sensual young woman made a smile creep across Annelisa's lips.

"I bet you find it hard to believe I ever wore these. Well, believe it. And someday when you're my age, you'll be able to remember when you dressed as a man. Now come down here so we can find some of Philip's clothes for you."

Methodically, the elderly woman pulled out each item of clothing from the trunk and handed it to Annelisa. In just minutes, her arms were full of everything she'd need to complete her current masquerade.

Pointing toward a dressing screen, Mrs. Jenkins said, "Go try these on and I'll look for boots and a hat."

In no time, Annelisa emerged a changed woman. Gone was her fashionable dress, replaced with a man's pants, shirt, and waistcoat, which thankfully fit quite well and seemed to hide the obvious features which pointed to her being a woman.

Standing in front of a mirror, Annelisa looked at the image staring back at her. From the neck down, she resembled any of the men in her social circle, but from the neck up...that was going to be a problem.

"Mrs. Jenkins," she said to the woman whose head was buried in a wardrobe. "What will I do about my face and hair?"

Annelisa fussed with her hair as she waited for the woman to deliver a solution. No matter what she did with it, she still looked like a female.

From inside the wardrobe, Mrs. Jenkins barked, "A wig!"

Turning toward her voice, Annelisa asked, "Do you have one?"

Her question was met by more rustling sounds and Annelisa turned back to look at her reflection. Why would Nikolai want her dressed like this? Was this all part of a plan to humiliate her? The thought stabbed at her, making her cringe. Would he do that?

Not that it would be any worse than what he'd already demanded of her. No, whatever he required she'd do if it meant keeping her freedom.

"Let's see how this looks."

Annelisa turned to see Mrs. Jenkins holding a coat and wig. She easily slid into the jacket and actually thought she looked somewhat dashing. The wig would be a different story, however. Darker than her light brown hair, it didn't seem able to hold all her hair, but with some judicious tugging and repositioning, it finally concealed the last of her truly feminine features.

Turning back to look at the finished product, she and the old woman grimaced. Even with her beautiful hair covered in a short wig and her body concealed by men's clothing, she still looked like a woman. Just a woman in men's clothes.

"Moustache!"

Spinning around, Annelisa watched as Mrs. Jenkins

returned to the stage trunk to pull out a fake moustache.

"How will this stay on my face?"

"Stage secrets. Glue that won't hurt you. Here, let's see how this looks."

Annelisa bent down to let her apply the fake hair to above her lip and cried out as she pressed it roughly to her skin.

"We need to make sure it stays on."

After a few tries, the moustache stuck and Annelisa turned to look at it in the mirror. She moved close to it until her nose almost touched its reflection and studied the area above her lip. Perhaps if another person didn't look too closely, they might just think she was a man.

"Voila!" Mrs. Jenkins exclaimed.

"Thank you so much for your help, Mrs. Jenkins."

Annelisa hugged her and hat in hand, started toward the stairs, knowing she had little time before she was expected at Nikolai's.

"Dear, before you go, remember something."

As she turned around to face the woman, Annelisa readied herself for what she feared she'd say. "Yes?"

"In the end, you have to be true to yourself."

"I will. Thank you."

Annelisa walked quickly down the road to Nikolai's house, acutely aware of the clothes that rubbed in all the wrong places. The boots Mrs. Jenkins had given her fit oddly, and every step was an effort to ensure she didn't fall flat on her face.

She was thankful no one passed her on the road as she began to think about her current situation. She hadn't been able to stop replaying their last time together as many times as she could find free moments. The feelings he'd caused in her had made her lose her composure, and as she made her way down the lane toward his home, she cringed.

Cried! Like a silly schoolgirl!

And then her ruse had failed miserably. Nikolai was no typical man, and if she intended on winning what had grown into a test of each one's intelligence, she would need more in her arsenal than a few tears, a pouty expression, and an imaginary disease.

His home came into view as she walked around a bend, and she stopped to steady herself for another of their meetings. What would he expect this time, their third time together? Nervously, she admitted to herself that the situation she found herself in was almost comical. That she worried about what he'd want her to do was silly considering that they'd already had sex once, twice if what he did their last time together was to be counted. What he'd expect would be making love in fulfillment of their agreement.

Wiping her palms on her pants, she began on her way again, chastising herself for the butterflies in her stomach. She wasn't some ninny who couldn't handle herself. She was capable and strong, and if this is what she must do to safeguard her freedom, then she would do it and without whining or simpering.

She just hoped if what she believed would occur that she could make it through without the benefit of anonymity her mask had provided her.

Each step she took toward his house was accompanied by the combination of her stomach jumping and her reassuring herself. By the time she'd reached his front door, she felt nauseous but emboldened.

An odd combination, to say the least.

She knocked once and then twice and waited. Looking left and right to ensure no one watched her visit his home, she wondered if she was early.

"Perhaps he was detained," she mumbled as her butterflies calmed themselves.

Annelisa waited for another minute and happily turned to begin her walk home. However it had happened, she'd been granted a reprieve. Suddenly, there was a spring in her step, and as she stepped down the path to the road, she took notice of the fresh smell in the air from the early spring flowers that lined the outer edges of the property.

What a lovely day, she thought as her foot touched the last stone on the pathway.

"Miss Fielding?"

The Russian accent of Nikolai's voice stopped her dead. Although she was sure it was all her imagination, it seemed as if the beautiful smell she'd just appreciated had entirely faded away and even the birds had stopped their singing.

Slowly, she turned and saw him standing in front of her with no coat on his back or hat on his head. Dressed only in a shirt and trousers, he seemed far simpler than a Russian noble and diplomat.

"Good afternoon, Count Shetkolov. I was just...I

knocked and waited but no one answered."

Nikolai nodded as if to relay his belief in her statement. "I made sure everyone was sent away for the afternoon. I was enjoying the beautiful day in the garden. Please join me."

Did she have a choice? Annelisa just hoped he wouldn't want to fulfill their bargain outdoors behind his house.

Nikolai waited for her to join him, and she took his outstretched hand to walk beside him. It felt warm and strong in hers. Earthy.

"I'm pleased you did as I asked. I knew you were a resourceful woman."

Annelisa stared at him and squinted her eyes in anger. "Was this all a ruse to make me look like a fool? Well, I hope you're happy. You got me to dress up like a man, so go ahead. Have your fun."

Nikolai stopped and turned her to face him. He took her hat off, and bent down to kiss her gently on the lips. "It was no such thing, Annelisa."

"Then did you just want to see me obey you? Was that it?"

The smile he flashed made her stomach flip, and she looked away just in case her blush was as severe as she imagined it was.

"As much as I have to admit I enjoy the idea of just once you doing as I say, it wasn't that."

Before she could ask any further, he guided her to a patch of soft grass and sat down. Annelisa nervously stared down at him, believing he intended to make love right there in the open.

"Sit. It's a lovely day. I thought we could spend our time out here."

"Out here? You want to...out here?"

Nikolai smiled as if she'd said something amusing and held out his hand again. "Sit, Annelisa."

Lowering herself to the ground, she sat on the cool grass and immediately surveyed the area around them to assess the privacy his garden afforded.

"Don't worry. The house closest to me over there is vacant most of the time. No one can see us here, no matter what we do."

If that was supposed to put her mind at ease, it didn't. If anything, his words only made her more nervous as they hinted to what he planned to do right there, in the grass, under the blue sky.

Annelisa felt like a naive schoolgirl. Hoping to calm what had blossomed into fear, she fiddled with the crease in her trousers. When Nikolai covered her hand with his, softly touching her leg, she closed her eyes and felt the sensations wash over her.

Nikolai moved his fingers back and forth across Annelisa's thigh, feeling the soft fabric of her pants under his fingertips. Her leg tensed under his hand, and he pressed lightly with his palm to calm her.

"Is it true that this government is being difficult with yours over Eastern issues?"

Damn, she had the uncanny ability to change his

focus at the worst moments. But he wasn't going to let her succeed this time.

Moving his hand up her leg, he stroked the fabric over where her thigh met her body. Her trembling told him now she would be the one who would struggle to remain focused.

"No, not at all. Your information is faulty, dear lady."

"Oh."

Nikolai inwardly smiled at the fact that he'd been able to distract her this time, if the flutter in her voice was any indication. He continued to drift his fingers over the crease of her thigh, pausing each time near her hip.

"So what have you done since I last saw you?"

Annelisa appeared to wrestle with her thoughts. "I...I...read a book. A wonderful book. On land and its economic value."

Unable to stop a laugh from escaping, he chuckled and said, "You are an interesting woman, Annelisa. While other women spend their time gossiping and scheming for husbands, you're reading books on economics."

"Why is that funny?"

Nikolai's hand drifted onto her lap. "It's not. But not everything worth knowing can be found in books."

He pressed his hand gently against her sex and watched her eyes grow wide. "I know of no book to teach you about this."

Flustered, she answered, "That's not true. I've read everything I can on the subject, so there is knowledge to be gleaned on it."

"What subject?" he asked, toying with her verbally

and physically.

"What?"

"What subject are you referring to?"

"What men and women do..."

Smiling, he turned her face toward him. "Making love. Or fucking, if you prefer."

Annelisa's cheeks turned a bright red and she averted her gaze from his. Nikolai couldn't decide which version of the woman he liked best: the confident seductress, which he knew was merely an act, the headstrong, intelligent young woman he and others saw in public, or this far more innocent woman who blushed at his raw language.

"There's no need for embarrassment."

Her eyes darted back to meet his. "I'm not embarrassed. But I don't see the need to play with me. That is what you're doing, isn't it?"

Nikolai unbuttoned the top buttons of her shirt and slid his hand in to caress the tops of her breasts. Leaning in toward her, he whispered, "I haven't begun to play, Annelisa."

Dipping his head, he planted soft kisses on the swell of her breasts, one then the other, feeling them grow warm at his touch.

"Why are you teasing me like this?" she asked, her voice sounding strangled.

Nikolai lifted his head and looked up at her. "No teasing. If I were teasing, I wouldn't be planning to be inside you in mere minutes."

The look on her face confused him. Was that fear or

desire he saw in it?

He ran his hands down her sides, happy to see her costume was authentic and there was no evidence of a corset. He wouldn't expect to find one, even if she'd worn a dress. He'd noticed that, ever the iconoclast, Annelisa preferred the artistic style over the restrictive, but more popular, corseted dress with its bustle.

With little effort, she could be out of her men's clothes and naked under him right there in the garden. A first for him, he was sure it would be an exceptional experience.

"But what if someone is watching, Nikolai?"

The fear in her voice registered on his heart. He had made sure their privacy was assured, but if she was truly afraid, he saw no need to torment her.

Lifting his face to hers, he kissed her mouth tenderly and stroked her cheek. "Your plea touches me, love. To make you happy, we'll leave nature to its own devices and go inside."

Annelisa nodded. "Thank you, Nikolai. I can only imagine what would happen to your reputation if we were found."

Smiling, he rose to his feet and took her hand to help her up. "I can't imagine making love to one's wife would be offensive to anyone in my circles."

She stopped dead and stared at him. "We are not married, Count Shetkolov. This arrangement allows me to keep my freedom, no more. In fact, other than cementing in my mind the opinion that you're a rogue, I can't figure out what benefit this bargain of ours gives you."

In a rush, Nikolai pulled her tightly to him and kissed

her passionately. When he was done, he lifted her chin and looked directly into her eyes. "We will be married if someone finds out about our meetings. And as for what I get, don't spend another moment on it. Just know our arrangement suits me just fine."

The stunned look on her face also suited him, and before she could answer, he whisked her into the house and closed the door behind them. There was a time for the verbal sparring she so excelled at, but now was not it. Now he wanted what he'd waited for since that night at the masquerade ball.

"I want you out of those clothes. This time I get to see every inch of you."

Nikolai didn't bother to wait for a response before he resumed kissing her. While his lips tended to hers, his hands tugged at her coat, waistcoat, and shirt before moving to her trousers. As each article of clothing fell to the floor, he moved to the next until she was left standing in her drawers and looking unbelievably charming. He made quick work of those, however, and in seconds she was close to as God intended.

She was breathtaking!

As he began stripping the layers of clothing from his body, he ordered, "Take your shoes and stockings off."

Annelisa slipped out of them and turned back to face him. "I'll have no choice but to marry you if someone happens upon us. All this clothing will be impossible to get on in time to lie."

Now entirely divested of his clothes, Nikolai let his gaze roam over Annelisa's beautiful body. Full breasts sat above a small waist, which flared temptingly to sensual hips and long, gorgeous legs. All those fools who refused to see past her intelligence and stubbornness didn't know what they were missing. Such a woman — intelligent, beautiful, and built to be loved by a man — was a rare find indeed.

He intended to make her his on a far more permanent basis.

"Come here," he said in a low voice full of need. "I want you."

As he'd done minutes earlier, he roughly pulled her to him, crushing her breasts to his body. Her pebbled nipples scraped against his skin, exciting him. His mouth devoured hers, his tongue snaking between her lips to mingle with hers.

Despite her inexperience, she met his passion eagerly and wrapped her arms around his neck, pulling him even closer to her. Her slick cunt pushed against the base of his cock, driving him crazy with need.

"Moya milaya," he groaned into her mouth as he squeezed her perfect ass in his hands. He slid a finger near her wet opening and teased her, and she ground her sex against his cock wantonly.

"Nikolai...yes...yes."

"Now I begin the work to ensure you never suffer from hysteria, my love."

Lifting her in his arms, he carried her to the chaise and gently laid her down. He positioned himself over her and leaned in to kiss her lips. She arched her body up toward his and pulled his hips into hers.

Nikolai pushed his body to hers, and in a moment of perfect pleasure, buried himself in her as she moaned sweetly, "Yes."

Eight

Annelisa was conscious of little more than the desperate desire for Nikolai. When he retreated from her body, she pulled him back to her, never wanting to be without him again.

This time there was no pain, only the sublime feeling of his body joined with hers, filling it completely. Her hands pressed into his back, kneading the taut muscles that flexed and relaxed with each thrust into her as she worked to hold him to her.

He stopped for a moment and looked down at her, his pale blue eyes filled with concern. "Annelisa?"

His accent blanketed every syllable, making him seem foreign and exotic. "What's wrong?"

Desperately wishing he'd return to being deep inside her, she shook her head and pressed her fingers into the small of his back. "Please don't stop."

Nikolai plunged into her again, grazing a spot

somewhere inside her that she instantly wished he would find again. A gasp escaped her throat, and he once more stopped.

"What is it?" he asked as he searched her face.

"Nothing. I love it. Please don't stop."

Lifting his body from hers, he hovered over her, still not convinced she was all right. "I don't want to hurt you. I know you're...inexperienced."

Annelisa smiled and tugged him back to her. "Don't worry, Nikolai. I'm not hurt."

Before he could worry any more, she rolled him over onto his back and leaned down to kiss him. Whispering in his ear, she teased, "Now I'll show you my knowledge of fucking."

Sure she saw a look of surprise cross his face for just a moment, she was pleased when his hauntingly beautiful eyes looked up at her, half-lidded and clouded over by need.

Nikolai buried his hand in her hair and passionately tugged her head toward him. His lips crushed against hers as his tongue mingled with hers in a kiss unlike anything she'd ever read about in any of her books.

He was so passionate, so commanding as he moved his hands to her waist to hold her in place as he teased her wet and needy cunt with his stiff cock. She couldn't move, even if she'd wanted to, and the feel of his strong hands pushing into the flesh of her hips as he played his erotic game excited her even more.

"So you possess knowledge? Show me," he said in a voice edged with need as he slowly pushed into her.

Annelisa stiffened in surprised as he touched that spot she'd so desperately wanted him to return to. Whatever knowledge she'd believed she had seemed to fade from her mind, replaced by the singular desire to feel him touch that spot over and over.

"Yesss," she moaned as he fulfilled her silent wish with each slow thrust of his cock.

The pace of his fucking was like sweet torture. Every plunge into her was followed by a slow withdrawal as her body desperately surrounded his, not wanting to experience the loss of him. Forceful and quick was replaced by slow again and again as he controlled the pace, holding her just where he wanted her.

"Nikolai...please."

As he continued, he smiled up at her. "More?"

"Faster. God, you're driving me mad!"

Suddenly, he sat up and she was on his lap, his cock still inside her and his face just inches away. "Ride me, Annelisa."

Unsure in her mind what to do, she let her body guide her as she began sliding up and down his shaft seeking the pleasure he'd given her just moments before. But in this position she couldn't feel what she so desperately wanted. The touch of his hand as he slid a finger between her cheeks made her flinch, and she tilted her hips.

That was it! There was that feeling!

"Faster, Nikolai...right there...fuck me," she begged as he began slamming into her, hitting that perfect spot each time.

And then she was conscious of only the most exquisite

feeling traveling from deep inside her to every inch of her body as she fell on top of him. Panting, she clung to him as he continued to push into her, extending the most wonderful sensation he'd created in her.

She heard him say her name over and over in a voice that sounded like it was miles away. And then just as he had that night in the Stewarts' garden, he came inside her, flooding her body with warmth.

"Annelisa?"

Lifting her head from his neck, she looked into his eyes as her fingers played with the damp hair at his nape. "Yes?"

Nikolai leaned forward and kissed her lips softly. "It's only a matter of time before we must marry if we continue to leave things to chance."

Annelisa knew he meant no harm by what he said, but the words "must marry" rang in her ears. She didn't want to marry someone because she had to, any more than she wanted someone to marry her because they felt they had to.

But what he said was true. She couldn't continue to forget to protect herself or she'd end up as the wife of a man who had no choice but to marry her.

Climbing off him, she quickly began dressing. "Then from now on we won't rely on chance."

Out of the corner of her eye, she saw the hurt her remark had registered cross his features. His response touched her emotions, but she couldn't worry about his feelings. She didn't want a man who saw her as an obligation.

As much as she preferred to avoid him now, she had no choice but to turn and face him. She may not want to marry him, but that didn't mean being intentionally thoughtless.

He sat on the settee, still naked from their lovemaking, looking entirely too good. For a brief moment, she let her gaze travel over his face and body, and once again her body responded to him. His blond hair was disheveled after all her pulling and playing with the ends. His goatee, which she realized she'd never noticed when he kissed her, was a shade darker than the hair on his head and more closely resembled the hair between his legs. And he sat looking up at her, legs splayed open, almost looking undignified as he seemed to study her.

Suddenly uncomfortable, she pulled at her waistcoat nervously. "What?"

His blue eyes scanned her from head to toe and back again before he spoke in a deep voice that touched her somewhere no other ever had.

"Come back in two days, and make sure you're dressed like this."

A sense of rebellion surged in her. "And if I don't?"

Nikolai stretched his arms over his head and clasped his hands behind his head, leaving nothing to obscure the view of his once again excited body.

"Then we go to the church and I never have to wait for you to come back. Your choice, moya milaya."

Annelisa couldn't decide if she loved or hated the smirk he wore. As he sat there, entirely exposed to her, he seemed so unguarded, yet at the same time he

exuded a power over the situation, the surroundings...
her that seemed so contradictory to his current state. For
a moment, she got lost in the vision of him before her.

"So which will it be, Annelisa?"

Shrinking her eyes into little slits, she glared down at
him, careful to keep her gaze focused on his face instead
of his raging erection. He was enjoying this!

"You know my feeling on marriage, Count Shetkolov,
so you have your answer."

Smiling the grin of the victorious, Nikolai said, "I'm
sure you'll understand if I don't escort you out."

"Afraid you'll offend one of your neighbors?"

He let out a laugh that even Annelisa had to admit
was contagious. "You underestimate my neighbors,
love."

Annelisa's mind flashed to old Mrs. Jenkins and the
look on her face if she saw a completely naked Nikolai.
Unable to suppress the chuckle from the thought, she said,
"I think you may overestimate your appeal, Nikolai."

After changing into her dress at Mrs. Jenkins and thankful
her old friend didn't seem to be too curious about her
afternoon, Annelisa began the walk home. Halfway there,
she realized she was still smiling and stopped short in the
road.

"What am I doing? Why am I smiling? The man is
blackmailing me to continue having sex with me!"

The rest of the way home she spent talking herself into
disliking Nikolai. He was too old. He looked so foreign

compared to every gentleman in her social circle. He was arrogant. And worst of all, he was too smart.

That flaw was the worst of his faults. Never before had she met a man who could outsmart her, yet Nikolai seemed to at every turn. Even the threat of feminine health problems couldn't dissuade him. The man was infuriating!

By the time she arrived home, she had convinced herself that he was by far the most vexing person she'd ever encountered, man or woman, and the most challenging opponent, hands down. Entering the house, however, she overheard her father in his study dealing with an actual opponent, and he was in no way like Nikolai.

"Fielding, you will amend our arrangement."

Annelisa heard her father slide his chair out from behind his desk.

"My Lord, I will do no such thing. Our arrangement was contingent upon your marriage to my daughter, and I agreed to fulfill my part to compensate you for any hardship you suffered when I withdrew my agreement to the marriage. You will get no more from me."

Her hands balled into fists as she listened to her father defend himself against the Earl of Swindon's extortion. If she were a man...

"You will and you know why. Do you want everyone else in England to know why also?"

Thornton Sutcliffe's barely veiled threat to tell everyone that she was a fallen woman struck her dumbfounded. Somehow he'd found out that she'd lost her virginity and now like the craven scoundrel he was, he was using it against her father to wrangle more money from him.

Annelisa heard her father's silence in reply to the Earl's despicable threat. Her heart broke from guilt as she waited to hear his response, knowing all too well what the next words out of his mouth would be.

"Please don't do this, my Lord. She's the apple of my eye, and your announcement would ruin her."

The Earl hissed his response. "Then I can be assured of your compliance, can't I, Fielding?"

Annelisa couldn't hear her father's usually strong voice as it dropped in defeat. Wracked with guilt for putting him in such a position, she slowly moved down the wall until she slipped into the dining room and held her hand to her mouth, sickened by the consequences of her actions.

Her poor father, forced to defend her against the likes of Thornton Sutcliffe! Regret overcame her, and she buried her face in her hands in the hopes of blocking it all out.

What a mess she'd made of everything! Both she and her father were being blackmailed, although Nikolai was nothing like the awful Earl of Swindon. But even worse, her dear father was forced to endure the humiliation of Sutcliffe's petty attacks.

Down the hallway, the door to the study opened and she heard the earl threaten, "Remember, Fielding, you have until Monday. If I don't hear from you by noon, everyone will know exactly why I chose not to marry your daughter."

Her blood boiled in anger and every cell in her body called out for justice. She fought back the urge to storm out and confront the rotten earl. She watched as he smugly walked to the front door, his dishonorable head held high as he basked in his success. Just as his hand reached the knob, he turned back and looked toward her with an expression of victory.

Turning toward her father, who stood in the doorway of the study, the earl barked, "Monday or else, Fielding!"

Andrew Fielding stood quietly as the front door slammed, his expression one of silent defeat.

Annelisa watched as her father slowly retreated into his study and closed the door. She so much wanted to go to him, but what would she say? How could she explain how sorry she was for all that she'd done?

But if she wasn't sure what to say to her father, she was perfectly clear as to what she wanted to say to the Earl of Swindon. Throwing caution to the wind, she stormed out of the house to catch up to the earl as he climbed into his carriage. She may be only a woman, but someone needed to put him in his place.

He saw her as she approached and seemed to relish the idea of the confrontation. From his perch inside the carriage, he smirked with an uncharacteristic grin, almost baiting her to give him a piece of her mind.

"My Lord, you won't get away with your blackmail. I won't let you."

Annelisa knew she was violating social conventions by speaking to a member of the peerage this way, but she didn't care. Even if he succeeded in wringing the last pound from her father, he'd know he was no better than a low life villain.

"You won't let me? Miss Fielding, you are a mere woman, and one I have on very good authority is too far beneath me to deserve any conversation with someone of my station."

Annelisa stepped back and struggled to keep her composure, feeling like she'd been slapped across the face. Something in her screamed for her to stand her ground.

"You are a cad, sir! And I am glad my father withdrew his approval for my marriage to you. You may be an earl, but to me you are a cad."

The offense of her words was written all over Thornton Sutcliffe's face, and Annelisa braced for his verbal attack. However, nothing could have prepared her for the vitriol that came from him next.

"And you are a common whore! Whatever I may have gotten for marrying you would never have been worth lowering myself to your level. You did me the greatest favor when you began your whoring, Annelisa."

Each word stung like a knifepoint digging into her skin. Before she could reply, the earl ordered his driver to leave, and Annelisa was left in a cloud of dust. Standing alone, she brushed the dirt from her hair and face and silently cursed the Earl of Swindon, wishing him nothing but a barren harpy, of the appropriate social standing, of course.

She hadn't been successful in convincing the

blackguard to end his wretched extortion, and she suspected it was just a matter of time before the entire countryside heard about her being a fallen woman. If anything, her outburst had only hastened the earl's release of his suspicions, and although she knew she should care, she didn't.

Walking back to the house, she mumbled to herself, "He deserved exactly what he got, the cad."

Annelisa locked herself in her room and lay down to forget about the whole awful event. She found herself wishing Nikolai were next to her, his arms around her as he promised in his Russian accent that everything would be fine.

How odd it was to think of him as comfort and security. She'd never looked to a man for help with any of life's troubles until recently, and now for a second time, she turned to Nikolai.

As much as she hated to admit it, he was quite charming, even for a blackmailer. And the feelings he created in her when they made love were unlike anything she'd ever experienced or even read about in her books. When he entered her, it was like the most wonderful part was being added to her.

Closing her eyes, she imagined his eyes—those stunning, pale blue eyes—and his sensual mouth, nearly hidden behind a goatee, the mouth that had introduced her body to more pleasure than she'd ever thought possible.

He definitely was very appealing.

However, something else was far more appealing.

Her freedom.

Nine

"I hope you're pleased with yourself. Some woman followed me all the way here. I thought I was going to have to outrun her."

Nikolai smiled at Annelisa, amused by the idea of a woman chasing after her. Running his hands down her back, he trailed them over her behind and gently pulled her to him. "You sound sweet."

"Why am I dressed like this again, Nikolai?"

Already excited, he pushed his cock against her and smiled. "I have a surprise for you."

"A surprise?"

He heard the concern in her voice and gently stroked her cheek. "Yes. We're going to a party."

Annelisa pushed herself away from him and stared up at him, her eyes wide with disbelief. "I'm not going anywhere. It's one thing for me to come here dressed in this costume, but I have no intention of meeting others like this."

"That's fine. I'll just speak to your father tomorrow, and we can begin planning for the ceremony."

Nikolai saw immediately the effect of his threat as she twisted her beautiful mouth into a scowl. Even dressed as a man, she looked adorable standing there completely frustrated.

"You know, that's not always going to work."

"Really? And why is that?"

Annelisa thought for a moment and by the look of irritation on her face, he saw she'd come to the same conclusion he had.

She either dealt with him this way or dealt with him as his wife. Either way, he won.

"Fine. Where are you taking me?"

Annelisa dropped herself onto the still lone piece of furniture in the parlor. Nikolai kneeled in front of her and slowly traced the seam of a pant leg up to the V between her legs. With his thumb, he drew little circles just where he knew would drive her crazy. After only a few strokes, she opened her legs more for him, her body telling him what she still refused to admit.

"Just a party with the other Russian diplomats."

Her eyes had closed with the movement of his fingers, but now they flew wide open. "Nikolai, no! They'll know I'm a woman!"

In one swift motion, he stood up and sat her on his lap facing him. Holding her by the waist, he gently pushed his erection toward her and fought back the urge to take her right there.

"Shhh. No one will know. Just don't cry out like that and no one will suspect a thing."

She dropped onto him, her head nestled in between his neck and shoulder, and mumbled, "Why are you doing this?"

In truth, he was doing this because the idea of her pretending to be someone else excited him. Just as the memory of her as a French coquette named Violet still stirred his desire, the idea of her dressing like a man made him want her even more.

"It will be fun. You'll see."

Nikolai kissed her neck softly and whispered, "We need a name for you. How does Albert sound?"

Annelisa lifted her head. "Albert?"

"Yes. It sounds perfect. Albert Fielding."

"No. Nikolai, please...someone will know."

Kissing her, he took her face in his hands. Her eyes remained closed as he said, "Annelisa, I would never let anything harm you. Trust me."

When she opened her eyes, he was sure he saw a look in them that told him she did trust him.

As much as sitting in his parlor with Annelisa on his lap pleased him, Nikolai knew it was time to go. A few more words of support, and he escorted her to the carriage.

Arriving at the Russian delegation party, Nikolai reminded himself to treat Annelisa as a man. Exiting the carriage, he waited on the sidewalk below but didn't extend his hand to help her down the stairs, despite the look of surprise she shot him.

"Come, Albert. We can't be late."

Annelisa stood on the top step waiting for him to help her, and he whispered, "I wouldn't give my hand to a man, Annelisa. Remember who you're supposed to be."

A look of recognition crossed her face and she whispered, "Oh," as she stepped down to the ground. "Nikolai, what if I forget? I've been a female for twenty-five years and a man for mere hours."

As they walked up the stairs of the stately home in front of them, Nikolai whispered instructions. "Try to lower your voice. And bow. Make sure your handshake is strong, but not too strong. And no giggling."

Annelisa turned to him and in a voice full of exasperation said, "I do not giggle, sir."

"Yes, you do. It's quite charming, in fact, especially when I'm making love to you. But as Albert, there is to be no giggling. Understand?"

"I don't giggle."

"Then that's one thing you won't have to worry about. Now when I introduce you to Count Borislav, shake his hand and say very little. If you can get by him, you should be all right."

"Please tell me that will be later, after I've had some time to practice, Nikolai. Please."

"No, you'll meet him first, as soon as we enter. Now let me see if your moustache is on properly."

Annelisa turned toward him and as he inspected above her lip, he took out his pocket watch to pretend to check the time. Looking down at the watch, he whispered,

"I want to be inside you now more than you can know. Remember that as we do this."

Nikolai saw how his words aroused her. "Ready, Albert?"

Just as he'd said, they met his superior, Count Vladimir Borislav, immediately upon entering and Nikolai watched with pride as Annelisa did just as he'd instructed. Safely past the Count, they began to mingle with the partygoers, and with each introduction he saw Annelisa's confidence increase.

Alone for a moment, she turned to him and boasted, "This is much easier than I thought. These people actually think I'm a man."

"More than you think. But your greatest test is coming this way."

"Greatest test? I thought the Count was my greatest test."

Nikolai turned his attention to the two women coming toward them and mumbled, "No, these are."

Nikolai bowed and shot Annelisa a look to do the same, which she hurriedly did, before he began the introductions.

"Ladies, how wonderful to see you again. Let me introduce you to Albert Fielding. Albert, these charming ladies are the sisters, the Countesses Borislav, Olga and Yelena."

"It's a pleasure to meet you, Countesses."

Nikolai watched as the two women scanned Annelisa from head to toe and back again. When he'd said they'd be her greatest test, he hadn't meant there would be any problem convincing them she was a man. The Countesses Borislav would see trousers and a jacket and automatically accept her as a man. In fact, they'd accept the fact all too well.

Notorious libertines, they'd be quite interested in a new male to pursue. More correctly, Yelena would be interested in a new man. Olga had long chased after Nikolai, much to his chagrin. With her eyes that seemed at times to be so big as to make her resemble a bug and her all too ample breasts that always seemed to be spilling out of her dresses, Countess Olga Borislav was just another potential mate he hoped his family wouldn't insist he choose.

"Oh, Nikolai, he's wonderful. Where have you been hiding him?" Yelena asked as her sister fixed her eyes on his crotch as she always did when they met.

"He's the nephew of a business associate. I knew he'd enjoy himself here."

Yelena cooed her agreement and wrapped her hand around Annelisa's arm to move her prey to a more private location in the corner of the room a few feet away.

"Count? Don't we...aren't we..." Annelisa stammered in fear as Yelena pulled her toward her goal.

"Yelena, I'm going to need him back, so you can only have him for a few minutes."

Nikolai saw Annelisa's eyes grow wide in terror. "Albert, just a few minutes."

Fear raced through Annelisa's body as she was hauled

off toward the corner of the room by this exceptionally eager woman. Damn, Nikolai! Why was he doing this? This woman obviously had designs on her — Albert — and planned to pursue them.

Once in the corner, the Countess began pawing at Annelisa's arms and neck, like an animal in heat. In no time, she saw the true horror of the situation. The woman wanted to kiss her!

"Countess Borislav, why don't we..." she began but was immediately cut off.

"Yelena. Call me Yelena, Albert."

Her sickeningly sweet voice, similar to her sister Olga's, nearly turned Annelisa's stomach.

"Very well, Yelena. Perhaps we can talk for a bit before we...do anything."

Before she knew it, Yelena had taken her hand and placed it just above the neckline of her dress, directly on the swell of her breast. Nearly panting from desire, her breasts rose and fell, nearly tumbling out of her dress with each inhale.

"What would you like to talk about, Albert?" With each word, her hands moved closer and closer to between Annelisa's legs.

Quickly, she grabbed her hands and held them tightly in hers. "Yelena, why don't you tell me how you know Nikolai."

Undeterred, she squeezed one of her hands out of Annelisa's grip and began stroking her forearm as she detailed how she and Olga knew Nikolai.

"Nikolai is an old friend of our family. He's also

Russian nobility. And as I'm sure you can tell, he's very attracted to my sister. The feeling is mutual. In fact, I wouldn't be surprised if an announcement about their engagement came quite soon."

Annelisa directed her attention to Nikolai and Olga just feet away. She quickly assessed that the woman was wholly unappealing and was in serious need of a new dressmaker, even more so than Yelena. But Annelisa's focus was riveted to Nikolai's face, which seemed to indicate he liked being alone with her.

For the first time, jealousy spiked inside her as she watched him smile and even laugh as the horrid woman touched his chest while she flirted shamelessly with him. He was enjoying himself with her while she was trapped with Yelena and her eager hands.

Tearing the woman's hands from her coat, Annelisa marched over to them and announced, "It's time we left, Nikolai."

From behind her she heard Yelena whine about the hour being early, and for a moment it seemed like Nikolai would throw her back into her arms. Thankfully, he turned to Olga and bid his goodbyes before following Annelisa to say goodnight to their host.

But Yelena was not to be put off so easily. Almost tackling Annelisa from behind, she spun her around and kissed her on the lips, much to Annelisa's shock. "I do hope to see you again soon, Albert."

By the time she reached the front steps, Annelisa was in a rage, but she struggled to keep it under control. Jealous over watching him with one sister and furious about being thrown as a bone to the other, she stormed toward the carriage only to find they must wait for it to arrive.

Nikolai walked at his usual leisurely pace, his long stride keeping close to her with little effort. As he joined her to wait for their carriage, he asked, "Did you have a pleasant time, Albert?"

"Don't speak to me."

"I thought you might enjoy the Countesses."

Annelisa turned to face him. "You knew they'd be here?"

"Of course. They attend all these diplomatic functions."

The anger began to grow in her to the point tears began to form in her eyes. He'd brought her here to see the woman he intended to marry. He'd brought his concubine to meet his future wife.

"I hate you!"

Then suddenly it dawned on her. Finally, a way out of their arrangement. If he were to marry Olga Borislav, then he couldn't blackmail her with the threat of telling her father what they'd done.

"I hope you'll be happy with the Countess. And now I've found a way to free myself from your blackmail."

"Happy with the Countess?"

"Yelena told me you are to be married. That means you can't threaten me with going to my father anymore."

The carriage pulled up in front of them, and Annelisa quickly got in and sat down. Nikolai joined her and as they began their trip home, he folded his arms across his chest.

"You're jealous. I'm flattered, Annelisa."

"Jealous? Absolutely not. Although I didn't take you for the type to like such a woman, I wish you well. I'm certainly not jealous."

"Yes, you are. But you have no reason to be. I will not be marrying Olga Borislav, no matter how much she wishes I would."

"I don't care."

"Then why are you so angry?"

"Why am I angry? You let that awful woman paw at me and she kissed me!"

In the dim light of the carriage, Annelisa saw Nikolai grin. Something in her snapped, and she lunged at him, arms swinging. He was much quicker and stronger and held her hands still as she continued to act out her anger.

"How could you?" she cried.

"Calm down. You'll hurt yourself."

As she wrestled against him, he pulled her onto his lap and forced her to sit down. When she continued to fight him, he warned, "Sit still or I swear I'll spank that pretty little bottom of yours."

Annelisa stilled, stunned into compliance. "You wouldn't."

"I will if you don't sit still. Don't say I didn't warn you."

Just as she was about to fight back, his lips were on hers kissing her more passionately than ever before. His tongue searched for hers, sending waves of pleasure straight to all the parts of her body she so desperately wished he'd kiss too. Mindless with anger, jealousy, and desire, she ground her body against his, begging for relief.

Throwing her hat across the carriage, Nikolai moved to her jacket and then her shirt, nearly tearing the buttons off as he worked to free her from it. His hands tore at her pants and he groaned, "Take them off. Now."

Desperate to be free of them and back on top of him, she wriggled out of her pants as Nikolai stripped his off to show his cock fully erect and ready. Wearing only her open shirt, she eagerly climbed onto his lap and slid up and down his cock, coating him with her juices.

"Remember when I told you I wanted to be inside you? I couldn't think of anything else all night. Only your wet cunt wrapped around my cock."

While he spoke, he thrust his hips off the seat, sliding through her slick folds as she wished he would just find the mark and bury himself deeply inside her.

She needed an answer first, though.

"Even when you were talking to that woman?"

"I didn't hear a word she said. The whole time she was talking, I was watching to see if you were all right and fantasizing about this. Didn't you see the smile on my face?"

Annelisa didn't know why, but his answer pleased her almost as much as what they were about to do. And she didn't understand exactly why that pleased her either.

Nikolai loved that Annelisa had been jealous. As she writhed around on his lap, alternately teasing him and then almost begging to be fucked, he watched her beautiful face register the emotions she felt, its loveliness not even obscured by the moustache and men's wig she wore.

In these intimate moments, she was so open, but he knew as soon as they were out of each other's arms, she'd return to denying her feelings for him. A twinge of anger bit at him, and he roughly yanked the moustache off her skin.

"Nikolai! That hurt!"

Immediately guilty, he whispered, "Let me make it better, love," and began tenderly flicking his tongue over the sensitive skin.

"Please don't tease me. I don't think I can handle it tonight."

Lifting her up, he found what he'd fantasized about for hours and slowly filled her until his cock was completely inside her.

"No more teasing, moya milaya."

For a moment, he was still, the motion of the carriage delivering the incredible sensations they both experienced. Her eyes looked into his, and for that moment she wasn't the Annelisa who complained about her time with him. She was the Annelisa who was completely his, body and soul.

He'd have to wait for her mind, but he'd take her

body and soul for now.

"Ride me, Annelisa. Show me how much you want me."

He half expected her to demand he show her how much he wanted her, which he would gladly have obliged, but instead he was pleasantly surprised when she began to fuck him with abandon. Her mouth sought out his, and he gave her everything she needed.

As her body crept closer to the edge, she whimpered his name against his lips, like a single word plea for him to show her how much he wanted her. Each time made him thrust deeper to touch that spot that gave her what she so desperately wanted.

She tightened around him and began to milk his cock toward his own release. There, in the dim light of the carriage as they rode toward home, she shuddered as her release took her over and his sent his seed deep into her. Exhausted, she laid her head on his shoulder and wrapped her arms around him.

For Nikolai, this was the closeness that came from his love for her. Making love—fucking—whatever they did was an extension of his feelings. He believed she loved him too, but as he sat there in the carriage, still joined with her and her holding him, he knew the spell would be broken as soon as he released her.

What would it take to make her admit her feelings?

Ten

Nikolai lay in bed drowsily thinking of his last time with Annelisa. Despite being less than two days earlier, the event seemed to want to fade from his memory, and he fought to relive the sweetness of their rendezvous.

God, she excited him! Just the thought of her riding him in their carriage, her passion in control of her, made him hard now. Even more, though, he wished she'd want to be with him as he wanted her.

Because no matter how many times she begged him not to stop while they made love, he knew she still regarded their time together as a means to an end.

Stroking his chin, he thought about how he could make her come to him. He didn't mind continuing their arrangement, but in truth, he knew it couldn't go on indefinitely. Hell, she may even be carrying his child at that moment, so their agreement would have to change to one of marriage. But he wanted her to want him, not out of obligation but out of love.

"Uprymaya," he grumbled as he closed his eyes in frustration.

It was unlikely she would admit she'd grown to care for him, even if she in fact had. Her independent streak was far too powerful to let feelings get in the way. No, if he ever wanted Annelisa to love him enough to admit it, he'd need something more than just giving her physical pleasure.

What she needs is a dose of her own medicine.

He'd told her to return that day, so if he intended to put a plan into motion, there was no better time than the present. When she arrived that afternoon, he'd begin the work needed to finally have her as his.

A pounding on the front door interrupted his thoughts, and he hurriedly got dressed. By the time he'd reached the main floor, his manservant had let a very upset Maksim in and he was frantically pacing through Nikolai's parlor, wringing his hands.

"Maksim, what brings you here so early this morning?" he asked as he took a seat on the settee.

"Nikolai, it's the worst news! There has been an attempt on the Tsar's life!"

Immediately, Nikolai stood and asked, "What do we know? Has he survived?"

"Yes, thank God! What has the world become, Nikolai?"

While Maksim fretted over the state of affairs in modern Russia, Nikolai rejoiced that his Tsar had survived yet another assassination attempt. This wouldn't be the last, though, he was sure. Alexander II's reign had introduced many changes to his beloved country — many changes that made discontent all the more possible. But for the moment, he was thankful the Tsar was safe.

Maksim handed Nikolai a letter. "This came for you at the office."

Nikolai read the message with a sense of regret. He'd been ordered to return home to deal with the implications of the attempt on the Tsar's life and was to leave immediately.

"Maksim, I've been called back to Russia. While I'm gone, I need you to continue our work with the members of Parliament who favor our ideas. Also, I'll be sending dispatches I'll need you to deliver to a number of people I've been meeting with."

"Of course, Nikolai. I'll be sure to keep you abreast of everything happening here."

Nikolai knew Maksim wouldn't be able to inform him of the most important person to him in England. Quickly, he realized he'd need to pay a visit to her father before he left and hope he could get a free moment to speak to her.

"Maksim, I need to make one stop before I leave. Arrange a coach for me. I'll only be a short time and I'll leave upon my return."

"I'll get to it immediately," Maksim said and left to make the necessary arrangements.

Nine a.m. was exceedingly early to be paying a visit to anyone, but as Nikolai pounded on the Fieldings' front door, he didn't care. He just hoped Annelisa would be available to talk.

The Fieldings' butler opened the door and stuck his head through the crack. "Sir?"

"I apologize for the hour, but I need to see your master."

The servant opened the door and stood aside for Nikolai to pass. "Of course, Count Shetkolov. If you'll wait here, I'll fetch Mr. Fielding immediately."

Nikolai watched the man hurry to the breakfast room and hoped Annelisa was there to hear him announce his arrival. Only a few minutes later, Andrew Fielding came out to greet him in the hallway.

"To what do I owe the pleasure of a visit on this morning, my friend?"

"May I speak to you in private, Andrew?"

Nodding, Andrew placed his hand on Nikolai's back to guide him to the study. "Of course, Nikolai. Is everything all right?"

As Andrew closed the door behind them, Nikolai explained the reason for his visit. Andrew sat behind his desk, his fingers steepled in front of him. "I'm sorry to hear of the attempt on the Tsar's life, Nikolai. How long will you be gone?"

"I don't know. But please know I have Maksim monitoring our friends and foes in Parliament. If you need to get a message to me, know you can trust him."

"Don't worry, friend. Take care of your man and be safe. These are troubled times, I'm afraid."

Nikolai extended his hand. "Thank you, Andrew. I'll

be sure to see you when I return. And if you could keep this news between us, I'd appreciate it."

As he left the study, he spied Annelisa standing in the doorway that led to the breakfast room, her face the picture of concern. He moved his head slightly to let her know to follow him outside and hoped she'd understand his signal.

Nikolai needn't have worried. Before he made it down the front steps, she was at his side peppering him with questions.

"What did you have to speak to my father about so early this morning? What could you have to discuss?"

"Someone attempted to assassinate Tsar Alexander this morning. I've been recalled to Russia."

Annelisa's gaze left his face, and she looked down at the ground. "I'm sorry, Nikolai. Is he going to be all right?"

"I believe so, but as a diplomat, I have to help ensure his reign continues to prosper."

"How long will you be gone?"

Nikolai swore he heard her voice hitch as she asked. "I don't know. Is that sadness in your voice?"

Immediately defensive, Annelisa's eyes grew wide. "That's ridiculous. I just wondered how long my reprieve from your blackmail would be. That's all."

Nikolai studied her face for the truth. How much she would miss him could be seen in her eyes, which seemed on the verge of tears.

Maybe she did care.

"Well, I pledge to continue my heartfelt efforts to

ensure you never suffer from hysteria as soon as I return, Annelisa. In the meantime, I'll be pleased to remember how much you despise marriage and trust you won't choose another in my absence."

Annelisa smiled. "Like I would be so foolish as to allow myself to become involved in a relationship with another man."

Nikolai began walking to his coach but turned around to look at her. "A relationship? Well, I promise that when I return it will be just that. I told you before that you won't get rid of me that easily."

Chuckling, she said, "As if I could ever be that lucky. Have a safe trip, Nikolai,"

As he rode away, he looked back to see her still standing there watching him leave. He was convinced more than ever that she cared. Now all he had to do was find a way to make her admit it.

Annelisa was torn between a feeling of victory over being freed from her arrangement with Nikolai and missing him as she watched his coach roll away from the house. The feeling of victory was short-lived as she admitted to herself that what had begun as blackmail had grown into a relationship. That she'd as much as admitted it to him just minutes before unnerved her, though.

She'd mastered the art of keeping men away, but to make one love her? That was a distinctly different story. He seemed to have some interest in her. He had, in fact, wanted to marry her when he'd found out about Violet's true identity.

But that had been out of obligation.

As the last sight of him faded from view, she turned to walk back to the house. For the first time in her life, the thought of trading her freedom for the love of a man crossed her mind.

Her thoughts filled with Nikolai, she made her way toward the stairs to go to her room, but her father caught her before she made it.

"Annelisa, come in to my study, please."

Since her stunt the night of the ball and her subsequent refusal to name the man who'd taken her virginity, their relationship had been at best strained. And now with Thornton Sutcliffe's blackmail, Annelisa felt worse than ever and so wished she and her father could return to the relationship they'd always had.

Her father sat in a chair near the fireplace and called to her to take a seat next to him. Unsure of what he could want to discuss with her, she sat down and waited for him to begin, her gaze settled on her lap.

For a long time, he said nothing, but when he finally spoke, his voice was the same as it had been before their recent problems.

"Annelisa, I don't know why you did what you did, but for what it's worth, I'm glad you won't be marrying the Earl of Swindon."

Looking up, she saw the face of the man who'd taken care of her for so long and she wanted to cry for all she'd put him through. Reaching over, she wrapped her arms around his neck and hugged him tightly.

"Thank you, Father. I'm so sorry what I've done has created such a mess for you. I never meant for any of it to hurt you."

Annelisa sat back in her chair and wiped her eyes. She'd waited so long to tell him how she felt, and the warm smile that met her words touched her heart.

"If you're referring to that scoundrel Sutcliffe, don't worry. Your father didn't get to where he is today without learning how to deal with the Thornton Sutcliffes of this world. I'm more concerned about you, dear."

Annelisa saw the concern in her father's eyes. "Oh, don't worry about me. As long as I know you understand why I didn't want to marry him, I can deal with whatever he does. I'm a lot like my father that way."

"I'm not worried about that, dear. I'm talking about your future."

"Please don't worry. I'll be fine."

"I just worry about you. Other girls are already married with children at your age. I know you're modern, but what will happen if you don't marry?"

Sure she wanted at the very least to calm his fears, Annelisa took his hands in hers. "I never said I wouldn't marry, Father. Just that I wanted to marry someone of my choosing who I love."

Andrew Fielding's face brightened. "That puts me at ease somewhat, dear, but do you have anyone in mind?"

Annelisa shook her head and smiled. "No, but don't give up on me yet. Perhaps there's a man out there who could love me."

"He'd be a lucky man, Annelisa. You have many gifts

to offer the right man."

"Thank you, Father."

Rising from his seat, he said, "Time for you to go. I have work to attend to. But there's one more thing. There's no need to be sad over Nikolai's leaving. He'll be back."

The blood rushed to her face, and she was sure her blush gave away far more than she'd prefer concerning her feelings for Nikolai. "Why would I be sad?"

"I've seen you two talking recently. He's a count, you know."

"Yes, I know," she said with a smile. "More matchmaking, Father?"

"Just food for thought, dear."

Annelisa left the study before her father had the chance to continue the discussion. Walking to her room, she chuckled at the idea of her father innocently thinking of Nikolai as a potential suitor.

"Annelisa, where have you been?"

Turning, she saw Cecile coming toward her from her room. Her face told her she had something on her mind.

"With Father in his study."

Catching up to her, Cecile pushed Annelisa into her room.

"Cecile, what are you doing?"

Before she knew it, Cecile had pushed her down onto the bed and stood glaring at her.

"Annelisa Fielding, you lied to me!"

Her mind racing to determine which lie her sister referred to, Annelisa quickly decided playing dumb was a far better plan than blindly choosing a lie and defending herself.

"Cecile, I have no idea what you're talking about. Calm down."

"I thought you trusted me. How could you have kept it from me?"

If she didn't get Cecile to lower her voice, everyone in the house would soon know what she meant. Taking her hand, Annelisa brought her sister to the bed and pulled her to sit with her.

"Please sit down. I promise we can talk about whatever you'd like. Just keep your voice down."

"How could you not tell me about your times with Count Shetkolov?" Cecile asked with a hurt look on her face. "I thought we told one another everything."

"How did you know?"

"I saw you leaving his house. What's going on? I thought you didn't like him."

"I never said I didn't like him, Cecile. He's an intelligent and honorable man."

"You said you weren't interested in him. That his good looks didn't matter to you."

"They didn't and I wasn't."

"Then what changed to make you go to his house without anyone else? What did the two of you do?"

Annelisa lifted her eyebrows in disbelief at her sister's naiveté. "Cecile, you really need to read those books in my bottom drawer. You're going to be married soon and need to know about what a man and woman do together."

Annelisa had hoped this would deter her sister's questioning, but she had no such luck. Cecile was not to be put off this time.

"Oh, no you don't, Annelisa. I'm not interested in talking about my future. I want to know what's going on with Nikolai and no more lying."

Annelisa stood up and began pacing back and forth across the room. To be honest, she was almost relieved to tell someone of her secret.

"Nikolai figured out it was me at the ball and offered to do the honorable thing and marry me. I declined his offer and he threatened to tell father everything. To make sure he didn't, I told him I'd do anything. So..."

"So you go to his house and have sex with him?"

Annelisa stopped pacing and turned toward her sister. "We make love, Cecile."

"Do you love him then?"

Cecile's question hung in the air like a huge question mark over Annelisa's head. Did she love him?

"Well?"

"I don't know."

After the words left her mouth, she exhaled and dropped her shoulders, as if the words had been a burden she was finally free of at last.

"I don't understand you, Annelisa. You didn't like the earl because he was odious, but now you don't know how you feel about Nikolai, even though he's very handsome, successful, and you've been sneaking off to be with him?"

"It's more complicated than that. I don't know how

he feels about me. He's never asked me to marry him again. What if he just wants me for sex?"

"Have you let him know you care for him?"

Annelisa silently shook her head.

"Then tell him."

"I can't. He's been recalled to Russia, and I don't know when he'll return."

Cecile stood up and wrapped her arms around her sister. "Then tell him when he gets back before another woman falls in love with those gorgeous blue eyes and steals him away forever."

Eleven

Annelisa waited in her father's study, her toes tapping the floor nervously in anticipation of Nikolai's arrival. His three week absence would end in mere minutes if his cable was correct, and her excitement at seeing him was nearly killing her.

To her surprise, the time away from him had only made her feelings increase, and she longed to see him again. She would take Cecile's advice and confess her feelings to him with the desperate hope that he cared for her in return.

Unable to sit still, she stood and walked to the window to look out at the garden. The memory of her refusal of his marriage proposal in that very garden made her wince. She'd been so cavalier that day.

Please let him be better than I was when I tell him how I feel.

"Andrew, how are you my friend?"

Nikolai's accent hit her deep inside, and she turned to see him standing in the doorway to the study. Her eyes traveled over his face and body, from his blue eyes and his goatee that made him seem so foreign and exotic, to his coat and trousers that covered the body she'd missed for the past three weeks.

"And Miss Fielding. What a lovely surprise to see you."

As Nikolai and her father moved to sit, Annelisa stood frozen to the spot in fear. Everything she hadn't been sure of bombarded her brain, nearly overwhelming her.

She couldn't deny it any longer. She loved him. But did he love her?

Annelisa watched as he and her father talked about the Tsar's safety and Nikolai's return to England. In truth, she only heard a fraction of their conversation as the sound of her heart's pounding seemed to drown out much in the room.

"You must be happy to be back, Nikolai. I know I'm happy to have you back so our plans for my company's expansion in Russia can commence."

"I'm pleased to be back, but I won't be staying long before I return once again to Russia."

Annelisa stepped forward. "Oh? Why?"

"I have wonderful news. I am to return home to marry the Countess Stravinsky in one week. I'll return to my post after the wedding, so don't worry, Andrew. Your plans will happen."

"Congratulations, Nikolai. This is wonderful news!"

As her father professed his happiness at Nikolai's impending marriage, Annelisa felt like the room was spinning around her. Married? Her Nikolai was marrying some Russian countess? Cecile had been right. Some other woman had fallen in love with those beautiful blue eyes and stolen him away from her.

As she stood there watching the man she loved beaming about marrying another woman, her stomach turned and she felt like she was going to be sick. Suddenly, there didn't seem to be enough air in the room and the dress she'd worn especially because he'd liked it before seemed like it would smother her.

Tears welled up in her eyes as the emotional disappointment enveloped her.

She'd lost him.

Before she began crying, Annelisa said, "Please excuse me, Father. I feel ill. Congratulations, sir," and quickly exited the room.

In the hallway, she stood with her back pressed against the wall, afraid that without the support, she'd collapse. As her father told Nikolai about Thornton Sutcliffe's blackmail, tears rolled down over her cheeks. Her Nikolai was another woman's.

For days Annelisa stayed in bed, truly sick over Nikolai's impending marriage to some countess whose name she couldn't remember. Cecile tried to console her, but little could be done. Finally, she suggested the impossible.

"Annelisa, you must tell him how you feel. Even if he

still marries Countess What's-Her-Name, he'll know you truly cared for him."

Her head buried in a pillow, Annelisa said, "He doesn't care for me, Cecile. Why would he care how I feel about him?"

"He might not, but you say he's an honorable man. He should know."

"He's not an honorable man! He never cared for me. He only used me until he found a suitable woman to marry!"

Cecile pulled her sister from the pillow. "Do you honestly believe that? Do you honestly believe he never cared at all?"

Annelisa wasn't sure what she believed. She'd made such a mess of everything, and now the one man she'd ever wanted to marry was marrying another woman.

"I don't know what I believe, Cecile. All I know is that I've lost him."

An hour later, with a great deal of help from Cecile, including the knowledge that he was in his neighborhood home that day, Annelisa set off for Nikolai's house one last time. She would tell him how she felt and hoped it at least make her feel better.

Something told her it would have the exact opposite effect.

As she made her way over the country road, a thought she'd never had before repeated in her head. Annelisa Fielding — spinster. For the first time, the idea that she'd be alone settled into her brain and tormented her. Worse was the knowledge that she'd be alone because of her own actions. Nikolai had asked her to marry him and she'd refused.

Why had she been so foolish?

Nikolai watched Annelisa through the front window as she stood at the edge of his property for what seemed like hours. He'd waited for days to see her since he hadn't had a chance to speak to her that day at her house, and his heart ached as he looked at the sad face she wore. It had taken all his diplomatic powers of persuasion to convince her sister to tell Annelisa to visit him, but there was no other way to get to see her, especially after he'd heard she was sick in bed for days.

He watched her finally make her move toward the house and then heard her soft knock at the door. When he opened it, he felt his heart miss a beat. She looked so sad.

"Come in."

Annelisa walked past him into the parlor, which still remained almost entirely empty without most of the furniture. With no seating choices, she sat down on the settee and he took his position next to her.

She remained silent, her eyes fixed on her folded hands in her lap, looking nothing like the Annelisa he'd known.

"I'm so happy you came, Annelisa."

Suddenly, the dam broke.

"Are you? Why? Why are you marrying another woman? I thought you cared for me. Was what we did merely physical? If it was, why did you ask me to marry you?"

Nikolai couldn't help but smile. This was the Annelisa he remembered.

"One question at a time. Yes, I am happy you came. I missed you. And what we did was never merely physical, not from the first time we were together at the masquerade ball. And I asked you to marry me because it was the honorable thing to do when I found out it was you I'd made love to that night."

Tears welled up in her eyes. "You didn't love me. It was just an obligation."

"No, I didn't love you when I asked you to marry me. I believed we could grow to love one another, but you didn't want to marry me."

Annelisa sniffled and stood to leave. "I have to go. I can't do this. I hope you'll be happy. Goodbye, Nikolai."

As she started to move past him, he grabbed her arm and yanked her down onto his lap. Stunned, she stared at him, her eyes wide with confusion.

"Uprymaya! Why does everything have to be a fight with you, Annelisa?"

"What are you doing? Let me go right now. You're engaged to someone else. Why would you tease me like this?"

Nikolai put his finger up to her mouth to silence her. "For once, I want you to listen without saying a word. I love you, Annelisa. I've loved you since that night in the Stewarts' garden. But I knew you didn't love me, and even when I believed you'd grown to feel something for me, I knew you wouldn't admit it."

"What are you saying?"

"There is no Countess Stravinsky I'm marrying. I mean, there is a countess with that name, but she's my mother's age and happily married to the Count Stravinsky."

Annelisa sat staring at him, stunned by his words. "Why did you lie? You broke my heart!"

Nikolai gently caressed her damp cheek. "I'm sorry. I needed a way to make you admit your feelings for me."

Leaping off his lap, Annelisa glared in anger at him. "How could you do that? I was sick in bed for days over you!"

He tried to pull her back to him, but she was already on her way to the door. Quickly, he caught her and held her to him as she struggled against his body.

"Annelisa, stop. I just told you I love you and I'm not marrying anyone else."

"Days, Nikolai! I was in bed for days thinking I'd lost you to another woman!"

Taking her face in his hands, he kissed her lips and whispered against them, "I love you, Annelisa. And I love that you cared enough to be sad for days when you thought you'd lost me."

"Ya tebya lyublyu," she whispered back.

Nikolai beamed at the words "I love you" in his own language coming from the woman he adored.

"Moya milaya."

"You always say that to me. I was so determined to

find out how to tell you I love you in Russian that I never found out what that means."

As he began removing her dress, he whispered, "It means, 'my sweet'."

Annelisa smiled. "I love you, Nikolai. I was devastated at the thought of losing you. You're the only man I've ever loved."

As she made her confession, he slid her dress down over her hips and let it puddle on the floor at her feet.

"Not to worry. As I told you that day I asked you to marry me, you won't get rid of me that easily."

He made quick work of her stockings and undergarments while he planted soft kisses over her stomach. When she was finally completely undressed, he looked up at her to see her watching him with almost frightened eyes.

"Annelisa?"

Twisting her face into a worried expression, she said quietly, "Every time I've ever been with you has been an act. I don't know..."

Nikolai rose to kiss her on the lips. Smiling, he answered, "I know, but I love this Annelisa, not Violet or you as Albert or even the Annelisa everyone else sees."

When he'd finished unbuttoning his shirt and pants, he slid out of them and stepped back to look at the woman he adored. Slowly, he trailed his fingertips over her skin, lingering on her nipples as they hardened under his touch.

"Nikolai..."

"No more talking. Let me show you what I've thought of every day since I last saw you."

Nikolai swept her up in his arms, and for the first time, took her up to his bedroom instead of that lone couch in the parlor. They made love as he knew they always would—openly and sweetly, with no masks or façade to shield either of them.

Afterward, as Annelisa rested her head on his chest, Nikolai thought about how he was going to tell his friend and future father-in-law he wanted to marry his daughter. He also thought about his talk with Thornton Sutcliffe earlier that day.

"Annelisa, I spoke to the Earl of Swindon today. He's been blackmailing your father, but I don't think he'll be doing that anymore."

"Good. It broke my heart to hear him say the things he did to him, and I told him what I thought of him to his face."

"You told the earl this?"

Annelisa sat up. "Yes, I did. I don't care who you noblemen think you are. It's not right to blackmail people. That goes for you too."

"Does it now? Well, I wouldn't have had to blackmail you if you'd said yes the first time I asked you to marry me."

"Correction, Count. The only time you've asked me."

Nikolai smiled at the most stubborn woman he'd ever met. "You're right. And I even bent down on one knee and you said no. I guess if I ever ask again, it would have to be something even bigger."

Quietly, she said, "Well, maybe not. It's the thought that counts. Perhaps you should try it again and see if it goes better this time."

Nikolai shook his head and frowned. "And I'd have to get permission to marry anyone other than Russian nobility, so that could take some time, if it ever happened."

Annelisa put her head down and sighed. "I understand."

"Thankfully, I had to return home just recently and received permission then."

When she looked up, Nikolai saw the look of surprise on her face. "Will you marry me, Annelisa Fielding?"

Annelisa fell on top of him and hugged him tightly as she said the words he'd longed to hear since that day in the garden. "Yes, yes, I'll marry you, Nikolai."

"And you want a husband now?"

"I don't know if I want a husband, but I want you. If that means I get a husband, then a husband I'll have."

Later, as they lay in bed together, Annelisa asked, "How did you convince the earl to stop blackmailing my father, Nikolai?"

"I threatened him."

Annelisa looked up at him. "That doesn't seem very diplomatic."

"He wasn't dealing with a diplomat. He was dealing with a man in love."

Snuggling up to him, she said, "I certainly hope if we ever have a son, he's just like you. But if we have a daughter, I want her to be just like me."

Nikolai kissed the top of her head. "God help me, let it be a boy. No amount of diplomacy would help me with two of you."

The End

Vampire Dreams

One

London, 1850

The dark streets of the city lay sprawled out in front of her, filled with both possible danger and salvation. As she ran, her feet pounding against the stones beneath them, her breathing came in pants that stole the moisture from her mouth. Her eyes frantically scanned for someplace to hide as she pushed her legs to run faster.

She could hear his feet as each one solidly hit the ground behind her. His stride much longer than hers, he was coming closer with each step.

If he caught her...

The pounding of her heart hammered in her ears as the blood pushed faster and faster through her body. Up ahead, she saw a door ajar in a rundown building. If it was empty, she might be able to find a place to hide and hopefully escape from the pain of what awaited her if he captured her.

She slipped through the doorway, but her cape caught on the doorknob, costing her precious moments. As she worked to free herself, she heard his footsteps slow down to a walk, a sign he was as sure as she that he'd won.

Finally, in desperation, she tore the fabric from the knob, and free to run once more, she turned and ran headlong into the chest of a man who stood silently watching her.

"Please save me! He's coming for me!"

Without a word, the stranger took her by the arm and led her to a table near the far wall. With his hands on her shoulders, he hesitated a moment and then spun her around.

His voice deep, he commanded, "Place your hands on the table and bend over."

Unsure if she'd chosen a fate as horrific as the one she'd fled from, she did as she'd been told and waited in terror for what was to come.

The noise of her stalker entering the building caused her to turn her head, but the voice behind her sternly warned, "Face forward."

She felt hands lift her cloak and dress, allowing the cool night air to hit the bare skin of her thighs. The feeling at once thrilled and shocked her, and she instinctively stood up to cover herself.

The man behind her forcibly pushed her back toward the table and leaned over her to whisper low in her ear, "Trust me," as he pushed his body firmly against her backside.

"Hey you! Where's the girl who came in here?"

With his hands on her hips, the man who gave her no choice but to trust him pushed his hips toward hers and thrust toward her still clothed body to simulate sex, complete with throaty groans.

"Hey! I asked you about the girl who came in here!"

Never looking back, Arden squeezed her eyes closed, shutting out the moonlight that streamed in through the window above, and waited for the attack she feared. Instead, she heard the man whose body continued to meet hers bark, "Go away! This whore's mine!"

Indignant at the use of the word whore to describe her, she started to push herself up but his hand held her by the neck and forced her to remain still on the table. A sound like a hiss came from her protector and the other man hurriedly ran out of the building.

A hardness brushed past her thighs and she realized while she'd escaped death, she now faced being raped by this stranger who had asked her to trust him. Over and over, his erection teased her. Fear turned to arousal as she felt his stiff cock press toward her and her body begin to want him. His hand on her neck eased almost to a caress as he continued to hold her down.

Noises behind them told her the original attacker had been chased off, and when the thrusts stopped, she pushed back against him, forcing him off her. Spinning around, she smoothed her dress and snapped, "You are no gentleman! Whore?"

The man stood looking at her, a small grin creeping onto his lips. In a voice far silkier than she'd heard from him before, he said, "You didn't need a gentleman."

Realizing he had no intention of apologizing for calling her a whore, she stubbornly tried to push past him, unsure where she would go, but he blocked her path solid as a stone.

"Let me go! I demand you step aside."

"I wouldn't be that gentleman you expect if I simply let you walk back out into a potentially dangerous situation, Miss..."

After a few moments, she saw the sense in his words and relented. "Miss Stephens," and then added, "Arden Stephens."

"Well, Miss Stephens, I feel responsible for seeing you safely home, so if you'll just give me the address, we'll be on our way."

Sighing deeply, she dropped her gaze to the ground. Now he'd realize just what kind of person she was. Homeless. He'd probably think she'd deserved being chased as a thief or pickpocket.

"Miss Stephens?"

Arden looked up into the brown eyes that seemed to search her face and felt the warmth of humiliation grow in her cheeks. Her gaze drifted over the fine cut of his clothes and his expensive coat, and she wrestled with how to explain that although she had no home, she was no street trollop to be looked down upon. She was just one of the unfortunate few whose father had died before his daughter had been blessed by a husband and whose mother had died of cholera in the last great outbreak.

"I don't have a home," she said quietly as she looked

directly into his eyes.

For a long moment, he remained silent. Arden waited for the pity or disgust, the two emotions her statement generally elicited.

"Well, dear lady, the gentleman in me feels compelled to remedy that situation. You'll come to my home, and although I expect it's beneath your station and gifts, I can offer you the position as my maid as my previous one has recently left my employ."

Arden looked up and studied the face of the person who'd been the kindest to her since her father had died nearly a month ago. His deep brown eyes appeared kind, but his face possessed a darkness that seemed contrary to them. She guessed he could be a few years older than her twenty years but noted how strong he'd proven himself so she corrected herself, realizing she couldn't place his age even as he stood no more than a foot away.

"I couldn't do that. I don't even know your name," she halfheartedly protested.

"Please allow me to introduce myself. My name is Brandon Ridley, and you seem to have few options better than my offer."

As he spoke, she paid special attention to his mouth. How beautiful his teeth looked! In fact, as she studied him closely now, he appeared thoroughly handsome and quite a gentleman.

With a nod of resignation, she agreed with his assessment of her present situation and accepted his offer adding, "But I should inform you, sir, that I have no experience as a maid, other than to take care of my late father."

She was pleased when he didn't express his sympathy at her father's passing. Her emotions were still quite raw and became impossible to control when people gave their condolences. She'd said her goodbyes and accepted the loss but truly wished she'd never have to think of it again.

"I'm quite sure you'll do just fine."

For the first time in weeks, Arden allowed herself to smile and actually chuckled when he confided, "Just keep an eye on the housekeeper. She's a spiteful old one."

As they walked, she congratulated herself on her apparent good fortune and then asked, "You have a maid and housekeeper? Isn't that superfluous?"

A surprised look crossed his face. "Superfluous? Definitely beneath your gifts," he mumbled to himself. Turning to look at her, he said, "No, Miss Stephens, I require both a housekeeper and maid. The housekeeper takes care of the house, and the maid takes care of me."

The way he said this struck her, but then she realized the house must mean the rest of his family. "How will your wife take to you bringing home a new maid? I know women prefer to run household staffs."

Casually, he answered, "I have no wife or children."

No wife or children but he requires a housekeeper and maid?

Arden stopped as he unlocked the front gate and began walking to the door of his home. Awestruck, she realized they'd walked blocks away from where they'd been into an exclusive part of London. His house, an enormous Georgian, stood before her, a sign of his obvious wealth, and the shame of the recent events of her life covered her.

Brandon stopped at the base of the steps and turned toward her. Beckoning her, he stood obviously confused by her reluctance.

"Miss Stephens?"

Arden knew she was more than the homeless girl Brandon Ridley was being charitable toward with a job as a maid. She may not be on his level, but pride was no reason to remain homeless.

Bowing to her own common sense, she entered through the gate and locked it behind her. As she joined him on the stairs, he smiled his beautiful smile again. "I hope you find my house everything you desire."

An hour later, she'd met the housekeeper, Mrs. Benson, and had seen instantly her new employer had spoken the truth. The rest of the staff had seemed pleasant, and Arden believed she had found somewhere she could stay, at least for the time being.

"I'll show you to your room, Miss Stephens."

Arden followed Brandon up the stairs to a second floor of bedrooms and a hallway that led to servants' quarters at the back of the house. When he stopped at a bedroom door, she stood confused.

"This will be your room. My room is at the end of the hall near the front of the house and that leads to the servants' area."

"Sir?"

"Good night, Miss Stephens."

Before she could ask if it would be better if she stayed

with the rest of the help in the servants' quarters, he turned and left her. As she watched him descend the stairs, Arden wondered just what exactly she'd agreed to.

Brandon reclined in his chair in his study and considered the evening's events. Saving Arden from her attacker had been a fortunate happenstance indeed. Although he'd been at that building for an entirely different reason, the potent scent of one like himself in pursuit of prey had encouraged him to stay to watch. However, just the sight of Arden had made him interrupt the chase. Her brown eyes staring up at him in desperation and her hands pressed to his chest as she pleaded for his help had ignited something in him making him want her for himself.

As he finished the last of his port, he remembered with pleasure the feel of her bent over in front of him. The feel of her hips under his hands. The softness of her body pressed against his. With no effort, she'd aroused him, even though the act had been entirely pretend. And if his acute sense of smell wasn't mistaken, she'd wanted him.

As he fantasized about her, he wondered what had happened to make her one of London's many homeless. Why had no one taken her for his wife? He thought of her wit combined with her obvious beauty and imagined many a young man vying for her hand. Young men like himself.

No. Not like me.

But now she was no longer homeless. She was safe in

his house as his maid. And even if he couldn't be the kind of man she deserved, he would make her his.

Two

Arden spent her first full day in her new home learning from the rest of Brandon's staff how he liked his house run. Mrs. Benson lectured her on such topics as dust and the importance of beating rugs correctly, while the older Mrs. Jandry, the cook, stood quietly cutting vegetables and preparing meals each time Arden passed through the kitchen.

By dinnertime, she hadn't seen him yet that day and casually inquired about his daily schedule from Mrs. Jandry.

"Does Mr. Ridley usually stay away from the house all day?"

Never lifting her eyes from the bread dough she was kneading, she replied, "The master is a night owl, to be sure. As his maid, you best become accustomed to his peculiar schedule."

Arden wondered exactly what she meant by "peculiar

schedule." She remembered Brandon saying the maid took care of him. Did that mean turning her days and nights upside down and becoming a night owl like him? And if so, when would she sleep—in the day?

Resolved to ask him about her concerns, she waited to see him, but by nine o'clock he was still absent and when the rest of the household retired to their rooms in the servants' quarters, she reluctantly climbed the stairs to her bedroom. Unsure if she was expected to know of his peculiar schedule, she remained awake until ten o'clock, but found herself too sleepy by then and retired for the evening also.

Extinguishing the gaslight, she lay back on her bed and relaxed in the darkness. The comfort of her new bed, unlike anything she'd had for weeks, felt so wonderful beneath her. As she drifted off to sleep, she wondered if her new job of being maid to a man who never stayed home was too good to be true.

Brandon knew by midnight all in the house would be asleep, including Arden. He remained at his desk in his study, waiting patiently as the minutes ticked away. When the grandfather clock in the parlor announced midnight, he quietly ascended the stairs to her bedroom.

Once inside her room, he stood with his back pressed to the door watching her. How beautiful she was in sleep! As beautiful as during waking hours. As the glow of the moon streamed in and bathed her in its light, he was reminded of the vision of her the night before and told himself she was a natural child of the night.

She remained asleep, and as he watched, aroused by her peacefulness, his passions created a storm in him he struggled to control. So innocent, yet so desirable.

He'd purposefully avoided her since waking, sure his need for her would be met by the response of a proper lady. No, he'd have her this way and wait for her to come to him.

Almost timidly, as if what he might find may cause him to lose control of his desire, he peeled back the blanket and sheet to reveal her body covered only by a thin white nightgown. Mere fabric was all that stood between his desires and sweet satisfaction.

He stopped a moment as she unconsciously recognized the change in her sleep, and when she stilled, he sat silently on the bed next to her to study her. She was so delicate — how would she respond to his touch?

Struggling to restrain himself, he gently touched the soft collar of her nightgown and tugged on the silk ribbon at her neck. Opened, it revealed a tease of what was to come. One by one, he untied the ribbons that held the fabric closed, until he'd revealed her beautiful breasts and body.

How he wanted her! That it must be like this for now he accepted, but he eagerly awaited the time when she'd choose to come to him. In a whisper, he spoke the chant that would awaken her as if in a dream.

When she opened her eyes and gazed up at him with a knowing look, his heart pounded against his chest in fear that the enchantment hadn't worked and she was

conscious of him. But soon he saw her eyes cloud over with passion as she reached out for him and searched for his mouth with hers.

The moment his lips touched hers, his cock hardened. The feel of her tongue touching his sent his fangs shooting into position, and he slowly ran his fingertips over a pearled nipple. Hypnotized, she watched as he removed his clothes with a mere thought and returned to her, his body desperate to be next to hers.

His mouth replaced his finger on her nipple, and he tenderly sucked as she arched up toward him wanting more. Like this, she was so willing and wanton, her desire meeting his. His fangs grazed her skin as he bit down on the base of her nipple, drawing a soft moan from her throat.

Her hands tugged at his hair, urging him to continue his sweet assault. The feel of her excited skin against his lips as he sucked aroused him more, and he yearned to have her in his mouth.

Trailing kisses over her stomach, he stopped just above her dark triangle and inhaled the scent he'd enjoyed the night he'd rescued her.

She had wanted him...

With little prodding, her legs fell open and his eyes feasted on her pink cunt and her swollen nub, moist and waiting for his mouth. Gently at first, he pressed his lips to her soft skin in the most erotic lover's kiss. Rewarded with a keening whimper, he slid his tongue between his lips and began softly flicking her excited clitoris.

Her fingers urged him on as they pressed into the

back of his head. Eager to feel her come apart beneath him, he slid a finger into her tight channel and stroked her tender flesh over the spot he knew would send her crashing into a million pieces.

Above him, he heard her excited pleas to bring her the sweet release she craved. Seconds later, as her insides began milking his finger, she exploded into his mouth. Sliding his finger out of her, he licked her juices, savoring the exquisite taste of her.

Now his cock would enjoy what his mouth had just pleasured. As he hovered over her, he looked down into her dreamy face and kissed her lips, letting her taste what he had.

"Now I'm going to fuck that delicious cunt, sweet Arden."

He positioned his cock at her entrance and slowly pushed into her, letting her become accustomed to his size before he began fucking her in earnest.

"Tell me what you want, Arden."

Obeying his command, she pulled him tightly to her and whispered in his ear, "Fuck me. Please."

The sound of such raw words coming from the mouth of his very ladylike maid nearly undid him, but after a few moments, he'd calmed himself and began plunging into her.

She met his every thrust with one of her own, at first shyly but then more passionately. With each thrust, he ached to sink his fangs into her neck, taking her blood into his body as she took him into hers. However, he'd wait for that. As he felt himself get close, he spoke to her.

"Sweet, Arden, you feel so tight around my cock. I'm going to fill you up. Tell me you want that."

"Yes!"

That one word sent him over the edge, and he shot his hot seed into her as she nursed his cock through her own orgasm. Sated, he rested on top of her and sweetly kissed her lips. She looked so beautiful as she looked up at him wearing an expression of pure satisfaction, and he so wished he could fall asleep with her in his arms. But that would have to wait until she willingly came to him. Until then, he'd take these secret moments with her.

"Sweet dreams, Arden," he whispered before he repeated the chant to send her back to sleep.

Carefully, he retied her nightgown's ribbons and tucked her into the sheet and blanket before he left to begin his night out. Hours later, after he'd taken care of the man who had chased her the night before, he drank from one of his usual women and fantasized about Arden's sweet blood flooding his throat as he buried himself deep inside her. Then she'd truly be his.

Arden awoke to the sound of the housekeeper's knuckles rapping on her bedroom door. Groggily, she sat up on the edge of the bed, still exhausted after what she reasoned must have been a restless night's sleep.

As she worked through her day, she awaited the time she'd see her employer again. She wanted to ask about what the cook had said, but more and more as the day wore on, she simply looked forward to seeing him after almost two days absent.

At eight o'clock her anticipation was finally eased when he called for her to bring his dinner. As she entered his dimly lit study, she hoped he would be able to help her understand just what her duties were, though he seemed entirely disinterested in her, attending to his paperwork and correspondence.

Arden stood patiently beside his desk and waited. Unaccustomed to being treated like this, she shifted her weight from one foot to the other and sighed. After she'd done this several times, almost without thinking, she saw him look up, his face indifferent.

"Yes?"

"Sir..." she hesitated. "Mr. Ridley, I was hoping I could ask you about our...arrangement."

Arden watched his face for any change but saw none. The charming gentleman who'd saved her just days earlier seemed to have vanished, replaced by a stranger who preferred to reply to neighbors' letters than discuss anything with her.

Moving his focus back to the papers on his desk, he said with an air of detachment, "Our arrangement?"

"Yes, sir. Mrs. Jandry mentioned that I'd better get used to your schedule, and as I'm to take care of you, I'd hoped you could tell me what your schedule is."

Brandon looked up from his papers and stared straight ahead. "I wouldn't get caught up in what my cook thinks you should do."

"Sir, how am I to take care of you if I don't know what my responsibilities are and when I'm expected to

perform them?"

Looking at her for the first time, he said, "You take care of me just fine, Miss Stephens," and then returned to the work in front of him.

Arden's exasperation rose up in her. "Will there be anything else, Mr. Ridley?"

"No."

She left his study confused and irritated without any further information about what his schedule was or what was expected of her. As she entered the kitchen, she was glad to find it empty, and she slumped down into a chair, her mind tortured by his behavior.

I've never met a more infuriating man! He runs hot and cold, one day saving me and providing me a position in his home, and the next he can't even be bothered to speak to me!

Arden waited until ten o'clock, hoping he would call her in to speak to him, but when his summons never came, she went to her room disappointed. Just as she had the night before, she fell asleep wondering just what her position in Brandon Ridley's house entailed.

Brandon sat in his study knowing Arden was just one floor away. It had taken every ounce of self-control he possessed to not offer her a seat next to him and enjoy a conversation as they had the night they'd met. But he couldn't trust himself yet.

He let his mind drift back to the night before and in seconds his cock began to strain against the front of his pants. She'd been so open, welcoming his touch and eager for him. The thought of how she'd felt around him made the hours he'd have to wait to visit her again torture.

Memory told him his reward for waiting would be sweet.

Once again, as the clock struck midnight, he climbed the stairs to her bedroom. Inside, he wasted little time before he'd undressed her, making sure to quietly chant his spell before to ensure she'd be awake and willing.

As he ran his hands over her full breasts, he yearned to see her beautiful eyes, full of desire, staring up at him.

"Open your eyes, sweet Arden."

Her eyes fluttered open, and he saw them clouded with passion as they'd been the night before.

"Tell me what you want, love."

As she wrapped her arms around his neck and pulled him close to her, she whispered, "Give me what I need, Brandon."

The sound of his name coming from her lips as she lay waiting for him to fuck her made his cock stiffen, and he shed his clothes instantly with just a thought.

"I wish only to please you, my sweet Arden."

He covered her mouth with his and slowly teased her with his tongue, flicking the tip along her lips each time he entered. She responded by sucking his tongue in a motion he wished he could feel on his cock.

A quick swipe of his finger along her wet seam told him her body craved the same as his. Positioning himself over her, he slid into her, feeling his balls rest against her body. He heard a small moan and looked to see her with her bottom lip between her teeth, a look of pain on her face.

"Take all of me, love. Give me all of you."

Cradling her face in his hands, he kissed her sweetly before he began to move in and out of her, enjoying the feel of his cock sliding against the slickness of her cunt. She wrapped her legs around him and he slid in even further. As he pumped in and out of her, he whispered in her ear, "Arden, say you'll be mine."

Eagerly, she panted, "Yes! Make me yours!"

Kissing up her neck, he stopped and rested his lips over the throbbing vein whose beat matched the rhythm of his fucking. His fangs descended, and he licked his lips in anticipation of the taste of her blood on his tongue.

"Mine."

His mouth clamped down on the column of her neck and his fangs pierced her skin, instantly delivering the delicious gift. Her blood, warm and sweet, flooded over his tongue and ran down the back of his throat, the taste more exquisite than he ever could have imagined.

Careful to take only what wouldn't harm her, he drank her essence slowly as he savored every drop. The feel of her giving him what he needed to exist caused him to lose the last bit of control, and with one last thrust, he came inside her.

She'd cried out as his fangs entered her and now as his orgasm brought hers, she cried out in ecstasy and dug her nails into his back. Carefully, he closed the tiny holes he'd drunk from and moved to look down at her. She looked almost angelic, and he thanked her for the gift she'd given him.

"Sweet Arden, from this point on, you are mine."

In the haze of the spell he had her under, she answered, "Yes, Brandon. Always yours."

The pull of her blood was strong in him now, drawing her to him and him to her. Only a few nights more and he hoped to show her his true feelings without controlling her.

Three

Arden was happy when Mrs. Benson told her Brandon had errands he required done, and as she set off to complete them, she noted the beautiful May morning. The warm breeze drifted over her skin, and the spring sun beat down, warming her face. For the first time in longer than she cared to think about, she was happy and safe, and she allowed herself to enjoy the freedom that came with the security of Brandon's home.

Looking down at the list he'd written out for her, she read over the words and felt a twinge of jealousy. Flower shop, confectioner, dressmaker's...her heart sank as she realized she was collecting gifts meant for a woman.

As she walked toward her first stop, she reminded herself that he hadn't even bothered to notice her the night before. And then there was the difference in their stations. Brandon Ridley was obviously wealthy, whereas, until just a few days ago, she had been homeless. And she was his maid. No matter what kind of romantic notions her young mind entertained, wealthy men didn't marry their household help.

It seemed strange to her that she should be jealous at all. True, Brandon was a very good looking man with a powerfully built body, but she hadn't thought of him as that until now. Or at least she didn't think she had.

The past few days had been confusing for her, and she hadn't been herself. Sure she wasn't sleeping as well as she should, she'd even considered asking the bitter old housekeeper for a sleeping draught in the hopes that maybe that would help. And now today, she felt sluggish again and lightheaded.

Her silly ideas of romance she was beginning to form for her employer would have to be banished from her mind if she intended to keep her position in his home. And for at least a short time, she needed her job.

After stops at each of her assigned errands, she found herself with arms full of flowers, handmade chocolates, and a beautiful red dress. By the time she'd returned to the house, she'd constructed a perfectly improper fantasy involving herself in the red dress and Brandon seducing her with the flowers and chocolates. Chastising herself for such ridiculous ideas, she wondered what had come over her to affect her mind like this.

As he had the day before, Brandon appeared at dinner time in his study. The cook had been instructed to prepare steak, and Arden served him expecting the same treatment as yesterday. She placed the tray on the table next to him and waited, as usual.

Brandon looked up at her and smiled broadly. "Miss Stephens, did you enjoy your time out today? Your cheeks look positively sun-kissed."

A stab of jealousy hit her as she remembered her day collecting gifts for him to give to another woman. "It was quite nice, Mr. Ridley. Thank you."

She cringed as she thanked him, as if she were showing her appreciation for him slighting her. She knew what she was thinking was silly but couldn't help how she felt.

He cut the piece of meat Mrs. Jandry had prepared into equal halves and ordered Arden to pull up the chair from the corner to the table and sit down. She did as instructed, confused and wondering what had caused this drastic change in him.

Motioning toward the plate, he said, "Please, enjoy, Miss Stephens."

He pushed one half of the steak toward her and handed her his knife and fork. Arden knew as a mere maid she couldn't let him sit there with no way to eat and moved to get up to get him another fork and knife.

Stopping her with his hand on hers, he said, "Please sit and eat. Mrs. Benson can get me what I need."

Arden wanted to protest, knowing she shouldn't eat with him, especially if Mrs. Benson would now be forced to do her job in her stead, but she liked the attention he gave her, so she sat back down and waited as he called for the housekeeper.

In mere moments, Mrs. Benson arrived with what he requested. Arden stared down at her food knowing the housekeeper's look of reproach faced her if she turned to look at her. Once they were alone again, she waited for him to begin eating and then took a small bite for herself.

As she enjoyed her food, he reached over to cut her steak. "You need more than that tiny piece." He stabbed the larger piece he'd cut for her and held it to her mouth. "Here. Eat," he ordered.

Her eyes wide with surprise, she looked up to see him ready to feed her. She reached for the fork, but he shook his head. "No. Let me take care of you like you do for me."

Taking the food in her mouth, she stared into his eyes, unsure of what was happening. Quietly, she said, "Mr. Ridley, sir, I don't seem to do much of anything to take care of you. And I obviously disappointed you in some way yesterday."

Brandon looked across the table at her downturned mouth. "I'm sorry for how I acted yesterday. You've done nothing to displease me, I assure you. You've been perfect, Arden."

His use of her name made her blush, and she looked away embarrassed, sure he clearly saw his effect on her. When he gently ordered her to eat, she smiled, making sure to keep her focus on the food in front of her.

After a few minutes of silence, he asked, "What did you think of the dress I had you pick up for me?"

Afraid that if she told him how much she admired the dress he'd know her feelings and how jealous she'd been, she joked, "I'm not sure red is your color."

A small smile crept onto his face, and Arden swore

she saw the look she'd seen on the faces of the men in love at the theatre years ago when her father had taken her. Common sense told her she must be wrong. Brandon Ridley was not in love with her. Of this, she was sure.

"I like your sense of humor, Arden."

Unable to keep herself from smiling, she beamed when he added, "And your smile."

When she'd finished eating, she rose to clear his plate. "Thank you very much for dinner, sir."

"Arden?"

Almost afraid to hear his next words, she met his gaze. "Yes, sir?"

"You may call me Brandon. It would make me very happy if you would."

Arden's legs felt like they had turned boneless and would give out they were so weak. Was he teasing her because he'd noticed how she'd grown to feel about him?

Barely able to speak, she managed to say, "Okay. Goodnight, Brandon."

By the time she went to bed, her cheeks were sore from smiling. As she climbed into bed, she knew one thing for sure about her time at Brandon's house. She was falling in love.

Brandon spent the hours after dinner alone in his study replaying the time he'd spent with Arden. His heart clenched hopefully at the thought that she'd been jealous over the red dress. Was their time together each night beginning to take effect?

He cringed at his intentional cruelty the day before, remembering the sad look on her beautiful face when she'd thought she'd disappointed him. Angry at himself for the slight, he vowed not to use her like that again.

She'd looked suspicious when he'd asked her to call him by his first name. She wasn't quite where he needed her to be to turn her. A new vampire needed to trust her sire, and he hadn't earned that yet. But he would, and tonight would be another step toward that.

The memory of how willingly she'd given herself to him each night touched his heart. When he decided the night he saved her to make her his forever, he never imagined she would make him so happy. He'd sired other vampires, having been led by his cock with those, never truly feeling anything more than desire for them. But Arden was different. She brought out more than the need to fuck in him. She made him care.

He remembered with pleasure how innocent she'd looked when he'd fed her, her pouty lips taking what he offered. Tonight he'd show her better things to do with her mouth.

Too eager to wait, Brandon climbed the stairs to her room before midnight, desperate to see the woman he quickly was falling in love with. Just as before, she lay sleeping and he slowly pulled back the covers to reveal her in her nightgown. Whispering his chant in her ear, he willed her awake. As her lovely eyes opened, she smiled, as if she'd been waiting for him to arrive, her Prince Charming to wake his Sleeping Beauty. Softly, he kissed her and began their nightly rite.

"How is my Arden tonight?" he whispered near her lips.

"Happy to see my Brandon."

He loved to hear her say his name, as if an angel from heaven was speaking to him. Stroking her face, he slid his thumb along the seam of her lips and his cock jumped when she took his finger into her mouth and began sucking. Her tongue licked the tip, and his eyes closed in ecstasy of what was to come.

"Love, you are everything I have long dreamed of."

She pulled him to her and wrapped her arms around his neck. "I need you. Please, Brandon."

The sound of need in her voice touched him, and he slid his finger inside her as she spread her legs for him. She was so wet and ready for him. Another finger joined the first and he pressed the pad of his thumb against her excited nub.

"Oh, yes! Please don't stop," she begged.

"Never, my love."

Slowly, he rubbed her in tiny circles as he fucked her with his fingers. In little time, he watched her bite down on her lip, ready to climax as she pushed down on his fingers as far as she could.

"Come for me, Arden," he softly commanded in her ear.

Her body did as he ordered, and she clamped down on his fingers as she shuddered through her orgasm, softly crying into his mouth as he kissed her. He stroked her to completion and bent down to kiss the little pink pearl in her dark triangle, feeling it still pulsate under his lips.

He returned to her mouth and kissed her softly. "Arden, come with me."

She sat up and followed him off the bed. He gently pushed down on her shoulders, and she knelt before him, her eyes looking up into his. Undoing his pants, he released his already stiff cock and watched her lick her lips.

"Do you know what I want, love?"

When she nodded, he asked, "Have you done this?"

She shook her head and explained, "I saw the women on the street do this for men at night."

For a moment, he thought about all the things she must have seen living on the street and pitied her. No one this wonderful should have to spend her nights around prostitutes. He loved the idea that she'd never done with anyone else what she was about to do to him.

He was pulled from his thoughts by her sliding her hand down his shaft. With a sweet glance up at him, she kissed the swollen tip of his cock, and an electric jolt traveled straight to his balls. Tenderly, she tongued the slit and his eyes rolled back in pleasure. He felt her wrap her lips around him and looked down to see her take the mushroom shaped crown of his cock into her mouth.

Inch by inch he watched his cock slip into her mouth, sure he'd never seen anything as erotic as the scene he now watched between his legs. With each retreat of her mouth, her hand pumped him and he drew closer and closer to the moment of release. The tightness of her

throat pressed close against the tip as she took all of him into her mouth and began to gag. Tenderly, he caressed her jaw as he pulled out of her. "You don't have to take all of me."

She looked up at him as if to tell him she wanted to make him happy, and he said softly, "I don't need all of that to be happy, Arden."

He watched as she began in earnest to satisfy him. She looked so gorgeous with his cock in her mouth, sucking him to completion. Each time her tongue slid over the spot just below the head, he jerked closer to release.

While she tenderly took care of him, he stroked her hair from her face. As he began to come, he heard her moan as he sent hot torrents down her throat. When he'd finished, she placed a small kiss on the tip of his cock and stood up to look at him.

"Arden, do you know what I want?"

She said nothing as she moved her hair to expose her neck and tilted her face away. Brandon pulled her face back toward his. "I want you to come to me on your own. Not in a dream. Will you come to me?"

He saw something inside her told her to be frightened of him, but what? Did she not believe he loved her? He took her face in his hands and cradled it as he kissed her. "Do not fear me. I'm yours and you're mine, remember?"

As she timidly nodded, he took her in his arms and his mouth touched her neck. In a moment, he found a pleasure as exquisite as the one he'd just experienced. Each drop, each pull made him love her even more.

After he'd made sure she was asleep, he returned downstairs to continue his night. There were plans to make for when she finally came to him.

Four

By the sixth day in Brandon's house, Arden worried she was losing her mind. She hadn't had a restful night's sleep since her first night there, she continued to feel dizzy and lightheaded, and for the past few nights she'd been having incredibly erotic dreams about him. As she practically sleepwalked through her day, she found her mind repeatedly turning to him. The color of his eyes. The way his hair curled up at his collar. How perfect his teeth looked when he smiled. How sensual he was when he chose to be.

Standing at the kitchen sink, Arden listened as Mrs. Jandry and Mrs. Benson stood toe to toe at the door to the pantry arguing over the cook's menu choices. Suddenly, everything seemed to swim before Arden's eyes, and she swayed, almost falling to the floor.

"Miss! Mrs. Benson! She's about to collapse!"

Both women hurried to catch her and helped her to

a chair.

"She's as pale as a ghost," the housekeeper said.

"I know. We need to get her to her bed right now."

"No, no. I'm fine," Arden said in a weak voice. "All I need is a few minutes in this chair."

"Upstairs right now," Mrs. Benson ordered in a tone that was less demanding than concerned.

Arden didn't bother protesting again and happily allowed the two older women to help her up the stairs to her room. In no time at all, she fell into a deep sleep.

"Miss Stephens? Wake up, miss. The doctor is here to see you."

Arden woke as Brandon's cook shook her gently by the shoulder. Slowly, she focused her eyes to see a strange man standing in her room.

"Miss, I'm the doctor. Are you feeling any better after your nap?"

"I don't know. I just always feel weak lately." Arden didn't feel the need to tell the doctor that an even bigger problem was what she was thinking about her employer.

The man stood by the edge of her bed. "Well, let's see what we can find out."

A thorough checkup revealed no obvious reason for any of her physical symptoms. The doctor suggested she remain in bed and left to discuss the case with Brandon.

Arden wondered if remaining in bed would mean more erotic dreams. It wasn't that they frightened her. In fact, quite the opposite was true. The dreams were everything she wished would happen with Brandon but never could when she was awake. How much she wished she could be the woman he desired as he did in her dreams—sensual, seductive, and loved by him!

Mrs. Jandry knocked at the door a short while later. As with others of her kind, she cooked when worried, preparing a tray she hoped would make Arden feel better.

Arden looked down at the tray of food and then looked up at the cook with a confused look on her face. "Mrs. Jandry, not that I don't appreciate it, but why have you brought me steak and wine?" she asked as she scooted herself into an upright position to eat.

"Doctor's orders, miss. He thinks you're mighty pale, and I have to agree. Now eat up so I don't have to worry about you."

Arden saw that the woman was trying to help, and it felt nice to have someone mother her. Since her mother died, she hadn't had anyone really take care of her. She'd done all the taking care of her father, especially at the end of his life, so Mrs. Jandry's fussing over her was a welcome change.

"All right, I promise to eat. Thank you."

As the cook turned to leave, she said, "The master has been concerned about you and wants to see you."

"He was worried?"

"Sure he was. He arranged for the doctor."

Arden felt guilty that she hadn't recognized Brandon would be kind enough to call for help. "Oh, then please ask him to come in."

Almost immediately, butterflies began their dance in her stomach. Brandon would be in her bedroom alone with her. Everything she'd dreamed about him had taken place in that very room!

Pulling the covers up, she straightened herself and prayed to God what she'd thought about him wasn't written all over her face. He gently knocked at the door and waited for her to allow him entrance. When he did come in, he looked somber and Arden worried he was unhappy with her.

"The doctor says you'll be fine in no time. How do you feel?"

She felt like a nervous wreck, not because of any sickness but because of him. Standing there next to her bed and staring down at her with those eyes that so often appeared to be searching for something in hers, he made her think of the fantasies her mind had been dreaming up every night. If he knew what she'd thought, he'd think her no better than the women of the streets she'd lived among for the past month.

She felt her cheeks become hot as she tried to answer. "I'm sorry to be such a hassle. I don't know what's wrong. I'm usually very healthy. I don't know why I feel so weak."

Brandon spied the tray of food Mrs. Jandry had left next to the bed. Picking it up, he sat down on the bed next to Arden and placed the tray on his lap. After he'd cut a piece of steak for her, she saw that he seemed intent on feeding her again.

"You don't have to feed me. I'm not too weak to pick up a fork," she joked.

In a low voice that touched her deep inside, he said,

"I don't have to do anything. I want to. Indulge me. It would make me feel better since I'm responsible."

In between bites, she asked, "How could you be responsible?"

He stopped as he stabbed a fork into a piece of meat and looked intently at her. "Arden, I am the master of this house. Everything is ultimately my responsibility." And then, after what seemed like hours of him staring at her, he added, "Especially you."

Arden wondered why he was being so attentive. He'd proven himself to be kind with his first gesture to her that night he saved her, but since then he'd been erratic in his ways, to say the least. After she finished eating and drinking some wine, which only served to make her feel more lightheaded, she thought he'd leave. Instead, after placing the tray outside the door, he returned to his seat beside her on the bed. Arden noticed with the loss of the tray there seemed to be no barrier between them.

"Brandon, I think I should rest," she said anxiously.

"Very well. However, I intend on sitting here while you do."

Arden knew he saw the shock on her face. What if she had a dream like the ones she'd had each night? What if she talked in her sleep and he found out what fantasies she had of him? He seemed to sense her unease and attempted to casually explain, "I need to take care of you. I can't afford to lose another maid."

Arden laid her head down on the pillow and closed her eyes for a moment before she turned back toward him. "What happened to your last maid?"

Hesitating, he finally answered, "She left for personal reasons."

Personal reasons? What does that mean?

As she drifted off to sleep, Arden wondered if the previous maid had gotten this kind of treatment from him. And if she had, why did she leave?

Brandon watched as she slept quietly, her face the picture of innocence. He knew what was happening, even if he didn't want to admit it. His nightly visits to Arden's bedroom were weakening her, and if he didn't turn her soon, she'd die. He'd thought he'd have more time, but understood now he had a choice to make—turn her into a being like himself or turn her away and let her live out her mortal life.

He found he could do neither. Nothing would make him happier than to have a companion to spend the rest of his years with, but was that his choice to make for her? Being a vampire was as much a cross to bear as a blessing. Would she ever be able to forgive him even if she did love him? None of the others had.

The alternative was even worse. In just the short time she'd been in his life, she'd brought something back that he'd been without for so long. Now each evening when he awoke, he had something—no, someone—to look forward to. And while he loved every moment he spent making love to her, it wasn't merely that he looked forward to since he could get that anywhere in London or any other place, for that matter. No, the kindness he

experienced with her made waking worthwhile now. He felt hollow at the thought of being without her and all the things she made him feel again.

The fear of her never understanding, never forgiving him for taking her life and replacing it with one of his choosing made the choice painful for him. He knew from experience with her predecessors that what he offered may not be what a young, beautiful woman wanted. To be attached forever to a man who'd seen almost two hundred years of life pass by was likely not a choice Arden would make either.

Gently, he stroked her hair, accepting what he would do in the end, but he feared losing the one person he'd grown to love in more years than he cared to remember. As he watched her sleep, a tiny smile formed on her lips at his touch. Could he go through with the choice he'd decided to make? The constant loneliness of his life could be ended with just one simple action. No more roaming the night in search of blood and the small moments of closeness that accompanied his feeding. He could have the blood of one he sired, as it was supposed to be, instead of unknown humans, whose blood could never sustain him as well as the blood of one of his own.

He wanted to believe she'd accept him — not run from him in fear and hatred — and finally give him what he'd hoped so long for. Had he finally found someone to be a companion?

Even now, however, as he looked at her innocently sleeping, he felt the overwhelming desire to drink from her. Just as in the past, his demons pressed against him, the monster barely contained beneath the veneer of a well-to-do Londoner.

He ran his tongue over his fangs and closed his eyes as the rush of desire raced through him. His body ached from the need she created in him. Reaching out to touch her face, his hand brushed her cheek and she leaned into it, looking for the kindness in her sleep she'd seen earlier from him. As her warm skin pressed against his, he knew that man held only a tenuous hold over the vampire he truly was.

The doctor had warned that she couldn't handle much more of whatever was attacking her system, and even in his ignorance he'd stumbled upon the reality Brandon knew he must accept. He would have to turn her within the next few nights or cease feeding from her. And that he could not do. What he received from her blood and each time he fed from her provided him more than sustenance, more than survival, and he couldn't force himself to let that go.

Brandon quietly slipped out of Arden's room and returned to his study. With everything on his mind, he poured himself a glass of port and tried to lose himself in the effect of the alcohol. As each sip slid down his throat, he sought some measure of escape from the choice he knew he'd make.

"As someone who's been a vampire for so long, you should know the alcohol never works like it did when you were human."

Startled, Brandon turned to see his sire standing in the doorway. "Vasilije, what are you doing here?"

"Whatever could be the matter with my Brandon?"

As he spoke, Vasilije glided across the room toward the man he'd turned so many years earlier. Brandon watched him push his long black hair from his face to reveal the beautiful features his sire had possessed for as long as he'd known him. Crystal blue eyes stared into his as he struggled to look away.

Vasilije stopped within a foot of Brandon and reached his pale fingers out to touch his face. "What is it that makes you want to drown yourself in this ineffective poison?"

Brandon turned away to escape his touch and moved to the chair behind his desk, hoping to put some distance between him and his visitor. The last thing he wanted was for Vasilije to know anything about Arden.

With the desk in front of him, he felt his control begin to build. "Why are you here, Vasilije?"

His sire sat down in a leather chair across from the desk and tilted his head back, eyeing the ceiling. "I'm bored, dear Brandon. London is so dreadfully boring this time of year." Vasilije lowered his gaze to meet Brandon's. "I crave excitement."

"I'm the last person you should call on if you seek excitement."

"I thought you might have some idea how I might entertain myself," Vasilije said leaning forward. "Anything new?"

Brandon prayed to God he hadn't heard anything of Arden. "Nothing that would interest you. Household staff changes, a minor loss in a business deal..."

"Good God, Brandon! You are the most boring vampire I know. What happened to that interesting young man I turned all those years ago?"

"He lived too many years and matured."

Flinging himself back in his seat, Vasilije waved away Brandon's words. "Do you remember the times we had, just the two of us, right after I sired you? Oh, how many of those zealous Puritan believers did we have? I miss those days."

"I don't. I was never as entertained by that as you."

Vasilije stood, his face twisted in disgust. "You really are quite suited to the repressed times of Victoria, aren't you?"

"You can go anywhere you want. If London is so boring, why not go somewhere else?" *Immediately, before Arden wakes up.*

Walking away, the older vampire said, "I think I just might, my dear Brandon. I won't bother extending an offer for you to join me as I can see you're supremely content drinking to your happiness."

Brandon smiled, hoping the visit had ended. "Goodbye, Vasilije."

Turning to face him, Vasilije returned the smile. "Never goodbye. And remember, I'll be around if you have any need to visit me."

As the front door closed, Brandon breathed a heavy sigh. He knew exactly what Vasilije had referred to. He knew about Arden, or at least knew he had met someone he would request to sire. Since as his sire Vasilije had the power to approve or deny his choice of Arden as one he wanted as his own, Brandon knew this visit was more a reminder of the rules of their world than a friendly call.

He also knew he wouldn't be able to put off his own visit to Vasilije any longer.

Five

Arden awoke on her own the next morning feeling much better. She hadn't had any dreams of Brandon, a fact she realized with disappointment, and for the first time in days had enjoyed a restful sleep. She looked around the room unhappy not to see him still sitting on the bed next to her. It was probably too much to expect anyone to stay for twelve hours, but she wished he had.

She had a vague memory of waking during the night to see him watching her, his eyes as always appearing as if they were searching her face for some answer. His face had been a mixture of worry and caring as he smiled to comfort her. As she replayed the memory in her mind, she heard no words, but had the sense that she was safe in his care.

Squeezing the sheets in her hands, she relished the sense of security she felt in his house. In addition to

having a home again, the events of the day before had shown her she had people who cared about her. Even Mrs. Benson had been uncharacteristically kind in response to her sickness. Most of all, Brandon's show of concern had convinced her that she could feel safe in her new home.

Once downstairs, Arden began her tasks as if nothing had happened the day before, hoping the entire episode could be forgotten. She'd often found in her short life that the best way to handle the difficulties life handed a person was to return to everyday activities as soon as possible instead of wallowing in those problems. It comforted her to know that the people around her cared, though.

Even though she knew Brandon's schedule by now, she'd secretly hoped he would come to see her when she began her day. While she straightened the mess he'd made in his study, she ran her fingers over the blotter stained with splotches of ink on his desk. She imagined him sitting in his heavy wooden chair, hunched over his desk as he wrote to another like him of weighty matters powerful men dealt with.

Arden tentatively placed herself in his seat and closed her eyes. Everything around her felt like him — dark and seductive. She ran her hands over the arms of the chair, feeling the smoothness of the polished wood against her palms.

A noise outside the door startled her, and she leapt out of his chair before anyone witnessed her inappropriate behavior. Hurriedly, she cleaned the room and left to return to the kitchen where she found Mrs. Jandry busy with her duties.

As she sat down at the table, she watched the cook, wondering how long she'd been with Brandon. "Mrs. Jandry, what is Mr. Ridley having tonight?"

While the cook detailed the menu for the evening, Arden waited patiently to move on to more interesting matters. When she'd finally finished explaining the dishes she was to prepare for him, Arden waited a moment and then asked, "How long have you served Mr. Ridley?"

The older woman spoke freely like she had never done before to Arden. As she listened, she hoped to hear something that would help her to know more about Brandon.

"I have been with the master for longer than I can believe. Is it possible I've been with him for twenty years? Yes, yes, it would be as poor Mr. Jandry has been gone as long."

The cook trailed off into a description of the disease that had taken her late husband. As she half listened, Arden questioned how old Brandon could be. How old had he been when Mrs. Jandry began as his cook? He looked within a few years of Arden, but twenty years as the master of the house would put him at decades older.

"Twenty years? So you were the cook to the senior Mr. Ridley?"

"No. Just the master," she answered as she chopped raw vegetables to dump into the broth she'd been simmering.

Arden's mind worked to figure out the puzzle of Brandon's age. *Twenty years as the master of the house yet as youthful in appearance as one born then?*

Her brain switching gears, she asked, "Mrs. Jandry, what became of the previous maid?"

Within seconds, the cook's affable disposition had iced over, her body stiffening as she stopped her chopping and then continued moments later.

"She left for personal reasons, miss."

Arden understood by her tone that she'd get no more about this from Mrs. Jandry, though she remained sure there was something to know about why her predecessor had left. Her question had effectively ended any conversation, so Arden kept her suspicions for another time and went about her business making sure everything was ready for Brandon's return.

When Mrs. Jandry began preparing his dinner tray, Arden knew he'd come home. Tray in hand, she entered his study, eager to see him. As she'd grown used to, he sat as his desk absorbed in his work, but the moment he saw her, he rose from his chair to take his dinner from her.

"Let me help you. Are you feeling better?"

His concern touched her, and she shyly smiled. "Thank you, sir. Yes, I'm fine now."

As he placed his dinner on the table, he shot her a look of disapproval. "What did we agree you'd call me?"

Arden felt her cheeks warm. "Brandon. I'm sorry, sir...Brandon."

The smile that greeted her made her insides melt. Obviously pleased, his gaze remained on her face, and she hoped he would repeat his offer to enjoy his dinner with her.

"I hope the doctor's remedies have made a difference. I see the color has returned to your cheeks."

Arden watched as he returned to his chair and began to eat. Crestfallen, she waited for him to excuse her.

"Yes, I feel much better today."

Silently, he dipped his spoon into his soup and brought it to his mouth. As he began to enjoy his dinner, he looked up to see her waiting for his next command.

"Thank you, Arden. Is there anything you need?"

Wishing she could tell him she wanted to stay, to enjoy his company, to ask about the maid before her, she merely shook her head and smiled.

"Then perhaps you would help me with something I need," he said looking up at her.

Before a more subdued answer came to her, she exclaimed, "Anything!"

"Sit with me then and keep me company. I find I need companionship, and I can't imagine anyone I'd like to spend time with more."

Arden knew her face showed how thrilled she was to be spending time with him again, but she felt no embarrassment. If anything, he seemed uncharacteristically shy himself for a moment. However, with a smile from him it passed and they began what she hoped would be an everyday ritual.

As they ate, they talked about her improving health and Mrs. Benson's surprising change toward her, and Arden chuckled at his almost juvenile mocking of his housekeeper. She saw her laughter had caused him to stop talking but before she could apologize for her improper

behavior, he confessed, "I love to hear you laugh."

Blushing, she dropped her gaze to the table. He lifted her chin with his finger until her eyes met his. His eyes had a longing to them like she'd never seen before.

"You have no reason to look away. Never be ashamed in front of me."

All at once, the incredible sensations she'd felt with him in her dreams passed through her body. Every touch of his hands, every caress of his lips, and every drag of his tongue over her most sensitive parts glimmered in his eyes, and her body responded to his gaze as she began to crave being close to him.

Her nipples tightened under her plain maid's uniform, pressing into the fabric and exciting her more. And an ache formed in the pit of her stomach followed by a need to have him inside her, filling her.

Brandon saw her desire grow in front of him and felt his own grow as his fangs lengthened in his mouth. She was ready. Tonight, she would be his. Tentatively, he leaned forward and touched his lips to hers. So soft, so willing against his, just as she'd been each night he'd visited her.

Afraid she might back away or run, he took her face in his hands and gently held her to him. Softly, his tongue slid between her half-open lips and searched for hers, teasing the tip when they touched.

She drew in a sharp breath in surprise but didn't pull away, instead almost imperceptibly moving her tongue over the sharp point of one fang. Brandon felt a jolt of excitement run through him straight to his cock as she innocently explored one of the most sensual parts of him. Unable to hold back, he moaned into her mouth, reveling in the feel of her tongue stroking him. His emotion startled her and as she pulled away, he willed his fangs to recede, not ready to take her where he planned to go just yet.

"Arden, look at me." Slowly she opened her eyes. "Do you like me?"

Like a soul desperate to enjoy what she'd been feeling, she nodded her answer, her eyes never straying from the lips she seemed to yearn to return to kissing.

"I've grown to care for you a great deal. Do you trust me?"

Without hesitation, she nodded again.

"I want to take you somewhere tonight. Say you'll come with me."

Breathlessly, she answered, "Yes."

Brandon smiled at her willingness to trust him and leaned in to kiss her again. "I have something for you, love. Keep your eyes closed."

As she sat patiently waiting, he retrieved the box of chocolates from near his desk and placed it on the table in front of them. "Open your mouth for me, Arden."

Obeying, she parted her lips and slowly moved her tongue to lick her lips in anticipation of his gift. As he placed the tiny candy on her tongue, her eyes opened wide and she smiled, savoring the delicious sweetness in her mouth.

"Oh, Brandon! It's delicious! Thank you!"

Innocently, she leaned forward to kiss him, and he tasted the sugar and milk on her tongue as she eagerly ran it over his. Brandon's heart filled with joy, and he wanted to make her happy again.

"I have something else for you. I want you to go upstairs to your room and put on the new dress I bought you."

He knew she'd thought the dress had been for another woman, and he saw the flash of recognition cross her face before she smiled wider.

"Go, and I'll be up to get you in a little while," he whispered near her mouth before kissing the tip of her nose.

Brandon watched as she excitedly left his study, his heart happy from their time together. All he had to do was make it through introducing her to Vasilije and she would be his. It had only been six months since he'd last made a request to his sire—the last time he'd chosen to sire one of his own. He accepted the protocol required for what he wanted to do with Arden, though the memory of his last attempt made presenting her to him something he dreaded.

He just hoped this time wouldn't end as his last visit had.

Six

Brandon waited outside Arden's bedroom door and tried to calm himself. His heart beat wildly as he envisioned what she'd look like in the dress he'd had made especially for her. He heard her go silent behind the door and knew it was time to go.

Three sharp raps on the door and she appeared in front of him, more beautiful than he ever could have imagined. The red dress fit perfectly, accentuating her luscious breasts and feminine body usually hidden behind her bland maid's uniform. As he stood staring at her, he wished he could bypass vampire law and take her as his right there at that very moment.

Arden smiled, but she made an expression that told him she was unsure of her new look. He reached out to take her hand, and twirling her in front of him, he stopped her to face him.

"You're every bit as stunning as I knew you would

be, Arden."

"Thank you so very much, Brandon. It's lovely. But where are we going?"

"I want to introduce you to someone. I promise we'll only stay a short while and then we can come home."

"Oh, we don't have to return early, do we? I'd love to have a night out."

"Then perhaps after you meet Vasilije we can take a carriage ride. Would you like that?"

Arden squeezed his hand in excitement. "Oh, I'd love that!"

As they waited for the carriage to stop at Vasilije's home, tension began to take hold of Brandon. He hoped this time would be a success and he'd approve of his choice. As his sire, his approval was necessary before he could take Arden as his own, but Vasilije was difficult to predict, as he'd learned the last time he petitioned for his approval to sire his previous maid, Celeste.

That time he'd chosen to withhold his approval and she'd left before he could convince her to return to his home. Looking at Arden, Brandon knew that unfortunate turn of events with Celeste was for the best as he never cared for her like he did for Arden. He just prayed Vasilije wouldn't disapprove of her.

Never before had he cared so much for the approval to sire a vampire for himself. The others had been to keep him company and fed. Arden was different. She was someone he could be devoted to.

Someone to love.

Taking her hand to ease her out of the carriage, he escorted her toward the massive mansion in front of them. Standing outside the door, he turned toward her and took her in his arms.

"Arden, although it's only been a short time that you've been in my life, I've grown to care for you a great deal. I hope you feel the same."

Looking up at him, she spoke the words he'd prayed to hear. "Yes, Brandon. I do care for you."

In a far more serious tone, he continued, "After tonight, I hope you'll be happy to be with me forever."

The door opened and they were shown into a sitting room to wait. The room spoke volumes about its owner. Furnished with expensive tapestries from around the world and priceless works of art, it showed like a shrine to the centuries Vasilije had walked the Earth. They sat on a sofa from the Louis XIV period, a further tribute to his holdings. Brandon held her hand and watched as she examined Vasilije's luxurious home. His sire was, in truth, no wealthier than he, but Brandon suddenly worried his home didn't stand up to the one she admired now.

"Vasilije's home is exquisite, is it not?"

"Yes it is, but I like yours better," she said, making him beam with happiness.

Brandon smiled, but his face quickly grew serious as he felt the presence of his sire. Looking up, he saw Vasilije enter the room and his stomach clenched.

Far older in years, the vampire who greeted him had never aged beyond his mid-twenties. Forever young, his body rippled with strength while his face appeared at once innocent and knowing. No lines or wrinkles marred his appearance to indicate the passage of time. Vasilije stood as a testament to the charmed facets of a vampire's existence.

Brandon looked to see Arden's face impressed by the man he jealously wished looked older or uglier. He winced as that jealousy stabbed at him, and he squeezed her hand possessively.

"My dear Brandon. Who do we have here?"

As he introduced Arden to his sire, he watched his eyes roam over her as if he were appraising a piece of fine art—or sizing up his next victim.

Vasilije took her hand, softly kissing the top of it, and looked into her eyes. "What a beautiful name, truly fitting for such a beautiful woman."

As the delicate dance to win his maker's approval began, Brandon wished for nothing more than to be finished with this night and home in her arms.

Arden shivered as Vasilije looked into her eyes. Uncertain why Brandon wanted her to meet this man, she felt his apprehension as he continued to squeeze her hand. So much had happened so quickly between them, and she didn't want to ruin that with the incorrect response to his friend. Was she to be friendly or merely respectful? By the look on his face as he watched his friend kiss her, she sensed respectful was the correct answer.

As Vasilije released her hand, she studied him closely. Tall, with jet black hair, he was striking with his regal nose and dark blue eyes. There was something almost hypnotic in his voice as he began to speak to Brandon in a tone that seemed to indicate his superiority but also his care.

She looked at Brandon, so dark and impressive himself, as he stood to speak to the man. How wonderful things had become between them in the short time she'd lived in his home. He'd obviously been planning this night for days, and she silently chided herself for ever being jealous. And as she watched him now as he looked over at her, she hoped he cared for her as she did him.

But her dreams made her hope for something much more than the proper love of a well-off English gentleman.

Something passionate.

Something that possessed her body and soul and made her unlike who she was when awake.

She sat waiting as they spoke in low tones about things obviously not meant for her to hear and closed her eyes to remember the lustful images that filled her dreams. His hands, so gentle yet commanding, as they cupped her breasts and his fingers pinched a nipple to an excited peak. His mouth pressed against the wetness between her legs with his tongue seductively lapping against her most sensitive spot and sending exquisite sensations throughout her body. His hardness...

Arden's eyes snapped open as she tried to make herself focus on her present surroundings instead of her wanton desires. Wiping the tiny beads of sweat that had formed across the tops of her breasts, she forced herself to examine Vasilije's well-appointed sitting room, with its imported tapestries and expensive furniture. It was no use. Repeatedly, her mind returned to all the things she wished Brandon to do to her.

As she sat trying to think of the mundane, a doubt crept into her mind. She was still just a maid, no matter how many red dresses she wore. What would someone like Brandon Ridley want with a mere maid when he could have a lady of worth equal to his station? Torturing herself with self-doubt, she looked over at him wishing he'd never brought her to this place. She had no business pretending to be something she wasn't. She was a homeless girl he'd taken pity on, no more.

A small frown formed on her face as a sense of shame began to cover her. God, she wished he'd return so they could leave! She belonged back at his home in her dowdy maid's uniform, not sitting in a red dress on display for his friend!

"Arden, what's wrong?"

She looked up to see him standing over her with a look of concern on his face. She put a fake smile on and shook her head.

"Nothing."

Brandon crouched down in front of her and steadied himself with his hand on her knee. Looking up into her eyes, he looked like she'd hurt him.

"Tell me what's wrong."

Arden hung her head and quietly said, "I don't belong here. I'm merely a homeless girl you took pity on with a job as your maid. Your friend probably wonders why you've brought someone like me to his beautiful house."

Lifting her chin with his fingertip, he met her tear-filled gaze. "I assure you I never took pity on you, Arden Stephens. From the moment I first looked down into those beautiful brown eyes, I've been enchanted. I offered you the job as my maid so I could have you near me. And Vasilije can see as clearly as I how lovely you are. It is I who doesn't deserve you, not the other way around."

Arden couldn't stop a smile from forming on her face. Looking down at the face of this amazing man who was saying such wonderful things, she wished they were at home in his study, just the two of them.

"Just give me a few more minutes with Vasilije and I promise we'll leave soon."

Brandon took her hands in his and brought them to his lips. "I love you, Arden."

As he walked away to rejoin his friend, she replayed his words over and over. *I love you.* Thrilled by his admission, her self-doubts faded from her mind and she returned to thinking of her fantasies. Would they make love that night? Would he be the same kind of lover as he was in her dreams?

"She's delightful, Brandon. But is she ready? She seems easily upset."

Brandon sensed the hint of disapproval in his sire's tone. Knowing he had the final say, he worked to reassure him as he had Arden.

"No need to worry. Trust me. She's fine."

Vasilije trained his blue eyes on Brandon's face.

"And why should I accede to your wishes this time? If I recall, you asked for the same permission with that other delicious looking treat not more than six months ago. And I knew she wasn't right for you, didn't I?"

Brandon struggled to control his temper. He knew Vasilije was right about Celeste. Still, his smugness irritated him.

"Arden's different."

Vasilije cocked one eyebrow and directed his gaze toward her. "And how is she different?"

Sure he couldn't trust his sire with the knowledge that she excited him more than any woman had in decades, he chose to focus on her unfortunate past and felt like a bastard as he did. "She has no family to be concerned about and was homeless when I found her."

Vasilije chuckled deeply as he turned to face him. "A stray? Don't you know not to take strays in, dear Brandon?"

"She's not a stray!" he snapped.

A long moment of tension remained between the two men until Vasilije turned toward Arden and moved to approach her.

"Well, let's make sure she's right for you then."

Brandon's chest tightened at the thought of how his sire would decide that. Following behind him, he tried to catch Arden's gaze, but Vasilije had gotten to her already.

Standing over her, he stared down into her eyes and began. "Arden, I'm so happy you've come here tonight. Do you enjoy it here?"

Brandon knew by the silky tone of his voice he was

hypnotizing her.

"Vasilije..."

Waving off his concern, he concentrated on Arden's eyes and continued. "Arden, how do you feel about Brandon?"

Afraid of what she'd answer, he said, "Vasilije, don't."

Turning his head, the older vampire chided him. "How can I be expected to allow you to bring her into our world if I don't know she can handle it?"

Brandon had seen him do this with another of his vampires and hated the idea of him having control over Arden.

"She's done nothing to warrant this."

Turning back toward her, he slid his finger along her jaw. "Don't worry. I promise I won't hurt her."

Brandon cringed at the idea that he could.

Vasilije repeated his question and Brandon saw a shy smile form on her lips.

"I love him."

"And why is that?"

"Because he's kind and takes care of me."

Brandon filled with guilt at her words. If he truly took care of her, he wouldn't let his sire do this.

"Arden, dear. Do you know what he is?"

Silently, she nodded, and Brandon wondered if she'd misunderstood the question.

"And what is he?"

"Vampire."

Brandon took a step back, stunned that she knew.

"And how do you know that?"

Arden smiled again. "He comes to me at night."

"And what happens when he visits you at night?"

Brandon's stomach clenched at the idea that his sire was going to know what he and Arden did together. Each visit with her held a special charm for him, and he didn't want to share those moments with Vasilije.

"Enough!"

The look of rage that Vasilije flashed toward him surprised Brandon, and he had to force himself to resist deferring to the one who'd made him what he was.

"Brandon, I grow weary of your interference."

"Vasilije, don't do this to her."

But his plea fell on deaf ears and Vasilije continued his questioning.

"Arden, tell me what happens when he visits you at night."

Looking down into his face, her beautiful eyes glazed over, she whispered, "He makes love to me and drinks from me."

Brandon closed his eyes in pain. He should be doing everything in his power to protect her from his sire's manipulations. Instead, he stood obediently as the shame of powerlessness washed over him.

"And you like when he does this?"

Shyly, she answered, "Yes. I love him."

Relieved and thrilled by her answer, Brandon opened his eyes and saw Arden's innocent face beaming from her admission. Gradually, the pain that had forced his eyes closed ebbed away and he found the strength he needed to protect her.

Running his hand over her cheek, Vasilije thanked her and turned to Brandon. "You're right. She's perfect."

Relieved she'd passed his sire's test, he looked over at her beautiful face staring straight ahead.

"So I'm going to take her."

Brandon whipped his head around to face Vasilije. "No! She's mine!"

"As your sire, I have right of first choice. You know that. And as I watched that beautiful mouth pledge her love to you, I couldn't help think how much I wanted that mouth filled with my cock."

"No! Don't do this!"

"Why not?"

"Vasilije, why would you do this? I've been obedient and loyal all these years. I'm alone, unlike you, and I want her for me." Brandon dropped his gaze to the floor. "Don't make me beg. Please."

His sire's mouth twisted into a cruel smile and Brandon worried he'd lost her. His mind raced through his choices. He could try to get her out, but she remained under his power. He had only one choice — kill his sire.

Brandon looked over at her his heart full of sadness. He couldn't lose her! If having her meant killing Vasilije, then that's what he had to do. Slowly, he moved toward him, unsure of how he'd do it, but sure he had to.

Desperation raced through him as his heart pounded against his chest. So many times for so many reasons he'd obeyed Vasilije, even when every fiber of his being had told him not to. He'd allowed him to lord his power over him, never possessing the strength of will or the true

desire to defy him.

Until now.

Rage like he'd never harbored for anyone surged within him. His hands began to shake in anticipation of what he knew he must do.

I can't let him have her.

Frantically, his eyes searched the room for what he'd need to do the deed. He zeroed in on a small antique table pushed into the corner.

Vasilije's attention was focused on Arden, but Brandon knew his power. Only a fool would underestimate his sire. But he had to get to that table.

Lightning fast, he lunged toward the corner of the room, catching him by surprise just long enough to reach his goal. Smashing the table off the wall, he hurriedly broke off one wooden leg as splinters flew everywhere.

He grasped the makeshift stake tightly in his trembling hand, raising it as he prepared to plunge it into his maker's heart. Vasilije stood facing him, the smug expression still on his face.

"You can't do it, Brandon. I'm your sire."

"Don't you mean won't? It's never been that I couldn't but that I wouldn't. But I can't let you have her, Vasilije. I love her."

"What a ridiculous idea! You act as if you'll only have one like her from this point on. Have you learned nothing in all the years with me?"

Brandon glanced over at Arden, who sat silently still under Vasilije's spell. All he wanted was her. No one else had ever made him so completely happy. He wasn't like others of his kind who collected women for their selfish pleasure. All he'd ever truly wished for was that one soul to share his years with, to erase the loneliness he'd lived with for so long.

And now he'd finally found her and Vasilije would take her from him to add to his menagerie of playthings.

"Let her be with me or I swear to God, I'll stake you."

"God? Now you bring God into it? Christ, Brandon. You sound like a simpering human."

As he spoke, Vasilije inched closer and closer to him.

"You'd kill your maker for one woman? What has happened to you?"

"Release her now and I'll take her away from here. We'll never bother you again."

"And if I don't you'll stake me?"

Brandon heard the disbelief in his voice mocking him. As much as he knew his sire possessed the power to defeat him, he had no choice. If he wouldn't give her up, he had to kill him.

"You may taunt me all you want, but I've made up my mind. I won't lose her to please you."

Before the last word had completely left his mouth, Brandon was defending himself from attack. By some miracle, the stake remained tightly in his hand, but in seconds he was flat on his back with the ancient and far more powerful vampire looming over him.

"You underestimated me, my child," Vasilije chided through gritted teeth.

"Not at all!"

With a grunt, Brandon raised his arm to thrust the

stake toward him, but Vasilije caught him by the wrist and held him fast to the floor.

"You can't win over me. Accept it."

The deep chuckle that punctuated the end of his sire's statement renewed his ire.

"I won't let you have her. Never!"

Wildly swinging his free hand, Brandon attempted to inflict some small pain on the one being that stood between him and his happiness, but Vasilije was too fast and quickly had both his wrists pinned to the ground.

Looking up into his sire's eyes, he saw all too clearly the cruelty that lay behind his beautiful facade.

"Do you remember that moment when I delivered you from your mortal life, Brandon? You were so innocent."

For a moment, Brandon's mind returned to the night he turned him into the creature he now was. "And I've been alone ever since. Whatever you think you gave me, you took away that innocence and replaced it with loneliness."

Vasilije dipped his head to Brandon's neck and grazed the skin with his teeth. "I gave you life," he said softly.

"Then allow me to have someone to share it with."

"Don't be maudlin. You can find others."

Brandon thrashed his body around, bucking wildly to throw Vasilije off him. His sudden movements surprised him, and Brandon saw his chance. In a flash, he'd rolled his sire onto his back and prepared to do what every vampire was forbidden to do — kill his maker.

His hand squeezed the wooden stake so hard pain radiated through his wrist and forearm. What he was about to do would make him a pariah in his world. But he had no choice.

He'd live as an outcast if he could have Arden.

Vasilije stared up at him in fear, the look on his face evidence that he finally understood. "Don't do this!"

"Let her go with me, and swear you'll leave us alone."

As Vasilije considered the demand, Brandon readied the stake to plunge into his chest. "Fine."

"Release her now."

Vasilije waved his hand and released her from his hypnotic spell as Brandon jumped to his feet and ran to her. Falling to his knees, he gazed up at her lovely face. "Are you okay?"

Arden nodded. "Would you take me home now? I'm tired of sitting here alone while you two talk."

"What about that carriage ride I promised you?"

"Can we do that another night? I'd rather go home."

He loved to hear her refer to his house as home. "Of course. Whatever you want."

Brandon escorted Arden to the door and stopped to bid farewell to his sire. Even now, as it seemed he would be allowed to safely leave with her, he worried Vasilije would attempt to once again ruin his chance for happiness.

"Thank you, Vasilije."

A look of arrogance came over his sire's face. "Just remember I am always your sire, Brandon. That doesn't change because I indulged you tonight. Remember that."

Brandon knew full well that he had bested Vasilije this night, but what the future held was uncertain. What was paramount was that he claim Arden as his as soon as possible to bind her to him and make her his forever.

As they rode home after saying their goodbyes, she whispered to him, "What happened back there? How did that table get broken?"

Pulling her close to him, he smiled and kissed her. "None of that means anything to us now."

Seven

Hours later, after more chocolate, kisses, and declarations of love, Brandon stood at her bedroom door ready to finally make her his. Everything was perfect. She loved him and somewhere deep in her mind, she knew what he was and accepted him.

Tonight she would come to him in his world and end his loneliness.

Taking her hand, he whispered, "Good night, love," and turned to walk to his bedroom one door down. Sensing her desire, he turned and said, "If you need me, come find me."

Ten minutes led to fifteen minutes and he wondered if he had made a mistake. He knew as much as he wanted her, if she didn't come to him, she'd never completely be his. As he waited, he listened for her, hoping she would give in to her desire.

A soft knock on the door was followed by her whisper. "Brandon."

Opening the door, he saw her standing there with a look of apprehension. "I need..."

"Let me give you what you need."

He took her by the hand and brought her close to his body. She felt so warm as her form melded to his. He knew she was frightened as her delicate hand trembled in his. Fear was the last emotion he wanted, though. That worked for his random victims, but he wanted the sensuous woman she'd been when he'd come to her before.

"Brandon, I..." she began and then stopped and lowered her eyes.

Trailing his finger over her throat, he said, "Don't be afraid. I would never hurt you, sweet Arden."

Slowly, he undressed her as she stood gazing up into his eyes with a look of pure love. When she was naked, he inhaled deeply, his breath catching in his throat. She was so beautiful. As his cock stiffened in response to the vision in front of him, his fangs exploded into his mouth.

His lips covered hers and just as before she ran her tongue across his fangs, teasing him. She pulled away to see what she knew she'd felt and looked carefully at them, watching them lengthen even then from the desire building in him.

Softly, she whispered, "Vampire."

Brandon didn't sense fear or disgust. The word sounded as if she were simply stating a fact that neither upset nor pleased her. He waited for her to speak again, but she said nothing, instead moving closer to his mouth and gently stroking a fang with her fingertip.

His breath left his body in a hiss as very quickly the last remnants of control began to evaporate. Grabbing her wrist, he struggled to keep her from going to a place she knew nothing of.

"Love, you're taking me somewhere you may not be ready for," he said in a raspy voice.

Innocently, she looked up at him. "Where?"

"Stroking my fangs is one of the most erotic things you can do to me. But I may not be able to control my desire for you if you continue," he cautioned.

"Then I've been forewarned," she said in a voice full of need.

As he continued to hold her by the wrist, Arden leaned into his mouth and slid her pink tongue between her lips to softly touch his fang. Desire shuddered through him as she repeatedly teased him, slowly stroking up from the sharp tip.

Something snapped inside him and he rushed to shed his clothes, wanting nothing more than to plunge inside her. His body felt like it was on fire with need for her. In seconds, he had her on his bed.

"God, I want to be inside you. Open your legs so I can see that beautiful cunt."

Smiling up at him, her eyes half-lidded from passion, she obeyed and he filled his eyes with the sight of the soft, pink skin his cock would soon devour. He ran his finger from her swollen nub to her wet entrance and slid it in to stroke her sensitive flesh.

"Tell me what you want."

"Take me. No more waiting. I want you like you are in my dreams."

Brandon knew exactly what she wanted and just before he filled her to the hilt, he whispered, "They weren't dreams. And this time, when my cock is deep inside your cunt, you'll truly become mine."

"Yes! Make me yours!"

Her pleas made the last of his control vanish, and he slid into her wet channel until their bodies met, flesh on flesh. Over and over, he thrust into her as she begged for more. Awake, she was so much more than he'd ever dreamed she could be, and her desire spurred him on.

He felt her body begin to tighten around his cock and waited for her release with his own, but just before his cock exploded into her, she snaked her tongue into his mouth to wildly flick it over his fangs.

Pure ecstasy washed over him as her orgasm milked his shaft while her tongue brought him a release so powerful everything seemed to fade away but her.

"Oh God...Arden..." he cried out as he sent his hot seed deep into her.

Over and over, she whimpered in his ear as he continued to pulse into her. When he'd finished, he sweetly kissed her forehead. If she would just give him the final thing he needed, she'd be his. Still inside her, he said softly, "Be with me as I am. Mine forever."

Arden's gaze met his and for a moment he feared he saw rejection. Had she misunderstood him or changed her mind? Without realizing, Brandon held his breath as he awaited her answer.

Silently, she turned her head and pulled her hair aside to reveal her neck. He needed no more answer and dipped his head to kiss the skin below her ear.

"I love you."

As she repeated those words to him, his fangs pierced her skin and he began to drink. As the blood poured down his throat, filling him with everything she was, he held her tightly against his body.

At the moment of completion, he brought his wrist to his mouth and opened it up for her to take him into her. He gently pressed it to her lips and urged her to drink. Brandon's cock surged as her mouth softly sucked on his wrist. Each sensual pull sent more of him into her, changing her into one of his kind.

Her sweet brown eyes stared into his as she drank from him, and he watched in awe as she began to transform in front of his eyes into a vampire like him. Gradually, the skin that had so recently been kissed by the sun began to pale to porcelain as she became a creature of the night. Never again would she have the rays of the sun on her face to pinken her skin. Her eyes too began their change to those of a vampire. For from this moment on, she would see as other nocturnal souls of their world.

When she lifted her mouth from his wrist, sated for the moment, he spied the tell-tale teeth of one like him — her canines drew to sharp points and dripped with his blood. Gently, he stroked his finger over them and watched her eyes close in ecstasy.

"Brandon..."

"Yes, love?"

Her eyes opened and she looked up at him, her face full of love. Reaching out to her, he tenderly touched her cheek.

"Promise me you won't leave me alone."

Brandon understood her fear. She'd lost everyone close to her and now she was in a new world, a completely different person from whom she'd been. He remembered his turning and silently pledged to do better by Arden than Vasilije had by him.

"You'll never be alone. I'm your sire, and you're mine to protect. I swear no one will ever hurt you again."

Arden leaned her head into his hand and closed her eyes as a tiny smile formed on her lips. "My Brandon."

Trailing kisses over her face and neck, he closed the pinholes he'd made. "Mine," he whispered to her as his tongue gently slid over her skin before they fell into a deep sleep.

As the sun set, Arden felt her body come alive and she turned to her right to find Brandon as she had every night since he'd sired her. He lay naked next to her, his muscular body excited by her touch. She ran her hands over the flat planes of his stomach to his hardened cock and gripped him. By the third stroke, his eyes were open and his fangs had dropped into his mouth.

"I love waking up with you," he said as he leaned over to kiss her.

"Evening, sire," she cooed, knowing her pet name

excited him.

"Come here," he ordered and pulled her on top of him.

"Brandon, I smell dinner. We don't want to keep Mrs. Benson waiting," she teased.

"Dinner can wait," he growled as he positioned her on him.

Straddling his hips, she rubbed herself on his hardened cock, enjoying the effect she had on him. Each evening as if they were newlyweds, they reveled in one another's body, and each time Arden fell even more in love with him.

She moaned next to his ear when he held her fast to him. "I love you."

Sliding into her, he said in a voice that signaled his need, "And I you."

Arden sighed as he touched the spot deep inside her that brought her ecstasy. Over and over, he stroked in and out of her body, creating the exquisite sensations that carried her to heaven each night.

"Oh God, Brandon!"

Her mouth eagerly sought out his, and she slid her tongue in to caress the inside of his mouth as his cock caressed the inside of her.

Brandon turned his head away from her and pulled her to his neck in an offering. "Drink, my sweet Arden."

As he plunged into her, satisfying her as completely as any woman could ever desire, she pressed her fangs into his skin and tasted the sweetness of his blood. As it hit her tongue and ran down her throat, nourishing her,

she drew from him the life only he could offer.

She knew he was close to coming and drank her fill as he exploded into her. Eager to feel the same sensations, she closed where she'd fed and offered him her neck.

"Take from me as I have from you. Let me nourish you, my love."

In an instant, his fangs were piercing her skin, and he tenderly drew from her vein as he held her close to him. She felt him grow hard inside her, and as he sucked the blood from her, she rode him, needy for the release their joining provided.

As he took her into him, he murmured against her skin, "Feel me as I take from you and give you myself."

With one last thrust, she came apart, holding his body to hers as waves of pleasure rolled over her. Later, as she lay with him still inside her, she professed her love to the man who'd first saved her life and then given her a new one.

The End

Turn the page to read Chapter 1 of
***Blood Avenged* (Sons of Navarus #1)**

Look for Blood Avenged and all the Sons of Navarus erotic paranormal romance series at all major retailers.

I am everything you desire.
I am everything you fear.
I am lust and appetite.
I am vampire.

One

The beat of the music slammed into his body like crushing blows from an angry attacker, each note reverberating in his bones. He sat perfectly still and let the beat thrum through him as he picked up the seductive scent wafting across the crowded room, carried by a thick cloud of cigarette smoke. Undetected by all but him, its subtle sweetness teased his nose with a promise of what was to come.

Scanning the room, he watched like a bird tracking its prey. All of humanity seemed to file past him. Desperate, drunk, and powerless, the crowd was a smorgasbord laid out especially for him. With no effort at all, he could have any of them. The brunette dancing between two men, her movements telegraphing that her sex was needy for what they offered. If he chose, in seconds, they'd be gone and she'd be his for the taking. The tanned, muscular male eyeing him from three tables away, who he sensed preferred what hung between his legs to what the brunette offered. The barely legal blond, whose wide green eyes betrayed just how much of life she hadn't experienced despite the lies her body told.

He could have any of them.

Vasilije watched his victim at the bar. Every bat of an eyelash he felt. Every clank of the ice against the glass he heard as if he were there himself. The distance between them meant nothing.

Through the tightly packed crowd, he saw the woman next to his target lean over, obscuring his view. He watched as she pressed her body next to the man's, a not-so-subtle hint to her interest.

The sweet scent remained, and Vasilije closed his eyes to enjoy it, not interested in the woman or her pathetic attempt to seduce his prey away.

He had no idea the vampire waited patiently for his moment. Vasilije liked the idea that ignorance was bliss. For now. In a few short minutes, another bliss would take them both over, and he'd have what he'd eyed for days.

The man made a move toward the door and every cell in Vasilije's body came alive. Two steps and he was in the thick of the crowd, their bodies pressing up against him as he brushed by them. He weaved through the group like a dark secret whispered from one person to another.

At the exit, he inhaled deeply, his sense of smell filtering out the putrid mixture of exhaust, perfume, and stale alcohol that hovered at the entrance to the street. Only his prey's scent remained, imprinted on him.

He was nearby.

Closing his eyes, Vasilije let his other senses take over. The sound of the man's shoes hitting the pavement echoed in his ears. The feel of his prey's blood pumping through his body throbbed against Vasilije's cool skin, matching his heartbeat.

So healthy. So alive.

He'd tracked him for days, his desire growing with each passing moment. It had taken little time for him to decide he would make him one of his kind. He stirred something inside that hadn't been touched for years.

Such a soul would be a perfect addition to his world.

He moved away from the noise of the club into the streets of London as he gained ground on his target. Now in his view, the man moved much faster. Did he sense the danger that lurked nearby? But it was no use. He would surrender this night.

Vasilije walked calmly, never losing sight of the man. He sensed his fear and took it into himself, relishing the sensation. How long had it been since he'd felt fear — true fear that stole one's breath away and paralyzed the limbs?

A quick left onto a darkened street and his prey broke into a full run, his fear morphing into pure terror that surged through Vasilije's veins. In his ears, he heard the man's heart pound faster and faster, his body reacting to his mind's screams.

Into the night air, he whispered, "Come to me," and waited for the man to make his way back to him. With each step, Vasilije moved closer, but the man remained out of reach.

Something or someone was helping him escape.

Quickly, Vasilije scanned the area, his eyes darting left and right in the darkness. Was there another of his kind close? He sensed no one, but someone was interrupting his pursuit.

Reluctantly, he accepted the situation and disappeared into thin air, reappearing just mere feet in front of the man. Stunned, he skidded to a stop against Vasilije's chest.

"No more running."

His hand moved to the man's chin and gently held him. Eyes filled with a fear he'd seen a thousand times before stared back at him, pleading for mercy from a being that possessed none.

His voice a deep timbre now, Vasilije began to hypnotize the man. "I've waited long enough for you."

To his surprise, the trick didn't work. The man's eyes grew wide and he opened his mouth to speak, but only weak cries came out. Why was he able to resist?

"Who are you?"

"Alex," he said, his voice almost a whimper.

"Alex, I want you to look into my eyes. Listen to my voice."

"Please don't kill me."

Vasilije stroked the man's cheek and leaned in next to his ear. "I'm going to give you a life you've never dreamed of, Alex."

"Please! Take all my money. Just let me go. I have a girlfriend. Tatiana. I don't want to die!"

Vasilije thought back to the only Tatiana he'd ever known in his over four hundred year existence.

Grimacing, he returned his focus to Alex's eyes and pushed his memory of the past out of his mind.

"Well, maybe I'll let you have her."

"Please don't do this!" the man begged, his blue eyes filling with tears.

Cradling his face in his hands, Vasilije concentrated on Alex, and slowly whatever had been protecting him slipped away. His lids became heavy, obscuring his eyes, and the fear left his mind and body.

"Alex." Vasilije let the name rest on his tongue as he hissed out the last syllable. "Mine."

The muscles in Alex's body gave in to his power and all fight evaporated from him. He slumped against the vampire's body as his mind finally succumbed to his persuasion.

Vasilije guided him to a building just a few steps away and leaned him against a stone wall. For a moment, he stilled to look at this human who had so captivated him, more than any other creature in years. His shoulder length blond hair shone like it had been touched each day by the sun. Vasilije gingerly touched the ends with his fingertips, feeling the sun's long forgotten warmth against his fingers.

His eyes moved over Alex's face, past his mouth and cheekbones to eyes hooded by slack lids. Within those slits were blue eyes that stared out passively at him. Eyes that saw what Vasilije commanded as he silently inserted ideas in to the man's mind.

Nothing about Alex was unique individually, and despite admiring his beauty, Vasilije couldn't say that was what had drawn him to the human. It was something else, something about him that created the impression of the forbidden.

But now he would be his.

Vasilije's fangs slid seductively into his mouth as he eyed the gentle throbbing of Alex's neck. In just a few moments, they would sink into his skin and sweet blood would fill him. The thought of it made his mouth water.

Unlike the rest of his fellow vampires, he wasn't forced to live under the restrictions of vampire law and obtain permission to turn a human. His sire had been taken from the Earth years ago, and without her, he was free to sire anyone he pleased.

He was truly a being beholden to no one.

Alex would join the hundreds of others scattered across the globe who counted him as their sire. Inside, he knew where each one was at any given moment, like a piece of himself inside another. When he desired to have them around, they were. And when he preferred a life of solitude, the choice of many vampires, he sent them away.

But they were never truly gone.

He would keep Alex with him until he'd completed his initiation period. To do any less would be cruel. A newly turned vampire needed his sire for virtually everything to survive. His blood would nourish him, like no other's could. A human might give him what he needed for a short time, but it could never be what his sire's was. And his knowledge would help Alex learn how to be a vampire and how to grow accustomed to the new life he'd given him.

Vasilije softly pressed his mouth to his neck, feeling the warmth of his skin against his lips. Alex turned his head in response, and Vasilije lifted his head. Staring deeply into his eyes, he silently instructed him to turn his head and obey.

His mouth returned to Alex's neck. As he watched the rhythmic pulse just under his skin, he slid his tongue over his fangs, enjoying the feel of their sharp points.

"Alex, from this moment on, I'm your sire. You belong to me."

Without moving his head, Alex moaned his unneeded agreement. For a long moment, the world around them stood still, as Vasilije pressed his fangs slowly into the tender skin. His canines pierced a vein and blood began to flood over his tongue. Its thickness oozed back toward his throat, the tangy taste sliding over his taste buds, exciting them.

How wonderful he tasted! As Alex's life flowed down Vasilije's throat, he fastened his mouth on his neck and pulled at the vein, careful to take only as much as he should. He'd bring Alex to the point of no return and then, as he lingered between life and death, he'd give him the first of many gifts a sire could provide.

Still human for the moment, Alex struggled against Vasilije's hold, but it was no use. A vampire so old, he had the strength of a bull and reflexes of a wild cat. At the first sign of resistance, he tightened his hold on the man's jaw and flung his leg over him, trapping his body between the wall and his own.

"It's futile to struggle," Vasilije whispered low in his ear. "Let it take you."

"Please..." Alex's voice faded to a groan as Vasilije's mouth tugged at his vein with more vigor.

"I want nothing else," Vasilije chuckled as he closed the holes he'd made in Alex's neck.

He carefully laid him on the ground, and as Alex fought to hold on to the last shred of his human life, Vasilije wiped the corners of his mouth. Licking the blood from his fingertips, he savored the taste as he knelt down beside the man who was to be his newest vampire.

Vasilije stroked the blond hair that would never again be touched by the warmth or light of the sun. His fingers glided over the sun kissed skin on Alex's face, which in moments would be reduced to a pallor common to those of the night. Even now, the warmth that had been present in his skin was gone.

Lifting his wrist to his mouth, Vasilije sunk his fangs into his skin to open a vein. Blood ran freely in a stream from his wrist, and he pulled Alex to him to begin the transition from human to vampire. Near death, his head had to be held to Vasilije's wrist, but as if it were his true nature, Alex began drinking seconds after tasting his sire's blood, eagerly sucking the liquid into his mouth.

For Vasilije, this was the part he enjoyed. To feed from the neck of a human could sustain him for a short time, but to take from another like him and give in return was a far more satisfying experience.

Alex's mouth sucked greedily at his wrist, drinking his sire's blood as readily as he'd drunk any liquid as a human. Vasilije watched the sensual scene, enjoying every moment. Blood stained lips pressed against his skin drew from him the most important gift a sire provided. As Alex swallowed every drop that spilled into his mouth, Vasilije watched his Adam's apple bob up and down in his throat. When he neared the end of the first feeding, Alex instinctively looked up to his sire to guide him.

Pulling his arm away, Vasilije let the ache in his wrist touch him inside, loving the sweet pain that accompanied feeding one of his own. Alex wiped his mouth and sat up next to him, unsure as all new vampires were.

"Come, Alex. I want to give you something."

Completely under his spell, his newest vampire followed him back to the club. Vasilije saw the brunette he'd admired earlier, without the two men she'd had before. Remembering how her body had felt against his as he'd pressed through the crowd, he approached her and with little effort, he had her nearly begging to leave with them.

By the time they arrived at his house, she had her hands all over Vasilije, but she wasn't for him.

Turning to Alex, he smiled. "She's yours for the night."

He eagerly took his gift to the couch and began undressing her. Vasilije sat back in his chair and in the dim light of the parlor, he saw his vampire bend her over and ram into her until she screamed out her orgasm. Unsatisfied, Alex pulled her head to his still hard cock and fucked her again as she eagerly swallowed everything he gave her.

Vasilije heard the familiar click of a vampire's teeth dropping as Alex came and in a flash was standing over him.

"No," he said in a deep voice like a growl.

"I'm hungry, and I know it would feel incredible to taste her now. You said she was mine."

"A vampire drinks from his sire whenever possible."

Before he could answer, Vasilije touched his wrist to Alex's mouth and the new vampire began feeding again. The brunette watched with eyes full of fear.

"Don't worry. I won't let him drink from you."

Vasilije watched the fear leave her eyes, replaced with their earlier lustful stare, now fastened on his own cock. Leaving Alex to feed, she crawled up to Vasilije and began rubbing the front of his pants. With little encouragement, she freed his cock and slid the engorged head between her lips. As her hand cupped and squeezed his balls, her mouth sucked his cock while Alex sucked excitedly at his wrist.

Looking down, Vasilije saw this was clearly not the first time this woman had sucked cock. Her tongue expertly slid under the crown, teasing the most sensitive part before she pushed her lips to gently clamp down on the base of his cock as her throat closed in around the head. The effect was incredible. Fighting the urge to come, he yanked her head off him and pulled her to her feet.

He'd said she was Alex's for the night, but now as his young vampire finished feeding for the second time in just a few hours, Alex grew sleepy and his head fell back against the couch. The brunette looked at Alex and then back to Vasilije before she went back to work on his cock, stroking him toward completion as she softly moaned next to his lips.

"Come," he whispered.

Following him to the floor, she pulled at his clothes before he removed them with a mere thought. He ran his hands over her body slowly and then ordered, "Get on your hands and knees."

She willingly did as he commanded, and in seconds she offered him whatever he wanted. Tonight he'd take simply fucking over anything else.

Vasilije placed his hands on her hips and held her tightly in place. His cock found her drenched cunt and he slammed into her, his balls smacking off her skin. She fought against his hold, backing up to meet his hard thrusts.

Fuck, she was eager!

No matter how hard he pounded into her, she met his body's movement equally with one as wanton of her own. Vasilije slid his finger and then a second one into her ass and began fucking her in both places, and she bucked against him like she wanted more.

Roughly, he pulled her up to his chest and continued fucking her cunt. His fangs slammed into his mouth as he ran his lips over her neck.

Alex may not be able to taste her, but there was no reason he shouldn't.

He bit into her and her moaning grew louder with each pull on her vein. The sounds of their fucking filled the room, and as he drew closer to coming, Vasilije slid his fingers down to her clit and began stroking her. His eyes closed, his mind focused on his cock filling her, his fingers teasing her, and the taste of her blood draining down his throat.

She cried out some words before she came, but he was too focused on the feel of her squeezing his cock to understand or care. Over and over, her body milked him until he filled her with his cum and she filled him with her blood.

When he finally slid out of her, she fell to the floor, her body exhausted from how he'd treated her. Hours later, after he'd fucked her until she begged to become his, a vampire like Alex, he dissolved her memory of everything she'd done and sent her home in a cab.

As dawn approached, Vasilije made sure Alex was safe from daylight in his own bedroom designed to be secure from the sun and crawled into bed for the day. He'd had a productive night, and as he laid his head on the pillow, he smiled at how good it was to be a vampire.